INCOGNITA

INCOGNITA

KRISTEN LIPPERT-MARTIN

carolrhoda LAB
MINNEAPOLIS

Carolrhoda Lab™
An imprint of Carolrhoda Books
A division of Lerner Publishing Group, Inc.
241 First Avenue North
Minneapolis, MN 55401 USA

For reading levels and more information, look up this title at www.lernerbooks.com.

Cover and interior images: © iStockphoto.com/Dutko (tattoo); © iStockphoto.com/ Alexander Chernyakov (fire); © iStockphoto.com/isitsharp (city).

Main body text set in Bembo Std 10.5/15.
Typeface provided by Monotype.

Library of Congress Cataloging-in-Publication Data

The Cataloging-in-Publication Data for *Incognita* is on file at the Library of Congress.
ISBN 978-1-5124-0577-4 (trade hardcover)
ISBN 978-1-5124-0896-6 (EB pdf)

LC record available at https://lccn.loc.gov/2015041824

Manufactured in the United States of America
1-39232-21109-3/10/2016

For Philip. Of course. Again.

CHAPTER 1

I pound on the thick glass of the boutique door with my fist, trying to get the sales clerk's attention, but he's determined to ignore me.

"Please! I'm desperate!"

He flicks his hands in my direction without looking at me—*shoo*—and continues to fuss over the headless silver mannequin that he's dressing in the display window.

I pace on the sidewalk, contemplate the looming disaster before me, and then realize there's only one thing to do: I must admit defeat and call Mrs. Fitzgerald.

I take out my phone. It doesn't even ring once before she picks up.

"Yes?"

That's how she always answers my calls. Not "Hello, Angel" or "Is everything okay?" Just a dry, humorless "Yes," as if I've interrupted her—which, given the intensity and complexity of her research work, I probably have. As usual, I try not to take it personally that my court-appointed guardian treats me no more warmly than she would treat a temporary lab assistant.

"The store is closed," I say into the phone. "They won't let me in."

I hear her typing in the background. A moment later she says, "Take out the credit card I gave you and hold it up for the clerk to see. Call me back if you have any other problems."

End call.

Nice chatting with you, too.

I walk back up to the boutique door, pull the card out of my wallet, and slap it against the glass.

"Hello? Can you help me now?"

The clerk turns and looks, his eyes widening as he takes in the gold lettering across the top of the black card. He nearly trips as he rushes to unlock the door. I guess it doesn't matter that I'm a seventeen-year-old girl in ripped jeans and a shabby tank top, rudely banging on the shop door right after closing time. I've got an elite credit card issued by invitation only, and that's all he needs to know.

The clerk opens the front door just wide enough to let me through, as if he's afraid a horde of people will try to rush in behind me.

"What do you need?"

"A dress."

"Well, naturally. I didn't imagine you came to Blake & Mikels for an oil change. What's the event?"

"Some sort of gala thing," I say, pulling the invitation from my back pocket. I unfold the thick vellum card and read off the full name for him. "The Metropolitan Museum Trustees Gala. And it starts in forty-five minutes, so if we could make this quick . . ."

He takes a deep, bracing breath. "Follow me."

We move deeper into the boutique, beyond a pair of black curtains, and into a circular room lined with mirrors. He points at the small pedestal in the center. "Up there. Let's get at it."

I step up onto the platform. For a full minute, he circles around me, squinting and tapping his lips with his index finger. It's like I'm in some sort of fashion MRI machine. I feel like I'm undergoing the most thorough examination I've ever had in my life—and that's saying something, considering that just a year ago, scientists were probing the deepest recesses of my brain on a regular basis.

He does two more full laps around me and then stops. "Got it. Be right back."

My phone rings while I'm waiting for him to return. I don't recognize the number, but that in itself tells me who's calling. Thomas rarely uses the same phone number twice. He's been able to get around the technology ban imposed on him by calling me from disposable phones. I hit the ignore button to buy myself just a little more time.

This gala event was his idea. It's going to be our first real date.

"We can consider it our high school prom," he said. "I didn't go to mine either. Not that I had your excellent excuse of someone drilling into my head to remove my memories. I was in Turkmenistan trying to hot-wire a two-wheeled goat cart."

After months of home detention, Thomas's lawyers have finally wrangled him a plea bargain in exchange for his complete cooperation with the federal investigators looking into his father's many cyber crimes. Starting tonight, there are no more restraining orders or ankle transmitters or federal injunctions prohibiting contact between us. No more overseers and intermediaries we're supposed to go through. Finally we get to go out on a regular date.

To the most exclusive party in Manhattan.

On an enormous private yacht docked near the Financial District.

Thomas's adoptive mother sits on the board of trustees for the Metropolitan Museum of Art, so the whole family is on the invite list for this gala, and Thomas is bringing me as his plus-one. This will be my first time meeting his parents.

I may have free-climbed half-built skyscrapers with no safety net dozens of times, but this is a whole different kind of scary, and if I make it through the evening without throwing up all the butterflies in my stomach, it will be a miracle.

My phone rings again. Same unknown number. This time I answer.

"Hey," I say quietly into my phone.

"I'm at your apartment," Thomas says. "Where, pray tell, are you?"

"I had a slight problem."

"What sort of slight problem?"

He's trying to keep his voice cool, but there's real worry driven deep into the cracks between the words.

"Just a wardrobe issue. I kind of—don't have a dress yet. Mrs. Fitzgerald sent me to Blake & Mikels."

"Ah. The ever charming Mrs. Fitzgerald. She always knows just what to do," he says dryly.

"Thomas, enough with that already. How can you dislike her so much when you've never even met her?"

"I'm just good at judging people. And stop that. I can hear you rolling your eyes."

"I'm not." Yes, I am.

"We should be to Blake & Mikels in fifteen minutes. And Angel . . ."

"Yes?"

"I cannot wait to see you."

I don't think I've ever smiled so hard in my life. "Same here."

I end the call and wait for the stylist to return, trying to look everywhere but in the mirror. It's still not an entirely comfortable thing, looking at myself. I feel like a puzzle that's been forced back together in spite of a few missing or mangled pieces. My therapist tells me that this is actually pretty normal for someone my age. Apparently, just because I had my mind tampered with doesn't mean I get a pass on the "figuring myself out" stage of life. She says I won't be able to trust the world until I can trust myself. I asked how long she thought that would take, and she said, "Possibly the rest of your life."

Super.

The stylist comes back, carrying a hanger with what looks like a spangly white slip dripping from it. "This is *the one*."

I take the hanger and examine the dress. What little there is of it.

"What's the problem?" he demands, registering the dismay that must show on my face.

"The back of the dress," I say. "It's kind of . . . not there."

"You have lovely shoulders. You should show them off."

"I don't think that's a good idea," I say. "Do you have anything else?"

"On short notice like this? You're lucky I had that."

"Well, I'm sorry, but this won't work."

No way am I walking into this gala with my wing tattoo exposed to the prying eyes of Manhattan's rich and famous. I mean, I doubt those people spend much time walking through East Harlem and looking at the graffiti scribbled onto the bus stops up there—but I'd still rather not draw too much attention to myself. Sure, I just had the tattoo re-inked to fill in the part that got lasered off while I was in the hospital, but that was for my own sake.

The clerk sighs, walks away again, and returns with a filmy white shawl draped over his arm. "Here. You can cover your exquisite designer gown with this if you must. I'll be just on the other side of the curtain."

I quickly shed my clothes like some grimy, molting urban insect and pull the dress into place. It's form-fitting but not too tight, long but not dragging on the floor. I arrange the shawl so that it conceals the two inked wings on my shoulders.

I spin on the pedestal, looking at the reflections of all the Angels in the mirrors around me. The dress is so light and insubstantial, even though I am not. But the contrast—maybe it works on me?

Yes, it kind of does.

I'm just about to let a smile sneak onto my face when the stylist draws the curtain aside to get a look at me. "Stunning," he says, sounding bored. "Although . . ." He points to the thick black watch I'm wearing. "You should take that ugly thing off. It really detracts from the overall look."

I shake my head. "It has to stay on." Mrs. Fitzgerald insists on that. It might look like a big ugly watch, but it's basically a panic button, in case there's some sort of emergency and, for whatever reason, I can't just call Mrs. Fitzgerald.

The stylist gives me another sigh from his seemingly endless supply. "Well, if you're all set, I can ring you up in the front."

"Actually, um, do you guys do makeup and hair by any chance?"

"You're kidding me, right? You really haven't prepared for this at all, have you?"

I shrug helplessly. "I've had a lot of other things on my mind lately."

"There are movie stars who wish they could attend the Metropolitan Museum Trustees Gala. There are people who would *kill* for an invitation."

I flinch at the word "kill," but he doesn't notice. He walks to the far side of the room and pulls a little trolley filled with makeup toward me. "Sit, sit."

He does my face, issuing orders at me periodically to look up, look down, don't blink, and above all DO NOT MOVE. He applies lipstick with such concentration you'd think he was defusing a bomb. Next, he rubs gel onto his palms and then seems to pull my short hair in several directions at once. I look in the mirror and see myself transformed.

While I'm staring at my reflection, wondering if anyone I used to know would recognize me—and wondering whether I'd want them to—the stylist takes care of my accessories. Within moments he's swept my regular clothes into what looks like a plastic garbage bag, transferred my wallet and phone to a bejeweled clutch, and placed a pair of strappy sandals in front of me. The heels are so high, I think they qualify as stepladders.

"I don't know about these shoes," I say as I step into them.

"Well, I *do* know about those shoes, and they are perfect for that dress."

I cautiously test them out. "I don't think I could run in these heels."

"Run? Why on earth would you need to run?"

"I mean, if the need arose to, say, flee for my life."

Before he can respond, a black SUV pulls up in front of the shop, and my phone buzzes. Time for me to thank this guy, hand over the credit card, avoid looking too closely at the receipt in case the price makes me puke, and get out of here.

I remind myself that I once scaled I-beams. And survived an assault by a team of elite soldiers. And took on the woman who killed my mother.

Surely I can handle my first real date.

CHAPTER 2

A driver in a black suit leaps from behind the wheel of the SUV and opens the rear door as I approach. Thomas gets out of the backseat. It's been four very long, very yearning-filled months since we last saw each other in person, and suddenly here he is, standing in front of me in a tuxedo.

I stop short, my breath trapped inside my chest. Thomas gives me a tentative wave, like he's nervous.

And all I can say is, "Your hair."

I've never seen him as a redhead. I kind of forgot he was one.

"Yep. The real me at last. What do you think?"

I walk up to him and hesitantly touch his hair. It's a deep, rich auburn. As I stare at it, tension ripples through my body like a low-magnitude earthquake. I pull my hand back and force myself not to see his biological mother in him, but I have to admit his hair does make me think of Evangeline Hodges.

She can't hurt me ever again.

I do my best to transform my clenched teeth into a smile.

"I like it a lot," I say, hoping I'm convincing, glad he's not able to see the images flashing through my mind—of Hodges in the police station, taunting me and telling me about the night she killed my mother. Of Hodges standing over me, gloating and exultant, because she believed I was dead at last.

I may have forgotten a lot of things but she will never be one of them.

Thomas pulls me into an embrace. "It's okay, Angel. I know it might remind you of her, but that's why I wanted you to see me like this. I want to drive those bad memories out with some good ones, starting tonight."

I laugh shakily. "Sounds like a plan." I would have held it all in—I would have lied to protect him—but knowing that I don't have to pretend makes me feel lighter. My heart swells in relief.

"Now it's my turn to have a look at you," he says. "This might take a while, so be patient as I ogle you." I don't know how a smirk can be sweet, but he's managing it right now. "You know, it's a sad thing, Angel."

"What is?"

"We're both so shockingly attractive that no one else will have us. We'd better stick together, then."

I really want to kiss him right now, but since the driver's still standing in front of us holding the car door open, now's probably not the moment for a make-out session. Thomas must be thinking the same thing, because he gestures toward our ride. "After you."

As I climb into the backseat, I catch myself studying the driver: memorizing the line of his jaw, the acne scars on his cheeks, the way his hair is cut into a sharply-defined V just above his collar. Why must I catalog these details the way I do? I'm still living like I'm back in the hospital, counting floor tiles. My therapist says this way of looking at the world will fade with time. The suspicion, the hypervigilance—I don't need to be in battle mode anymore. I'm safe now.

It's hard to change my ways, though.

Inside the car, I stash the bag with my street clothes under my seat and smile at Thomas when he slides in next to me. The driver shuts the door, hops back in the car, and pulls away from the curb just as Thomas takes my hand. "Am I allowed to kiss you?"

"I think it will mess up my lipstick."

"What if I promise not to go anywhere near your lipstick?" he says, kissing my neck.

I feel like there's a wick running through the middle of me and he just lit it.

Unfortunately, I don't get to savor the moment for long before I remember something. "Oh! Before we get there, I promised Virgil I'd—well, he wants to talk to you. I guess he feels the need to do the 'dad' thing, seeing as this is our first date."

"Really?" I can't tell if Thomas is actually skeptical of Virgil's paternal instincts or just irked that our kissing is over already.

"I mean, he does try," I say in Virgil's defense. "Even if it's super awkward."

"Just as long as I don't have to talk to that creepy Mrs. Fitzgerald."

I don't know why this comment sets me on edge. Maybe because he's saying something I feel too but don't want to admit? I have trouble sorting out mere discomfort from actual distrust. Admittedly, Mrs. Fitzgerald is very odd. And off-putting. She doesn't make much eye contact, wears the same ratty brown sweater nearly every day, and eats anchovies straight out of the can as an afternoon snack.

I say the one thing about my guardian that is as positive as it is undeniable. "Mrs. Fitzgerald is brilliant."

"I know she's brilliant. That's what weirds me out about her. Why would some world-class neuroscientist want to work as a babysitter?"

"Thomas! She's not my babysitter. She's my legal guardian." Virgil says he can't officially acknowledge me as his daughter yet. He still fears for my safety. And though he probably wouldn't admit to believing in something as unscientific as a curse, I suspect he also figures that anything that brings me closer to the Claymore family brings me closer to disaster. Based on my previous experience with the Claymores—what I remember of it—I can't disagree.

"No, I didn't mean she was *your* babysitter," Thomas says quickly.

"She's not Virgil's babysitter either," I insist. "She's his caregiver. His health is very fragile and he needs someone competent to handle all his daily medical needs."

"Sure, I get that. I can understand a team of nurses, but she's like Nobel Prize levels of genius. She could probably have her own research lab if she wanted."

"I can't even imagine what Virgil pays her," I say.

"Money is not usually a motivator for that sort of person."

"Okay, so she *is* a little strange. That's not a crime. Look, I have to take my lead from Virgil. If he trusts her, I should too."

"You said 'should,' which means you really don't."

"I—I do. I'm working on it, anyway."

"I know you don't have much choice about her being in your life. It's just . . . I practically have sinister-motive radar, and everything you've told me about her raises question marks. Like, what Chinese American woman has a name like Fitzgerald?"

"I don't know. Maybe she's adopted, or she married someone with that name," I say, though I can't imagine her being married to anyone or anything except her work.

"She wasn't adopted. She got her PhD in theoretical biotechnology from Peking University and came to the U.S. eighteen years ago."

"How do you know that?"

I really don't know much about Mrs. Fitzgerald at all except that she's worked for Virgil for more than a decade. And she saw Evangeline Hodges for what she was long before anyone else did. One of the first things my father said to me when I met him in person was, "I should have listened to Grace about that woman."

"Found out everything I could about her, which wasn't much. That's what worries me. She has almost no online fingerprint at all, and that's usually a sign that something's been erased."

"So much for that technology ban on you, I guess," I say. Officially, Thomas isn't allowed anywhere near a computer or a phone. But clearly the FBI agents who are monitoring him have underestimated his resourcefulness.

I can't deny I share the same worries that Thomas does. I take solace in how the Feds hover over us the way they do, not that I can say I ever feel totally safe. Thomas is on the Feds' watch list because of his past involvement with and future potential for criminal mastermindism. Meanwhile, I have all kinds of untapped superpowers from the Velocius project lurking inside my brain, and I doubt very much the Feds want me to figure out what they are. Point is, they want to keep both Thomas and me under their thumb, for different reasons.

"If Mrs. Fitzgerald is hiding anything sinister," I say, "she must be awfully good at it, seeing as the Feds have made three random, surprise visits to Virgil's house in the last month."

Thomas's eyebrows soar. "You didn't tell me that."

"I don't know much about it, other than that they searched all of Virgil's computers. I'm guessing they were making sure that there were no remaining backup files with information from the Velocius project."

"And Virgil cooperated?"

"A hundred percent. He gave their computer forensics teams complete access to everything. And his computer is connected to Erskine Claymore's mainframe, and even the off-site data storage for all of Claymore Industries."

"Whoa."

"Yeah. I suspect Virgil hasn't mentioned any of this to his father. The point is, the Feds examined Mrs. Fitzgerald's computer too. If she were up to anything sketchy, how could she keep it from them?"

"Please. People who know how to hide things can make it look like they're not hiding things. I do it—"

I give him a fierce, shaming look.

"*Used to do it*, I mean." He laces our fingers together and leans his shoulder against mine. "Anyway, speaking of reasons to be paranoid, let's get this chat with Virgil out of the way so we can get on with our amazing night together."

He kisses my hand gently.

I brush a piece of his red hair back from his forehead. He's right—I'm already starting to push away the bad associations with that color.

I take my phone out of the small clutch that I unwillingly received in exchange for the mangy string bag I was carrying when I arrived at Blake & Mikels. I punch in the number for Virgil. I think I might be the only person who has this number. Aside from Mrs. Fitzgerald, but she hardly leaves his side, so she doesn't need to call him.

I see Virgil's face on the screen. He blinks, but his lips do not move. The ALS has robbed him of the use of those muscles. His vocal interface—the translation device he relies on to communicate—speaks for him. "Hello. Don't you two look wonderful."

"Good evening, Mr. Claymore," Thomas says in his most mature, "impress the parent" voice. "We do look wonderful. Well, Angel more than me, but I look pretty dashing if I do say so myself."

"I hope you have a fun night, but I just wanted to say . . . please be careful."

"That shouldn't be a problem," Thomas says. "Seeing as there's no person in all of New York City who's watched more carefully than Angel. Sometimes her protective detail is so close she can smell their breath."

Talking via Virgil's vocal interface means there's a slight delay before each thing he says. I know it's not his fault, given his physical limitations, but all the strained pauses pretty much sum up our relationship. We're working on understanding each other, on figuring out how to be a father and daughter, but it takes a bucketload of patience.

At my request, he did change the voice to sound less like the voice translators the soldiers at the hospital used. The first few times he talked to me, my blood pressure spiked and my mouth went dry. Not the ideal beginning to my life as a member of the Claymore family.

"The federal agents will have an easier time doing their job if Angel doesn't keep trying to dodge them. I've had yet another complaint from them this week, Angel."

"Duly noted," I say meekly. "I will never, ever do it again."

I look out the back window, trying to spot the tail that usually follows me. I can usually shake them when I'm on foot, and I'll admit I enjoy putting the Feds through their paces. Some days I practically do parkour to lose them. The subtle difference between "protected" and "monitored" is lost on me, and lately—just in the last few days—I can feel the weight of even more eyes than usual.

"Also," Virgil says, "I know that you, young man, will be on your best behavior in all possible ways tonight. Not that Angel couldn't handle things if you weren't."

"Sir, the fact that Angel could probably kill me six different ways is an unnecessary incentive for me to be a gentleman. I care about her very much. And I respect her like crazy."

"We'll be back by one," I add.

"Nice try," Virgil says. "Midnight."

"Fine. *Dad.*"

His face shows no emotion because it can't. Instead he closes his eyes for a long moment. That's his version of a smile.

I find myself smiling too. "We have to go now. See you later!"

I end the call and shift myself closer to Thomas. My foot accidentally knocks into his ankle and hits something hard.

Something that feels very much like an electronic monitor.

I lift the bottom of his pant leg, and there it is.

"Angel—"

"I thought you were supposed to get this taken off a few days ago. I thought that's why we could finally see each other and go out together in public. I thought that's what was making this night so special."

He holds up his hands in a gesture that's half *calm down* and half *don't kill me.* "Let me explain."

"Please do."

"Um. There's been a slight delay on my plea bargain? I think that's the best way to put it."

"A delay? Why?"

"It's just, you know, the Feds work slowly."

"Okay, so what does that mean for right now? For tonight, I mean."

"It means that technically, for the moment, the terms of the original agreement are still in effect." He says it quickly, like he's reciting possible side effects at the end of a drug commercial.

"All the terms? Including the 'no contact with Sarah Ramos' part?"

"Um. Possibly?"

"And you're jeopardizing your plea deal *why*? Just so we could go to some fancy party together? That's crazy."

"It's not crazy. I want to have a normal date. No, not a normal date: I want to have a spectacular date. With you. I wanted this to be our prom night and your birthday and maybe Mardi Gras thrown in. I wanted to give you everything you've missed out on, and I don't care about the stupid restraining order. So maybe I might have sort of—"

"Lied to me," I say.

"*Withheld certain irrelevant details* is more like it. The point is, my heart was and remains in the right place."

I take a deep breath. I have a lot of experience with being deceived. I know Thomas didn't mean to hurt me, but I also don't have a lot of spare benefits for all my doubts.

"Do your parents know about this?" I ask.

"Well, yes. I am allowed to be out at the party tonight. That part's not the problem. It's just—"

"You're not allowed to be with me."

He grimaces. "Right."

I slump back against the seat and pull my filmy shawl tightly around me. All along, in the back of my mind, I kept expecting something to go wrong with these plans. That's why I put off getting ready until the last possible minute. It had seemed like tempting fate. My brain is hardwired to expect the worst, to distrust happiness. And for good reason.

"Angel. Don't get like that. It'll be fine."

"And what if the Feds just happen to see handsome you and fabulous me together at this gala thing? Did you think about that possibility? They'll probably find some other way to punish you."

"I don't care. I'll deal with the consequences tomorrow. Besides, I've grown fond of Nessie."

"Nessie?"

"Yes, that's what it says here, see?" He taps the metal anklet. "NESE1798. I hope that doesn't indicate my ranking. I'd hate to think there were 1,797 other potential threats far more dangerous than me out there."

"We're here, sir," the driver says as the SUV comes to a stop in front of a dock. The place is swarming with security, not to mention expensive cars and limousines. Volleys of camera flashes are going off on both sides of the main entrance.

The yacht is lit up with strings of white lights that look like stars on a leash. I can see people walking up the gangplank, women in ball gowns and men in black tie. One woman is actually wearing a tiara. On deck, waiters in white waistcoats are scurrying toward the center of the yacht, balancing silver platters full of champagne flutes.

"We shouldn't do this," I say.

"You said 'shouldn't,' which means you still want to."

I face Thomas. Handsome, redheaded Thomas, who is looking so apologetic and hopeful that I feel the anger drain away from the glare half-formed on my face.

"You are truly far too gorgeous to waste tonight," he says. "It would be a crime for you not to go."

"No, it would be an actual crime for *us* to go, at least as far as the Feds are concerned."

Thomas leans toward me until our faces are inches apart. "We deserve this, Angel."

That I can't argue with. After all we went through and all the months of waiting, we deserve to have one evening of fun. We deserve something special that no one can take away.

"Okay, look," I say, "we're already here, and I'm in a dress that costs as much as a semester of college tuition, so here's what we'll do. You get out now, and I'll tell the driver to take me around the block a few times and drop me off in ten minutes. Maybe if we don't show up together, it won't be so obvious. I mean, this is a very crowded party. We can kind of get lost in there, right?"

"Deal. I'll make nice with a few of my mom's friends, stuff a few hors d'oeuvres in my face, and then I'll meet you on the lower deck"—he looks down at his watch—"in around half an hour. Starboard side." He gives me a quick kiss, then leans back and studies my face. "Everything's going to be okay, Angel."

Something about the way he says that makes me worry. I kiss him again, hard enough to smother the fear. When I pull back from him, he looks happily dazed. I wipe my lipstick off his mouth.

"See you inside in a few minutes," I say.

I watch him get out of the car and walk toward the security guards at the entrance. Out of the corner of my eye, I see a sudden movement. A young guy in a hoodie, maybe seventeen or eighteen, steps out from behind a nearby building onto the sidewalk, in full view, staring at the back of the SUV.

I'd be inclined to think he's just watching the spectacle of all these rich people and celebrities arriving at the dock for the party, but that wouldn't explain why this is the fourth or fifth time I've seen him this week. And why he always makes a point of showing himself, like he's waiting for permission to approach me.

Well, he's not getting it tonight.

CHAPTER 3

There are some words I've only ever encountered in a thesaurus. Up until this moment, "opulent" was one of them.

I look around, trying to keep my mouth from dropping open every time I turn my head, but it's nearly impossible not to be impressed. There's a six-foot-long ice sculpture of the Brooklyn Bridge sitting on the bar at the far end of the room. I overhear someone saying that the tulips decorating the tables were flown in on a private jet from Holland earlier in the day. All the food seems to be very tiny and much of it is pierced by long, silver skewers. A waiter walks by with a tray and offers me a lamb "lollipop," but I decline for fear that "lollipop" is some euphemism for eyeball or an even worse part of the lamb.

Almost everyone is wearing black, and I worry my shiny white dress makes me stick out in all the wrong ways, until a woman stumbles past me clutching a bottle of champagne by the neck. "Great dress!"

"Oh, thank you." The thought, *That woman looks just like*

so-and-so, gives way to the realization, *That actually is so-and-so*. By now she's swallowed up by the crowd. I hear music start up—I recognize a popular song that Thomas and I agree is overplayed. As I step out onto the main deck, I expect to see a DJ, but instead I see the actual band who sings the song. Playing like they're a wedding band, just carrying on in the background, completely unnoticed.

I feel like Alice in Wonderland, if Alice had fallen down the rabbit hole and landed on a yacht docked along the East River where a lot of people are talking very seriously about the latest art installation at the Met, which is made out of milk jugs, wire hangers, and ten thousand breath mints.

And yet, even with all the wow-factors piled on top of each other, after ten minutes of gaping, I'm bored. The one person I want to talk to is on the other side of the room, shaking hands with a series of middle-aged people who I imagine are friends of his parents. Thomas's mother, dressed in a plum-colored suit, is petite and energetic. She doles out hugs and vigorous handshakes to the throngs of people surrounding her, laughing and looking like she's having a wonderful time. Thomas's father, on the other hand, is gripping his martini glass and looking as though he wishes he were anywhere else, prison included. I guess I won't be meeting them tonight after all, which comes as both a relief and a disappointment.

I watch as Thomas's mother whispers something into his ear. Thomas nods and then dutifully shakes a few more hands, but all the while, he's scanning the room.

The moment our eyes meet, every opulent detail of this party drops away. The noise and laughter and the shimmering gowns—all of it grows fuzzy and dim. There's just this tunnel connecting us, and I wish I could walk through it to reach him.

I feel . . . *happy.*

It's such a simple feeling, but getting here has been anything but simple for me. I was so alone for so long that lonely became normal for me. I lived in the shadows, fearful, trying not to get caught. I was a walking secret, and the only peace I ever knew, my only sense of safety, came from solitude.

But now I can look at Thomas and feel happy.

Thomas's mother leads him by the arm toward another group of her friends and colleagues. He sneaks another look at me, rolling his eyes. He points to his watch and holds up a hand. *Five minutes.*

I nod, my face achy from smiling, but as I watch him, he's suddenly transfixed by something on the opposite side of the room. He throws a worried glance in my direction. No, not just worried. Panicked.

I try to figure out what he's looking at, craning my neck to somehow see over or through the mass of people now congregating by the door to the deck.

Someone's coming in, flanked by men in dark suits with ear pieces. Bodyguards? Secret Service? For a moment, I worry that Thomas is in big trouble. Maybe the FBI is reneging on their deal.

At last I get a clear view. Instantly I know how a champagne bubble must feel as it pops. A moment ago, I was feeling effervescent, and now . . .

My grandfather, Erskine Claymore, has just arrived.

My heart starts beating a snare drum rhythm, and for a moment the world seems to pause. I worry that my shock at seeing Claymore is triggering my Velocius abilities, so I try to snap myself out of it. I promised my FBI handlers that I wouldn't use the crazy mind-enhancing technology that Dr. Wilson and Company put in my head, and even if I hadn't made that promise, I don't want my thoughts jumping to hyper speed ever again. Because I know that every time it happens, I'm subtracting years from my life.

So I fight to stay calm, as the grandfather I've never met—the man who's made several fortunes by trampling people like me underfoot—approaches. He doesn't look anywhere near eighty-two years old. His snow-white hair is full and stylishly cut. His eyes—green like mine—sparkle behind a pair of boyish wire-rim glasses. Dressed impeccably in a pale gray suit and red bow tie, he gives off a warm, generous, charming vibe. He catches people in his gravitational pull with every step—hugging, clasping hands, and generally working the room like the incredibly important, influential man that he is. I can't believe it didn't occur to me that he might be at an event like this.

And now he's making his way toward me.

No, I'm imagining that.

He's just chatting with people as he walks across the room. But he *is* coming this way. An impromptu receiving line is forming, and I'm right in the middle of it.

If I bolt now, I'll draw attention to myself. So I stay frozen in place. He won't recognize me. At least, he shouldn't. Hodges went out of her way to get rid of me so he'd never even know I existed, and Virgil has been very careful to keep us from meeting. There are no images of my face floating around on the Internet—no social media profiles, no close-up photos snapped by admirers during my lawbreaking days. Still, Erskine Claymore is a man with astronomical resources at his disposal. I'm about to find out whether he's somehow managed to discover who I am.

He reaches out for my hand and gives it a squeeze.

"Lovely to meet you," he says as his gaze drifts toward the next face.

As soon as my grandfather is a few feet past me, I look around, but Thomas is gone. Or at least I can't see him among all the people bumping into me as they shuffle to get near Claymore. I move toward the stairs as fast as I can, swimming upstream against the flow of people.

Thomas told me to meet him on the starboard side, and it's only just occurring to me that I have no idea if that's the left or right. I figure I've got a fifty-fifty chance and go to the left side of the boat, lower deck. It's so crowded I can hardly make my way through the clusters of people, all of whom are glinting with jewels.

Five minutes becomes ten. Then fifteen. I lean over the railing and look up at the buildings, several of which are probably owned by Erksine Claymore.

Still no Thomas.

My shoulders sag and the shawl slips down on one side. Behind me, I hear a girl's voice say, "So. You a friend of Thomas's or something?"

Startled, I turn around. Standing on the deck is a girl my age in a bright yellow cocktail dress. She has wavy blonde hair with streaks of dark blue. Her full, round cheeks and slightly upturned nose make her look a little younger than she probably is, but her raspy voice makes her sound like an old blues singer.

"I noticed him searching for someone in the crowd while I was talking to him. Are you dating or whatever?"

Her expression is at once sneering and wounded. I immediately wonder if she's an ex-girlfriend.

"Who wants to know?" I ask.

"I used to go to school with Thomas." She puts out her hand for me to shake. "Cassidy Hicks. Resident mean girl of Dorchester Academy. That's a fancy private school in Connecticut, in case you haven't heard of it."

I actually *have* heard of it. I went to a fancy private school too, not that I'm going to bother mentioning this to her.

I ignore her outstretched hand. She lets it drop but turns up the wattage on her sneer. "I didn't think Thomas went for exotic types."

My eyes automatically narrow. "Exotic? Is that a code word for something?"

"Oh, relax. If I wanted to insult you, I'd just do it."

Yeah. Definitely a mean girl.

Good thing I'm a scary girl.

I smile. "And if I wanted to snap you in half and toss you into the river, I'd just do that too."

I step around her, but before I can get very far she says, "Well, in case you're curious, I just saw Thomas leave with a couple friends."

I turn back. "What did the friends look like?"

She shrugs, twirling a piece of her hair. "Just two guys in suits. They were propping him up as he walked so I figure he sneaked too many drinks."

"When was that?"

"I don't know. Like five, ten minutes ago maybe."

As I push past her, my shawl falls even farther down my shoulder. I hear her give a little gasp, but I don't have time to dwell on it. A very bad feeling is swelling inside me. I climb the stairs to the main deck and thread my way through the crowd. When I'm back on the deck near the yacht entrance, I take my phone out and dial the number Thomas last used to call me.

No answer.

I rush down the gangplank as fast as my sky-high shoes will allow. A security guard lifts a rope to let me out. Some photographers are still milling around. They snap a few shots of me before deciding I'm not anyone tabloid-worthy.

"Excuse me," I say to the security guard, "there was a guy in a tux, red hair, with two other men. They just left a few minutes ago. Did you see which way they went?"

He blinks rapidly and without looking at me says, "No, sorry."

Judging by the flat tone and the lack of eye contact, the people who took Thomas slipped this guy some money and told him not to mention seeing them.

"That kid with the red hair? His mother is on the board of trustees for this event. Do you understand what I'm saying? Rich, important people will want to know where he went."

After a second he tips his head to the right and covers his mouth like he's coughing. "Toward the parking garage near the south dock."

"The guys with him, what did they look like?"

He ducks his head and says, "Tall, dark-haired, pale skin, spoke with some kind of accent."

I almost blurt out a "thank you" but decide he doesn't deserve such politeness. I rush down the sidewalk and back onto the street. High heels and cobblestones are a bad combination, so I reach down and slip my shoes off one at a time, carrying them in one hand as I rush down the street. I hold my dress up a little so I can jog.

"Thomas!"

His name echoes off the brick buildings on either side and bounces back at me.

There's nothing going on down here at this time of night. No restaurants or bars open. This is a place for tourists and right now, it's empty. I pass the parking garage the security guard mentioned, but the gate is down.

The lapping water and distant horns of the city make me feel even more alone. And scared. I know Thomas wouldn't leave without telling me. Not unless he was trying to protect me. And the Feds wouldn't hustle him away like that, right out from under his parents' noses—plus I'm pretty sure most FBI agents do not have accents. Something is very wrong.

The wind makes my dress flap violently, and I have a hard time keeping my shawl from blowing away. Where could they have gone? Manhattan ends right here at the water's edge.

I see a crumpled cocktail napkin near the entrance to the south dock and dash toward it. A tall metal grate covers the entrance. There's no way someone could have gotten around or over it, and even if they did, there'd be nowhere to go except into the East River. The only two boats tied to the dock are small, empty tugs that are both dark and empty.

I stoop to pick up the napkin. It's got the Metropolitan Museum logo on it.

"Thomas! Thom—"

Something loops around my neck, rough and tight, choking me.

My eyes water as I gag and struggle to tear the rope away from my throat. The next thing I feel is my feet lifting off the sidewalk. Someone hustles me toward the river where the two tug boats are knocking against the dock. The water comes at me fast. I plunge into a sudden coldness.

I've gone under. I look up and glimpse one of my high heels floating on the top of the water above my head. I try to swim toward the surface, but the rope tightens and something drags me farther down into the greenish-black depths. I think it's an anchor.

CHAPTER 4

The rope squeezes my neck, and the world stops.

It's not death, yet. It's that moment people talk about when everything you feel and remember and wanted but didn't get is crushed into a split second that cannot possibly hold it all. And yet it does. All your life is pushing up against your death like it's trying to get the last word in before falling silent forever.

I feel no cold, no anything. The rope constricting around my neck seems to pause. I'm suspended in liquid like some lab specimen in a jar, trying to keep my eyes open in the dark, dirty water.

My brain is searching, processing, trying to calculate my options and coming up empty. I continue to sink and the rope continues to tighten. Bubbles rise in front of my face—the last of my air fleeing my lungs like rats leaving a sinking ship. My Velocius abilities have kicked in to sustain me, helping me last a bit longer than I might otherwise, but they can't make me immortal. And the person who put this rope around my neck knows that.

I look up. The last bleak ball of light recedes.

Good-bye, Thomas.

Good-bye, Virgil.

Good-bye, Mrs. Fitzgerald.

Are these are my only good-byes? Am I leaving only three people behind? I feel like someone is missing . . . a friend I've never said good-bye to . . .

Someone I've forgotten.

Did the surgeries erase this person from my memory, from my life?

No . . . I think this might have been a friend I lost even before I ended up in that hospital. I remember nothing about her except a feeling of betrayal. But who betrayed whom? I don't know. Doesn't matter. Forgiveness is easy when you're dying.

Just as my mind starts to transition to resignation that this is the end, I feel the rope constrict once again. My sinking halts and starts to reverse. I'm going back up. At first I think I'm imagining it, but the light above me is growing brighter and less fuzzy. I ascend toward life, toward air. With the last bit of strength I have, I reach up, grab the rope, and pull, which takes some of the force off my neck.

A moment later, I burst out of the water and take my biggest breath since the day I was born. I land on my side on the dock, my hand underneath me awkwardly. My wrist turns too far, and the pain shocks me into full alertness. My neck burns. I pull the rope up over my head and toss it away. The anchor takes the rope back down again, and I see that it's attached to the nearby tug.

I can't see anything at first. I lie on the rough concrete, my dress like plastic wrap around me. And clear plastic wrap at that. Fortunately someone puts a jacket around my shoulders. I look up into a face I recognize. It's the boy I'd seen watching me as I arrived at the party.

"You gonna live or what?" he says in a heavy Brooklyn accent as he smacks me hard on the back.

I cough the last of the river water from my lungs. "Thank you," I blurt out. My eyes are finally able to focus.

He's my height, thin but muscular and his arms seem almost as long as his legs. He's coiled-spring tense and fidgety but yet still . . . genial? Shy? I can't quite get a read on him. It's like his body language is telling me two opposite things at the same time. What I first took for shadows around his eyes are actually purple-turning-green bruises, and there's a deep cut on the bridge of his nose and a dozen other small, partially-healed nicks on his chin, cheeks, and forehead. He looks as if he recently flew through a windshield.

"Who—are—"

"We'll get to that in a minute."

He pulls me to my feet and though I'm still drenched and dizzily gulping air, I try to assess what kind of threat he might be. I suppose his saving my life wins him a lot of points, but following me around for days set him back a bit.

"Come on," he says. "Let's get out of here before those goons come back and try to give you another taste of the East River."

"Friends of yours?" I ask.

"Never saw 'em before."

"How many were there?"

"Two. And they might be back, so I don't suggest staying out in the open like this."

"What did they look like?"

"Big. Now come on. We gotta get moving."

The wet satin plastered to my legs makes it hard for me to walk. I lift the skirt and take a few confused steps, not sure if I want to go with this kid or run the other way. I look down at my wrist and see that my watch has stopped. I wonder if the panic button will still work . . . My gaze drifts down into the water, knowing that my phone, even if I could retrieve it, is ruined. The thought strikes me that I've now lost the only way I had to reach Thomas. Terror unspools in my chest along with a flush of guilt. I feel like somehow I made this happen just because I'd dared to be happy.

"I said, come on!" When I look up, the kid is starting to jog toward the nearest shadow provided by a blocky brick warehouse. He motions for me to follow. I raise my skirt almost daintily and run to catch up, my wet feet making a slapping noise on the street as I go. The jacket the kid gave me has quickly turned into a sopping towel and there are streaks of blood and snot on the cuffs, but at least it's keeping me covered.

"What's your name?" I ask as I trip along behind him.

He doesn't answer. His head is whipping back and forth, his arms pumping at his sides. He seems to be heading back in the general direction of the yacht.

I try another angle. "Before you saw me get thrown into the river, did you see anybody else around here? A redheaded guy, my age, and a couple of other guys?"

"Nope. Just you and the guys who tossed you off the dock."

He turns sharply into a narrow passage between two warehouses that are probably a hundred years old. Everything down here has a faint, fishy scent, like it's been baked into the bricks and the sidewalks. By now it's dawning on me that he's not taking me toward Thomas. "Where are we going?"

"We need to lay low for a bit."

I stop running. "Um, no, I don't think so."

He skids to a halt and looks back at me. "Look—"

"I appreciate your help, but I have no idea who you are or why you've been following me"—his eyes widen, like he didn't expect me to recognize him—"and you don't seem keen to tell me. So if you can't explain what's going on, frankly, I have other things I need to deal with right now." I take his jacket off and throw it back to him. He looks confused and even a little hurt, like I'm abandoning him, but every moment that passes is time I'm wasting. I turn around and walk back toward the street. I don't know how I'm going to track down Thomas, but I'm going to start by finding someone who can lend me a phone. I need to call the police, and then I need to call Mrs. Fitzgerald so she can alert the Feds . . .

I'm shivering. Maybe from fear, but mostly from exposure. I might as well be walking around in my underwear right now. Wet underwear, to be exact.

"Wait!" the guy calls out.

But I'm not going to wait. That dunk in the river has washed away all illusions I might have had about building trust and taking an ordinary approach to life. This moment, this frenzied fear and anger I feel—it's like I've been thrown back in time, to a person and a place I once knew far too well. A girl who understood how life really works. People like me have to fight for every scrap of happiness and even then, it can be taken away in a matter of moments. Maybe people like me don't get happy endings.

I feel a tug on my arm. "Hold on a second—"

"No!" I shout. "Just leave me alone."

He withdraws like I slapped him across the face.

We hear a screech of brakes and turn to see a white delivery van pull up near the dock where I was so recently tossed into the water. Both of us instinctively step back into the safety of the shadows.

"Those are the guys," he says. "Told you they'd probably be back."

We crouch behind a couple garbage cans. I glance back and forth between the kid's face and the van. The kid looks more afraid than angry, which is the direct opposite of how I feel right now, even if the effect is the same: We wait and watch, both of us rigid and intensely focused.

I'm wondering if maybe we're cut from the same traumatized cloth.

Someone in the van leans out the window and shines a search-light around near the dock gate. I feel like some deep sea fish, watching the lights of a submarine cutting through the ocean gloom. After another minute, the van pulls away slowly and drives off.

I stand up and succumb to a post–"close call" bout of shivering.

"Looks like we're clear," the kid says, his voice soft and sad. "You know, if you want to go now." He puts his hands in his pockets and looks down, doing his best impression of a freshly kicked puppy.

I take a few steps out onto the sidewalk. Then I spin and sigh. Might as well try this one more time.

"Can you at least tell me why you've been following me? And why you pulled me out of the river?"

He probes one of the cuts on his upper lip with his tongue as he thinks about answering. His shirt is pretty wet, and I notice I'm not the only one shivering.

"I've been following you because I was hoping you could help me. And obviously I pulled you out of the river because I figured if you died you weren't gonna be able to do that."

"What? How am I supposed to help you?"

"I need some answers."

"From me? Answers about what?"

"I don't even know," he says. "I came here two weeks ago because of this." He reaches into his pocket and pulls out a phone, which he hands to me. "Took this off a guy who—let's just say we weren't pals. It's dead now, but there was this weird text message on it about dry cleaning."

"Call me crazy, but I'm not seeing an obvious connection to me."

"It was a code. If I had a way to charge the phone, I could show you, but I think I remember it pretty well. Something like 'When you're ready to pick up the dry cleaning, it's at . . .' and then it gave an address. So I went to that address a couple weeks back and saw you coming out."

I gape at him. "What?"

"Yeah. The apartment building on Riverside? That's where you live, right?"

No one knows that address except me and Virgil and Mrs. Fitzgerald. And Thomas.

Plus the Feds, of course.

And those are all people I'm supposed to trust.

But if someone mentioned the location of my apartment in

a coded text, that means . . . what? That even more people are watching me? And what do those people want with me?

"Anyway, I'm guessing that text went to more than one person," the guy continues. "Those guys who just tried to do you in, they probably tailed you from your apartment."

"So what does that mean? That *I'm* the dry cleaning getting picked up? You think this was some kind of assassination assignment?"

"Unless you actually do run a dry cleaning business."

"Who sent the text? Do you remember the phone number or . . ."

"It was someone named Grace Fitzgerald."

I nearly stop breathing. "That can't be. Or . . . maybe she didn't realize what she was doing . . ."

As soon as I say it, I know it's ridiculous. Mrs. Fitzgerald is the most deliberate person I know. She can rattle off pi to the twentieth digit and recite articles to Virgil full of highly technical details. She does *not* make mistakes, especially with sensitive information like my address.

I need to put a hand on the side of the building because it feels like the ground just suddenly shifted under me.

Mrs. Fitzgerald gave my address to an assassin.

I look at the watch clamped on my wrist. The very thing that's supposed to summon help when I need it suddenly feels like a snake wrapped around my arm. I'm glad I didn't try activating the panic button, alerting Mrs. Fitzgerald that I'm in trouble.

The guy moves back and forth in front of me like he's not sure which direction I'm going to fall. "So . . . somebody you know, I'm guessing?"

"She's my legal guardian."

"Yeah. Well, scratch her off your Christmas card list this year because she just sold you out."

"I just . . . She's always been so—strange, yes, but my father trusts her so completely." With good reason. She's worked for Virgil devotedly for years. And if she wanted to have me killed, her opportunities have been plentiful. Why do it now and in such a strange, roundabout way?

"People are unbelievable dirtbags sometimes, eh?" the guy says.

A barge blows its horn mournfully in the distance. Last ferry to Staten Island for the night. It's been almost an hour since Thomas disappeared from the party. I feel like he's slipping farther and farther away and now nothing is making sense.

I press the power button on the guy's stolen phone, but predictably, nothing happens. "So where did you get this phone? And why did you care about finding the address?" And what a shame he didn't grab the charger while he was at it.

"Long story."

"Sorry, don't have time for long stories."

"Well, mine's gonna take a while."

"Then I'll have to hear it later." I shove the phone back at him. "Right now I need to find someone. It's an emergency."

He takes the phone and nods, not meeting my eyes. "Sure, it's cool. I don't know where I came from, who I am, or how to get home, and I was thinking you might be able to give me some clue about at least one of those things. But, hey, we all got our own problems, right?"

That's a familiar list of unknowns. It lines up pretty well with the list I had a year ago.

He shakes his head and smiles down at the sidewalk. He's trying very hard to seem like he doesn't care and that's what makes it so much harder to walk away. Behind that forced smile is someone scared out of his mind.

"Do you—do you know your name?"

"Mikey."

"Mikey what?"

"Don't remember."

I exhale and close my eyes. "That's what I figured."

As much as I want to turn and leave, I can't stand the idea of brushing him off when he's asking for help. There are some decisions that you can't make just for your own safety or convenience without some part of you screaming "Hypocrite!" Didn't I once stand where Mikey is now, asking for help from a stranger? And Thomas gave it to me. Now I'm just walking away.

Sure, I've got good reasons. Thomas *is* that good reason. I have to find him. That's what's important right now. But still . . .

I make a decision and open my eyes. "So what happened to you? You were in a fight or an accident, weren't you?"

"Both." He leans against the brick wall of the alley. "I'll warn you right now, it's a pretty whacked out story."

"I'm sure I can handle it. Got a few whacked out stories of my own, as a matter of fact."

He takes a deep breath like he's squaring up to lift a huge barbell over his head.

"Three weeks ago, I'm in—I don't know what you'd call it, like reform school but in a hospital. They gave me these drugs and did all this stuff to me—I can't even describe it because I barely remember it. They told me they were helping me and it was either this or go to juvie. So I guess I must've picked the hospital. Seemed like a better deal, you know?"

Yeah, I know.

"Obviously I got some history, and I'm sure it ain't good if they won't tell me what it is. Anyway, I'm trying to mind my own business, keep my head low, do whatever they tell me, so I can get out of there and get on with my life."

"Get a fresh start," I say.

The words are a shot of novocaine; my mouth goes numb as I say them.

"Yeah. Exactly. It was pretty much the same routine every day until these guys in suits show up and say they're shutting the place down. They don't say why, just that we're done. Treatment's over. We're all being transferred someplace else."

I try to listen carefully but it's hard because I'm so cold and I have a terrible feeling I know where this story is going. I look toward the river, glassy black dotted with the shifting lights reflected off it.

"Twenty-four hours later I'm on a bus and we're heading up the Pennsylvania Turnpike to this halfway house outside Philadelphia. We never made it."

"What happened?"

"The address they gave the bus driver. It was, like, the middle of nowhere. Cows and corn and all that. The guy thought he was lost and then . . ."

Mikey looks suddenly like a little kid trying to work up the courage to check his closet for monsters.

"You're probably not going to believe me but . . ."

He puts both hands on his head, his jaw clenched. He's

determined to get through the story even though he also looks like it's the last thing he wants to do.

"This black SUV pulls up next to us, and I hear this loud pop. I didn't know what happened. Thought maybe a tire blew out. Suddenly we're swerving all over the road. I can see the driver slumped over the wheel. The bus flips onto its side into a ditch. There's about five or six kids on the bus and a couple security escorts. I was in the backseat and I kind of hid back there because I got this really bad feeling about this, that it maybe wasn't just an accident."

He squints. Larry, the doctor who helped perform my surgeries, once told me that I squinted a lot during memory modification procedures. He said people do that when they remember bad things—to try to limit the glare of a painful memory. But you can't close your eyes to things inside your mind.

He glances up briefly and clears his throat.

"The other kids with me, they're moaning and calling for help. A couple of the guards tried to get up. I'm just real still, trying to figure out if I'm hurt and how bad. Through the back door, I watch these three guys get out of the SUV and climb up onto the side of the bus. At first I think maybe they're gonna pull us out, but then they start walking along the side of the bus and they . . ."

He's swallowing, like there's lump after lump of rock-hard emotion catching in his throat. He closes his eyes and makes his finger and thumb into a gun. He points down toward the pavement.

"They just start firing down through the windows, shooting people at point-blank range. 'Til everyone's dead."

"Except you."

"Right."

"What did you do?"

"Well, I wasn't going to stay there and wait to get shot. What am I, stupid? So I kicked open the emergency door at the back of the bus and slid out. I ran into the rows of corn. I ran hard, but this guy started chasing me, he was right on me like *that*. He takes a shot at me and then tackles me. Puts this Glock right in my face."

"And?"

He shrugs and ducks his head like *no big deal*. I can see that his skin is prickling from the cold river wind.

"I got away," he says.

"That's it? Just 'I got away'?"

"Yeah."

"How?"

"Let's just say that I'm good with my hands."

I point to the phone he's holding. "And how did you get that?"

"Took it off the guy who tried to shoot me and whose butt I subsequently kicked. Now I'm just trying to figure out what's going on. Actually, forget that. I don't even want to know anymore. I just want to go home. Assuming I've got one."

Even as he says it, I feel like some gate is dropping, separating me from him. It's not that I don't believe his story, it's not that I don't care, it's that I don't want to get involved. But I'm barely back from this battlefield myself, and I don't think I'm up for another tour of duty. It's selfish, I know it is. And yet, with Thomas missing, and with people trying to kill me, I just don't think I have the capacity to delve into this kid's situation. Not at the moment, anyway.

Mikey shifts his weight back and forth. He runs his hand over his sleek, black hair. "I know none of this is your problem . . ."

"Look, I do want to help if I can," I say. "Now's just a really bad time. But you know where I live—come look for me in a couple days."

"Yeah, sure. Assuming we both live that long," he says morosely.

I take a few steps back toward the street. Mikey's still-wet jacket lands on the ground in front of me.

"Here. Take this. Not safe walking around looking like that. Some guys are pigs."

I hesitate a moment but then pull it on. "Thanks."

"Hey," Mikey says suddenly, like something's just occurred to him. "Did you ask me about a redhead kid earlier?"

I freeze. "Yeah. That's who I need to find."

"He your boyfriend or something?"

I sigh impatiently. "Is that relevant?"

"I mean, was he at that party thing with you?"

"Yes . . ."

"I saw him get hustled off the yacht. I was watching for you to come out."

It would've been helpful if he'd mentioned this earlier, but I bite back my frustration. "So you saw the guys who grabbed him? Was it the same set of guys who threw me in the river?"

He rubs his chin. "Nah. The guys who threw you into the river were real pros. The other guys with the redhead were . . . let's just say they were a lot less impressive overall."

I pull my skirt up and start jogging back toward the yacht.

He's right behind me. "You're not gonna go looking for them on your own, are you?"

"No, I should—I'll just go to the cops and tell them what I saw—no, better yet, you can come with me and tell them what *you* saw."

"Whoa, whoa, whoa." He grabs my jacket—his jacket—and pulls me up short. "I'm not going to any cops."

"Why not?"

He's suddenly looking so jittery, for a moment I think he's going to bolt. "I just . . . Everything in my body is, like, allergic to cops. I get these feelings, you know? Not memories, but like an aftertaste, almost?"

I should keep moving. If he can't help me, if he *won't* help me, I'm not obligated to worry about him. Thomas's safety should be my priority. Second only to my own safety.

But I hear myself saying, "Yeah. I know what that's like."

"They told me that I wouldn't remember anything from my past, but sometimes I do," he says. "Did that happen to you?"

"Yeah. A bit."

He looks up at the sky. "Soon as I got here, to New York, I felt like . . . like I belonged here. You know?" He points toward the river, toward Brooklyn. "I feel like I'm so close, but I just can't get there."

I look across the river. I don't know what he sees over there, but I know how he feels while he's looking. I know that ache. I know that longing for something that you're not even sure exists.

"Okay," I say.

"Okay what?"

"I'll do what I can. You help me find my boyfriend, I'll try to help you find out where you came from."

"Really?" He looks down. "I appreciate it. It's Sarah, right? I heard your doorman call you that one day."

"I go by Angel." I shake his hand. "You up for a little search and rescue?"

He nods eagerly.

I stand there shivering, trying to think. For once, I'm tempted to try using my Velocius abilities, just to see if that'll help me come up with some plan. But I'm not even sure how to trigger Velocius. These powers seem to choose the appropriate moment, not the other way around, and though I can control them in that moment, I haven't tried actually kick-starting the process. It's like I know how to fly the plane once it's in the air, but I don't know how to take off.

"Has your boy got a phone on him?" asks Mikey.

"Yes, but he wasn't answering it, and I don't know the number now that my phone is in the river."

"Too bad. We could have tracked that phone tag."

Track the tag . . . "His ankle monitor!"

"His what?"

"He's wearing an ankle monitor. It must have a GPS tag, right? That's what they're designed for."

"An ankle monitor?" A wide, approving smile spreads over Mikey's face. "What did he do?"

"It's a really, *really* long story, but the Feds are keeping tabs on him at the moment. They'd be able to find him, right?"

"I don't think getting the Feds involved is a good idea."

"Why?"

"First, they're the same as cops, only slightly better-dressed. And second, aren't *you* supposed to have a bunch of Feds watching out for you 24/7?"

I shoot him a sharp look. "How do you know that?"

"I been following you for two weeks. I see those losers all the time. You gotta wonder, where were they when you got thrown in the river?"

That's a really good question. I reflexively search the street. There's rarely a time when I can't spot them, especially when I'm out in public. Mikey's right. Those guys who tried to drown me should never have gotten that close to me.

"If your own bodyguards suddenly vanished when they're supposed to be looking out for you, just long enough for someone to try and drown you, I got my doubts that the rest of the FBI is gonna be in your corner."

"Fair point," I acknowledge. "But if we're not going to the Feds or the cops, how am I going to find Thomas?"

He answers by waving at me to follow him. We jog a block or so, back toward the yacht, staying in the shadows until we come out near the place where I saw him earlier this evening. The whole street is blocked off with NYPD sawhorses. Half a dozen limousines are parked on each side, their drivers standing out on the sidewalk chatting among themselves.

"See that?" Mikey points toward the far end of the street, at a police cruiser with a very tired-looking cop inside. "Probably doing overtime or pulled the short straw for security duty for this fancy party," he says.

"I thought you weren't on board with asking the cops for help," I say.

An unmistakable twinkle appears in his eye. "We're not gonna ask for their help. We're gonna take it."

CHAPTER 5

The empty stalls of an outdoor fish market block our view of the yacht, but I can hear that the party is still going strong. But where we are, behind the security barricades, the only human beings in sight are the drivers of the shiny black limos.

"Every cop car has a computer in it so they can look up license plates and arrest warrants," Mikey tells me. "We just need to look up your boy's ankle monitor in the probation registry, and it'll give us his location."

"So we're somehow going to trick them into giving us that information? Or do I just saunter up and ask nicely? I mean, I assume I'm the one who's gonna have to talk to them, considering your cop allergy."

"Ha. No. Talking to the cops is not a good idea for either of us, especially you. They'd probably want to take you home, which is exactly where that Fitzgerald lady told those assassins to find you."

Again, I have to agree. I'm probably safer being MIA at the moment. "So what's your plan?"

"We need to get that cop out of that car so we can use his computer."

"Oh, is that all?"

"Yeah. You create some kind of distraction and make sure the driver gets out of the car. I'm gonna go around the block and come back from that direction. Soon as you see me coming toward you, go." He slaps me so hard on the back it makes me cough. Guess there was still river water in my lungs after all.

"Good luck."

I wait two minutes and then see Mikey come around the corner, slipping past a sawhorse and walking up the street toward me. When he gets within ten yards of the police car, I step out under the glare of the streetlight onto the sidewalk and walk as fast as my wet satin skirt will allow.

Mikey makes eye contact with me and nods.

I dart into the street in front of the cop car, then let myself go limp and fall to the pavement. The driver immediately gets out and says, "Whoa, you all right?"

Mikey dashes over to the car, opens the passenger door quietly, and slips into the front seat, staying as low as he can.

I push myself up onto my side and put one hand to my forehead. "I just got all dizzy for a second."

"Hold on. Don't try to get up. Let's get you checked out."

The cop takes a small flashlight from his belt and shines it quickly in each eye. It blinds me for a second and when I'm able to focus my eyes again, I see a second cop walking up the street holding two cups of coffee.

We weren't counting on two of them. Mikey's still inside the police car, hunched over the laptop that's mounted onto the dashboard.

"What do you got there, Jon?" the second cop calls out. "Party girl escaped from the yacht?"

I quickly stand and then pretend to lose my balance again, swaying on my feet. The second cop puts the coffees on the trunk of the car and walks toward me. As I throw in a bit of moaning for added effect, they discuss calling an ambulance.

I see Mikey pop up like a gopher inside the cop car, his eyes huge.

"Yeah. Call it in," the second cop says. "I don't want any blowback if she chokes on her own vomit. Hey, you famous or anything?"

"Me? No. I, uh . . ." I glance toward the cruiser. Now Mikey's shaking his head frantically. I think he's saying *no ambulance*.

But the cop is already reaching for the radio attached to his collar. I grab at it, like I'm flailing wildly.

"No, I'm okay! Really. I'm fine. I just need to get a cab or something." The radio comes unclipped and swings loose behind his back. "Oh, I'm so sorry!"

The second cop is now reaching for his radio. "I'll call it."

"No! Really! I can walk!"

My eyes zero in on the first cop's utility belt—specifically the small canister next to his handcuffs. Pepper spray.

The first cop says, "Dispatch standby for a—"

"I am so sorry about this," I say, right before I grab the pepper spray from his belt and blast him in the face. I try to spray the second cop too, but he ducks behind the trunk of the car before I can reach him. A second later, he steps back out in the open, gun drawn.

"Drop it," he says.

"Okay. That was really dumb of me. I'm sorry," I say, laying the pepper spray down on the street.

The first cop is really, really not happy with me, judging by the choice words he manages to choke out as he lies curled up on the ground, his hands pressed to his eyes.

And now the second cop notices Mikey inside the car. He moves the gun back and forth, alternately making me and Mikey his target. "You, out of the front seat! Hands on the top of the car! Now!"

But Mikey doesn't have time to answer before a white van plows through the sawhorses blocking the street entrance. The same white van we saw near the dock, looking for my body.

It screeches up to us, blocking the police car in, and I have to drop to the pavement and roll toward the car not to get run over. The cop hardly has any time to react before the driver leans out the window and takes a shot at me.

He misses. The cop fires at him and the driver fires back, hitting the cop.

I recognize the guy holding the gun. That jawline and pockmarked skin—he was the limo driver who took Thomas and me to the party.

He points the gun at me again.

Suddenly Mikey appears, leaping off the roof of the police car and kicking the guy's arm just as he fires.

The van slams into reverse and spins around. I run to the sidewalk as it peels away. The cop who got shot is lying on the ground, his hands across his chest. The other cop is still gagging from the pepper spray.

"Come on! Let's get out of here!" Mikey shouts at me, opening the door to the cop car.

"We're stealing a cop car? Are you insane?" Granted, I've done equally insane things—scaling construction cranes, for starters—but I thought the idea was *not* to attract the NYPD's notice.

"You see another available getaway vehicle?"

"Fine!"

I'm about to get into the cruiser when something important occurs to me.

"We can't just leave these guys here," I say. "They'll radio for backup and give our descriptions. Then every cop in the city will be after us."

"You think we should waste them?"

"What? No! I mean we should take them with us!"

I lean over the cop who's been shot. There's a big hole in the front of the cop's shirt, but no blood. Clearly he's wearing a protective vest. Still, he's doubled over in pain. Maybe the bullet broke a rib or something. Mikey joins me, swearing under his breath, and helps me hoist both cops into the car. He makes a point of collecting their guns and radios.

"What are we going to do with them?" he asks as we stuff the second cop into the backseat.

"We'll figure that out once we're out of here!"

Once both cops are in the back, Mikey jumps into the driver's seat, and I slide in next to him. After tucking one gun in his waistband and handing the other to me, he turns the key in the ignition. I immediately shove the second gun into the glove compartment.

Mikey speeds away, nearly plowing into the back of a parked limo before veering into the center of the street. Once we're past the overturned sawhorses, he experimentally flicks a few buttons till he manages to get the lights and siren going. The cars in front of us move to the side.

"Man, you didn't skimp on that pepper spray, did you?" Mikey says. "My eyes are watering so bad, I can hardly see. Shut that slider window."

He points behind us to the plastic wall that separates the front and back seats of the cruiser. There's a small port window in the center.

I look into the backseat. The pepper spray fumes have both cops nearly incapacitated. The cop who got shot has his hands on his chest and he's breathing in and out like he's running a marathon. I find a bottle of water in my door's cup holder and toss it into the lap of the cop I maced. He starts rinsing his eyes immediately.

Now I shut the port window all the way. "Thanks for stepping in back there," I say to Mikey.

"No problem. I save your life once, I save your life again, maybe eventually if we keep hanging out long enough you'll save mine. By the way, I couldn't help but notice that once again, there were no Feds swooping in to rescue you."

"Yeah, I noticed that too. And I've seen one of the guys in the van before," I say. "The one who shot at me. He was Thomas's driver when he picked me up to go to the party."

"Seriously? That's—weird."

"Weird's one way to put it."

"Bad" is another word that comes to mind. It means the people who want me dead haven't just been following me from a distance like Mikey has. At least one of them has been very, very close by.

"You think those guys are working with the ones who grabbed your boy?" Mikey asks.

"If they're not, it'd be a pretty huge coincidence that he got kidnapped and I got targeted on the same day."

That doesn't explain what these people want with either of us. Or how they even knew we were connected. Only Virgil and Mrs. Fitzgerald knew about our relationship.

Which brings us back to Mrs. Fitzgerald.

"So what now?" Mikey asks.

"We find a quiet place to dump these guys," I say. "Then once we've used the computer and ditched this car somewhere, we can call 9-1-1 and tell the NYPD where to find their officers."

"Don't be such a girl. They'll be fine."

"I *am* a girl, and that's what we're doing."

Mikey drives another few blocks, running lights with obvious relish. Eventually he pulls over in front of an old brick building with a large metal gate lowered over what looks like a garage opening.

"Where are we?"

"No idea, but it looks like a nice, out-of-the-way place to leave a couple cops."

He pops the trunk and jumps out. After a moment's hesitation, I take the gun out of the glove compartment and follow him. He's rooting around in the trunk now.

"No doubt they have bolt cutters in their bag of tricks back here. Ah, here we go. And zip ties too. It's our lucky day."

Mikey uses the bolt cutters to snap the padlock off the sliding gate. He raises the metal door, then turns back to the cruiser. Pointing his stolen gun at the cops in the backseat, he nods at me. "Open the door. We'll tie them up inside."

I open the back door and say to the cops, "Can you walk?"

Both of them nod, though the cop who got pepper sprayed is still coughing and spitting, his eyes still shut tight.

The cop who took a slug in the vest—his name tag says "J. Reitman"—starts to speak. "Why don't you—"

"No talking," Mikey barks. "Just get out."

Mikey grabs the guy by the arm, and I take the other one. We steer them into the garage. There are fence sections stacked against every wall and a bunch of blowtorches and welding masks lined up on one of the worktables.

Mikey looks around and says, "What the heck is this place?"

"Welding workshop, I guess."

Just then, Officer Reitman elbows me hard in the chin. Not a direct hit or else my teeth would be clattering all over the floor right now. I stagger a little but keep my grip on him.

Mikey fires the gun into the floor next to the cop's boot. His expression is cold and flat as sheet metal. "Next one goes in your head, you got it?"

The cop nods.

"Easy," I hiss at Mikey. "Let's just tie them up and get out of here."

"Wait." Mikey flicks the gun toward Reitman's chest. "First . . . take your boots off. Your uniform. Everything."

I shoot him a questioning look.

He leans toward me and whispers, "We need something to wear if we're gonna ride around in a police car."

"Oh, so now we're going to impersonate cops? Great."

"You can't keep wearing that wet nightgown around the city," Mikey says, meaning my ruined designer dress.

I let my shoulders drop. Which makes my dress straps fall. I hoist them back up, realizing he's got a point.

The two cops strip down to their underwear. Mikey and I hurriedly dress. Both cops are way bigger than either of us, plus their outfits are meant to accommodate bulletproof vests. I'm swimming in Officer Reitman's shirt, and even using the very last notch in his utility belt leaves his empty holster sitting so low on my hips, the whole thing could slide down any second and trip me like a lasso.

"No one is going to believe we're really cops," I say. "We're gonna look like we're dressing up for Halloween."

Mikey snaps the cop's hat in place, pulling the brim low, and loops his thumbs over his utility belt. "Then we'll have to fill in the rest of the uniform with attitude."

"You can wear all the attitude you want, but we leave the guns here," I say, leveling a nonnegotiable stare at him.

"They weren't going to listen to us unless they thought I meant business. I wouldn't have really shot them."

"Are you sure about that? You looked like you were capable of anything just then."

He glances down at the cops and then back at me, as if he's only just realized that guns can be dangerous. "I don't . . . I don't want to hurt anyone. Even a cop. I feel like . . . maybe that used to be who I am, but I don't want to be that guy anymore."

"Leave the guns here then. It'll show these guys that we aren't trying to hurt them or anybody else."

He puts the safety on his gun and hands it to me, suddenly anxious to be rid of it. I pop the bullet cartridges out of both weapons and throw them into a bucket of water near one of the welding stations. The guns themselves find a new home on a high shelf, well out of the cops' reach.

I take a quick inventory of my remaining accessories, all attached to the utility belt: pepper spray, handcuffs, a small silver whistle, and a mini flashlight. I've made do with less.

I make eye contact with Officer Reitman. His face is actually strangely calm—not afraid, not angry. Just puzzled.

"I'm really sorry about this," I say.

I reposition his name tag over the bullet hole in his shirt, and we rush out the door.

CHAPTER 6

As we head for the cruiser, I pull the police hat on, trying to summon some kind of cop-like vibe that might make me look a little less ridiculous. Mikey gets to the car first and slides in on the passenger's side. "Figured you can drive while I use the laptop."

I start the car and pull out onto the street. The car lurches forward faster than I'm expecting. I slam on the brakes. Mikey has to brace himself against the dashboard.

"You do know how to drive, don't you?"

The car jerks and comes to a hard stop as I test out the gas pedal and brakes, trying to get the feel of it. "Of course. I'm just not used to driving a car this big."

He gives me a skeptical look and then pulls on his seat belt. Once I'm cruising along relatively steadily, he says, "Your boy. Thomas? What's his last name?"

I tell him. He types it into the computer. We wait while the system processes the request. Thirty seconds pass. A minute. Finally, Mikey says, "No hits. You sure that's his real name?"

A bolt of alarm goes through me. Is it possible Thomas lied to me about his name? Why would he do that?

No.

I don't believe it.

I trust him.

"Try it again," I say and spell the name out for him.

"That's what I typed," Mikey says. "I'm telling you, it's not here."

"So this felony we just committed was all for nothing then? There's no other way to look him up?"

"Not unless you have the individual tag code."

"The tag code?"

"Yeah. The serial number on his actual ankle monitor. Don't suppose you know that?"

"NESE1798."

"Okay, that's a little weird."

"He mentioned it earlier this evening."

"You guys need to go see a movie once in a while and find something better to talk about."

I can feel the fear and tension and chaos of the evening coursing through me. It's like my adrenaline has turned to acid and it's burning from the inside. The incomprehensible chatter on the police scanner isn't helping me focus. I turn the volume all the way down, muting out the rapid-fire voices and confusing terms.

"Got it," Mikey says.

"Where is he?"

"Upper East Side. Eighty-Eighth and Second Avenue."

I exhale in relief.

Ahead, the traffic light changes to yellow and I slow down. Mikey shakes his head, leans forward, and flicks on the lights and sirens.

"No more traffic lights for us, sweetheart. Punch it."

Fifteen minutes pass with Mikey giving me turn-by-turn directions. I'm wondering when the moment will be right for me to mention that I've actually only driven a car about five times, and none of those times were at night or at a speed above twenty-five miles an hour. Virgil thinks driving is an important life skill, but I don't agree. When I was a kid, almost no one I knew had a car, and those who did seemed to spend their whole lives finding parking spots.

Thinking of my old life reminds me of those thoughts that spilled from my mind in the moments after I went into the river. I was half-remembering someone who'd been important to me, but who?

I don't have time to dwell on it right now because I need every ounce of concentration to drive. Even though the lights and sirens are fraying my already white-hot nerves, I must admit they're making it way easier to navigate city traffic. Everyone just moves out of the way so I don't have to worry about running into other vehicles.

"We're getting close. Two more blocks," Mikey finally says, and I kill the lights and sirens so that we don't tip off Thomas's captors to our approach.

"Turn right up there," Mikey says. "Sheesh, you drive like an old lady."

"Where?"

"Right here, right here! You're going past it!"

"Well, give me some more warning!"

I make a too-fast turn that throws him against his window. He looks down at the laptop screen. "Hold up! Stop!"

I slam on the brakes and everything in the car, mostly a bunch of wrappers and empty coffee cups, slides forward.

"This is the place," he says, pointing to the left side of the street.

"What is it?"

The whole building is cocooned in scaffolding, and there's a construction sign in front. In the dark, that's about as much as I can see.

"I think it's a church." As soon as he says it, I spot the very top of the steeple poking out from the metal webbing that surrounds it.

"What if they took the anklet off him and just chucked it in here?" I ask.

"If they'd done that, the database would show that the anklet had been tampered with, and the security company would put out an alert."

"What security company?"

"The police don't actually monitor these ankle transmitters— they contract out to a security company."

"How do you know so much about these things?" A little tickle of worry about Mikey makes me wonder about who he really is—or was—and where he came from.

He points to the screen. "Because when I looked up the tag number in the police probation registry, that sent me to another site with all that information. What, you don't believe me? See for yourself. The company sends the cops an alert if the ankle monitor has been cut or damaged because they assume that means the person is on the run."

"Okay." I tamp down on my suspicions and take a deep, hopeful breath.

"So it's still on him. Which means he's here."

"Or else his body's here. I suppose it's also possible they cut his leg off and just left it here."

"Thanks, that makes me feel better."

That's when I notice the white van parked at the end of the block.

I stiffen. "I don't think they just left pieces of him here. I think they're inside with him." Mikey raises his eyebrows, confused. I point toward the van. "Does that look familiar?"

"Sure does."

"Come on."

Mikey and I get out of the cruiser and stare up at the dark church. Mikey says quietly, "So how do we get in?"

I scan the facade, looking for options. "Well, I think we should split up. Thomas could be anywhere in the building, and we can cover more ground separately. Plus, if one of us runs into trouble . . ."

"The other one might get away?"

"Or, you know, find a way to help."

I spot what seems to be a set of blocked-off stairs on the side of the church. The steps lead down—maybe to a basement? "How about you try heading down there?" I say, pointing.

"Where are you going to go?"

"I guess I'll go—" I crane my neck and look toward the scaffolding encasing the steeple. "Up."

CHAPTER 7

I haven't done any serious climbing since I returned to New York. It took me a long time to recover from my injuries after Virgil got me out of the hospital. Fun fact: my Velocius abilities might speed up my thinking and even sustain me when I'm on the brink of death, but they do nothing for healing. I still heal at the same rate as everyone else: slowly.

I'm about to find out if my muscles have healed enough to get me thirty feet off the ground.

I put my hands around the scaffolding bars, find a foothold, and start pulling myself up. The steeple is six stories up. In the old days, it would have taken me only a few minutes to reach it, but my limbs feel heavy and clumsy and my hands hurt like crazy. All my climbing calluses are gone. I grunt and grope, ten feet up, fifteen. And as I climb, I start to wonder . . . will this trigger a memory?

I hope not. I don't need the distraction.

For a while, right after I returned to New York, memories were coming back to me on almost a daily basis. A lot of what I remembered was about my mom. Simple snippets, like sitting next to her on the bus. She would let me stand on the seat and pull the cord to signal for our stop. I loved doing that. I loved *remembering* doing that. I'd found these little gifts of memory when I least expected it, like pennies on the sidewalk, and I felt lucky to stumble across them.

But eventually my steady flow of returning memories became more of a trickle. I hit a plateau and couldn't remember more. Until one day, I was walking by this playground just as it was getting dark and on a whim, I grabbed hold of the monkey bars. As I swung from one side to the other, I got this glimpse of my old life. I was talking to someone, arguing with someone about whether it was possible to climb up a crane tower.

That's how I realized: When I climbed, things came back to me. Something about the motion would jar things loose. I think that's why I was able to remember so much back in the hospital.

Twenty feet up the side of this building, my hunch gets confirmed. I'm suddenly slammed with a memory. And not a good one . . .

I'm in the police station, just minutes after I attacked Evangeline Hodges— after she told me what she did to my mother.

I'm lying on my side, my cheek pressed to a floor coated with hair and cigarette ash. My hands are still shackled to my waist. The place where they put the taser against my body burns and itches. Hodges is sitting in a chair, using one arm to support the opposite elbow. I hear one of the cops say something about her collarbone being broken. He tries to console her: "At least that reward you offered did the job."

"The person who called in the tip didn't ask for the reward," another cop replies.

"Good," Hodges says. "Saves my employer a bit of money at least."

"Can't imagine passing up a hundred thousand dollars," the cop replies. "Whoever turned her in must have really hated her."

The paramedics arrive. I don't know how much time passes. It's like I'm watching this happening to someone else.

Maybe I'm already dead. I hope so.

They lift me up. I feel the straps tightening around my body as they secure me to a gurney.

Hodges leans over me—gives me one last, triumphant look. "You're about to take a very long trip to a very cold place."

I won't let myself cry.

In the ambulance, though, after they load me in and close the doors, I can't hold back the tears anymore. They pool within my eye sockets, and somewhere down the road, the ambulance hits a pothole, jostling me, and the pools overflow.

The only way I can keep it together is to focus on one thing: somebody I trusted turned me in, and there's only one person it could be.

A flock of pigeons bursts out of the steeple and flies straight into my face. One of my hands slips off the scaffolding planks, and both my feet follow suit. I drop and swing free by one hand before managing to loop my leg around one of the poles and then finally balance my weight on a sliver of planking.

I didn't come this far to be killed by a bunch of birds.

I hoist one aching leg over the stone wall surrounding the belfry. Inside the steeple there's no actual bell, just a makeshift floor of loose plywood sheets covering the rafters. I test the nearest board before putting my full weight on it. Then I take a few light steps, avoiding the worst of the pigeon poop and using whatever I can as a handhold in case the wood gives out beneath me.

I slide over to the door built into the belfry wall.

Locked. Of course.

But I notice a slight gap in the boards beneath my feet. I pry up a slab of wood, trying to be as quiet as possible. Below me, I see a single point of light moving back and forth. It's got to be a flashlight. I quietly slip down through the opening and into the rafters, trying to get a better look. It's hard to see anything because the inside of the church is filled with as much scaffolding as the outside, with canvas sheets draped here and there to protect the murals on the walls.

I drop down, using the interior scaffolding like stairs until I come to a balcony that probably housed an organ at one point. It's very Phantom of the Opera up here. At the end of the corridor there's a door leading to a staircase. I come out into the mezzanine at the back of the church. Someone is speaking angrily in a language I don't recognize. As I peek over the railing, I see a flash of red—the top of Thomas's head.

He's on the ground floor, tied to a chair. Standing in front of him are three men in dark suits, just like the security guard described. One of those men is preparing a syringe.

Thomas is struggling, but they've got him lashed so tightly that there's not much point. The man with the syringe ties off the veins in Thomas's arm, taps lightly to pick a vein, and injects him.

Thomas screams in pain. I fight the urge get down there as fast as I can. Those guys have guns and I don't. I can't let them hear me coming. I need to assess the situation before I make a move.

"What was that? What did you just put in me?" Thomas says through clenched teeth.

The guy slaps Thomas on the side of the head and holds a small metal object in front of Thomas's nose. Now he speaks in English. "You see this? This is the key to your future. You bring us what we want, we give you what you need."

Suddenly there's a rustling movement off to the side. With a boom, a twenty-foot section of the scaffolding topples over onto the nearby pews. Dust rises, and pieces of pipe and plastic sheeting continue to rain down for another few seconds. One of the guys raises his gun toward the heap of broken scaffolding, and another pans his flashlight over the area.

The flashlight beam lands on the name tag of a stolen NYPD uniform as Mikey steps out from behind the fallen scaffolding.

Mikey wasn't kidding about being good with his hands. He lays one guy out with one punch and then catches another guy right in the face with a second strike.

Now's my chance to move. I slip down through an opening in the floor. Nearby I spot an unused piece of scaffolding pipe, maybe four feet long, lying against the wall. I grab it and move toward the front of the church.

The guy who just injected Thomas is backing away from Mikey, his back to me. He snatches a gun out of his belt. "Don't come any closer!" he shouts at Mikey.

I smack him across the back with the pipe.

When he hits the floor, Mikey kicks him in the gut just to make sure he stays down.

Meanwhile I kneel in front of Thomas. He doesn't smile when he sees me. In fact his face practically collapses.

"Angel?" He shakes his head. "You're not supposed to be here."

CHAPTER 8

This wasn't quite the welcome I was expecting.

I get to work untying Thomas. "Are you okay?"

"Uh . . . yeah. Hey, can you grab that key on the floor?"

He points to a small object lying a few feet away, near the base of a column. "I need that. Wait, first kiss me."

I do.

"Okay, now get the key."

The key is attached to a little red barrel with a number embossed on the side. It looks like the key to a locker.

I look over at the men on the floor. They all seem to be out cold. Mikey pokes one of them with his boot and gets no reaction.

"What did they just do to you?" I say. "Who are these guys?"

"Let's get out of here first. Why are you wearing a police uniform? And who's this guy?"

"What makes you think I'm not V. Abrams, NYPD?" says Mikey, pointing to his name tag.

Thomas looks Mikey up and down. He takes in the cuts and

bruises on Mikey's face. The hair. The ill-fitting uniform. The fact that he's wearing his police hat like it's a beret, sort of cocked to one side.

I step in before he can say anything offensive. "Thomas, meet Mikey." I lean in close to Thomas and whisper, "He's like me."

"He was at the hospital with you?"

"No, a different hospital apparently. He can't remember a lot of his past and someone tried to kill him a couple weeks ago."

"Great. A test-subject class reunion. How did you find him?"

"He found me. When you disappeared, I went looking for you and nearly ended up dead in the river. He pulled me out."

"You fell into the river?"

"I didn't fall. Someone pushed me."

"Who?"

"Don't know," I say. "Didn't see who it was."

"Where was your security detail? Why didn't the Feds protect you?"

"They seem to have conveniently disappeared at the exact moment I actually needed protection."

He shakes his head, looking half tired, half furious. "That doesn't make any sense . . ."

"Add it to the list."

As soon as I finally get all the duct tape off his ankles and wrists, I want to hold him and tell him that I'm so glad he's all right. But he immediately pulls his arm close to his body and rocks back and forth on the chair.

"What was that stuff they put in you?" I say.

"Whatever it is, it hurts like crazy. I felt that stuff go all the way up to here." He puts his hand over his heart. "And now my whole arm is burning. But they said there's an antidote. They've got it stored in a locker somewhere. That's what the key's for."

"Antidote?"

"Yeah."

"You only need antidotes for poison."

Thomas takes a deep breath. "It's not necessarily poison poison. I mean, I don't think it's lethal. I think it's . . . going to mess with my brain somehow."

I get so mad I have trouble getting my hands to work. They instinctively clench into fists.

"Thomas, I'm so—"

"It's not your fault," he cuts me off. "All this is something to do with 8-Bit. Not you, okay?"

I wasn't expecting Thomas's dead biological father to factor into any of this. "Are you sure?"

"Yes, I'm sure. 8-Bit was working on a project for these guys before he died, and he never delivered."

"The project 8-Bit was working on before he died was Velocius," I say.

"It can't be that," Thomas says.

"Why not?"

"Because these guys are low-budget mooks. If someone was after Velocius data, they would've sent someone a heck of a lot classier. And besides, there is no Velocius data anymore. It's all gone."

"So we were told," I say, looking over at Mikey—living proof that there's a lot about these programs that we still don't know.

"No, it's gone," Thomas says. "Not that I can convince the Feds of that. If I could, they wouldn't keep—"

He stops himself and looks down, still clutching his arm, though the pain that crosses his face might be there for a different reason.

"Wouldn't keep what?" I say. "Tell me or I'll tie you back up."

He rubs the place on his arm where he got injected. "They keep hounding me, asking me if 8-Bit had some secret backup data stored somewhere, pressuring me to give it to them."

"Pressuring you how?"

"You know, threatening me with eternal house arrest and endless probation and no sprinkles on my ice cream and . . ." He bites his split lip. "Never seeing you ever again."

"Is that why your plea deal got delayed? The Feds think you've got some secret stash of Velocius files that you're hiding from them?"

"It's not that wild of an accusation," he says. "They knew how 8-Bit worked. He kept backup files on every job he did. He always wanted to have some dirt on the guys he worked for. You work with scum, you need a way to protect yourself when they inevitably turn on you."

"But you don't, right? You don't have anything."

"Of course I don't," he says. "And I've been telling the Feds that, but they won't let up. They say they've got evidence that someone uploaded some data via satellite link a few hours before you were rescued—"

I cut him off. "You're just telling me this now?"

"My lawyer told me that the Feds were lying, just playing some last-minute game, on the off chance that I'd actually cough something up."

I grit my teeth. "Okay, we can talk about that later. For now let's focus on getting help."

"From whom?"

I instinctively touch my watch. But of course I can't use that. Not if Mrs. Fitzgerald is working against me. "Well, these guys injected you with an unknown substance, so a hospital might be a good start."

"If we do that, my FBI buddies will be swarming my hospital bed in no time. And if the Feds find out these guys kidnapped me, they'll see that as proof that I've been holding out, that I've got something 8-Bit tried to keep from them. Which means I'm never gonna get rid of them. Once I turn eighteen, they might even go from threatening me to actually throwing me in jail."

"But, Thomas . . ." I look down at the puncture mark in his arm. "You might need medical help."

"It could just be a bluff," he says, rolling his sleeve back down and buttoning his cuff. He grabs his tuxedo jacket off the back of the chair and looks around the floor for something. "Dang. I lost my bow tie."

"What if it's not a bluff, though?"

"Look. If it were a poison, wouldn't I start feeling sick?"

"Didn't you just say you had a horrible burning sensation from your elbow to your heart?"

"Yeah, but other than that, I feel totally fine," he says, buttoning his shirt cuffs. "I'll be okay. Let's just get out of here and pretend this whole situation never happened. No need to overthink it."

This sends a pang of anxiety through me. Thomas overthinks everything. He is not the kind of guy who casually dismisses a mystery like this. He doesn't shrug and say oh, well. He always wants to find the answers.

Suddenly one of the kidnappers' phones starts ringing.

"Maybe one of us should answer that," I say. "Maybe we can find out who these guys are."

"I told you," Thomas says. "It doesn't matter. Just leave it."

He tries to pull me toward the door but I stand my ground.

Meanwhile Mikey pats down the unconscious kidnappers and finds the phone in the inner pocket of one guy's suit coat. "How do you say hello in Russian or whatever?"

"I think they were actually Czech," Thomas says. "So I doubt you can pull this off . . ."

"If whoever it is starts speaking anything other than English, then just grunt or something," I cut in. "You seem like an accomplished grunter."

Mikey puts the phone to his ear, presses the button to answer, and then listens. His steely expression doesn't change at all, though he nods and makes a few sounds like mmmm and tchah.

I hate being in limbo like this, not knowing what's going on or what to do next—while Mikey seems thoroughly, infuriatingly in control of the situation. I literally climb the wall for a minute, just to burn off some of my nervous energy, until Mikey finally ends the call. He tosses the phone onto the floor and then steps on it. The sound of the glass crunching beneath his boot turns my stomach for some reason.

"Well?" I say a little more sharply than I mean to.

"The good news is the dude spoke English. He said 'the boss' was expecting results soon and then he called me a couple names. Apparently this guy," Mikey kicks the guy he took the phone from, "hasn't got much brain power and needs to be reminded that he's not gonna get paid unless he finishes the job."

"What else did he say?" Thomas asks.

"Something about eight pieces."

"Was it 8-Bit?" I say.

"Yeah. That's it!"

Thomas and I look at each other. I'm fighting off swells of dread, but Thomas looks almost relieved somehow.

Mikey gives a big smile. He points to the small locker key in Thomas's hand.

"Most important: I found out where that belongs. But the place is not gonna be easy to find."

CHAPTER 9

Thomas stares down at the key in the center of his palm and then makes a fist around it.

"A bowling alley?" he says. "Are you sure?"

"Yep," Mikey answers.

"Repeat the guy's exact words," Thomas says.

I don't understand why he's grilling Mikey on this point, but Mikey reluctantly concedes. "Well, okay, he didn't say it was a bowling alley, but I could tell from the background noise that that's where he was calling from. I could hear the balls rolling and that sound of pins knocking over, you know? It's a distinct sound." He looks at me. "I used to play all the time. I think."

I see Thomas wince in pain again. Time to get moving.

We head toward the door that Mikey came through at the side of the church. As we weave through the scaffolding blocking off the front of the church, Mikey says, "So, you got some ideas about where we should go?"

"We?" Thomas says, turning around to look at Mikey. "I'm not sure we need you at this point. How about we find a place to drop you off?"

"But . . . I can't remember anything, and I'm hoping she'll help me," Mikey says, suddenly sounding vulnerable again.

"Yeah, that's very sad and all, but I'm not sure that you bring anything to the proceedings."

Mikey shrugs. "I'm good with my hands. I could help you, maybe?"

"I don't need someone who's good with his hands. I need someone who's good with his brain, and yours seems to have a lot of missing pieces right now. Sorry, but we don't have time to babysit you."

"Thomas," I say as we jog down the stone steps. "Hold on." While Thomas is right about Mikey—we don't know anything about him and this is a bad time to be taking chances—Mikey has not been without his uses. He's the biggest reason I found Thomas at all . . . and the only reason I'm not currently sitting at the bottom of the river with an anchor around my neck.

"We can't afford to 'hold on.' Who even is this kid? How do you know he's not the one who chucked you in the water to begin with?"

Mikey looks at me, half in panic and half in outrage. "I didn't! Tell him!"

I put my hand up, hoping I can calm things down, and say to Thomas, "I understand your concern, but if he threw me in, why did he fish me back out?"

"I don't know. I don't know what angle he's working, where he came from, or who he's working for," Thomas says.

"I'm not working for anybody! And I didn't throw her in the water. I was just following her because I wanted to talk!"

"I think we should keep him," I say.

"Angel! He's not a stray dog."

"No, actually, that's exactly what he is. It's what I once was to you, Thomas. And you let me follow you to safety."

"Okay, true, but you were a cute stray dog. This guy, not so much."

"Hey! I'm right here, you know!"

"It's just for now," I tell Thomas. "If he does give us any reason to doubt him, he leaves. Simple as that. Agreed?"

By now we've reached the police car. Given that Mikey and I are dressed as cops and Thomas is in a tuxedo, it's pretty clear that Thomas should be the perp sitting in the backseat, but when Mikey opens the front passenger door of the police car, Thomas's eyes fasten on the computer.

He points at Mikey. "You, stand back. I need to get my hands on this baby right now."

"Your girlfriend?"

"He's talking about the computer," I clarify.

Thomas is already sliding into the front seat. "What is that awful smell?"

"Could be pepper spray," I say.

"Pepper spray?"

"You weren't the only one having some fun with new friends tonight," I say.

Mikey opens the passenger door to get in.

"Hold up," says Thomas. "Don't get too comfortable. I think we need to ditch this ride and find a new one."

"Aw, no, not the cruiser!" Mikey whines.

Thomas waves his hand toward Mikey like he's swatting a fly. "At some point, the police are going to figure out that you've got this car and cut the engine remotely."

"They can do that?" Mikey says.

"Yes, they can do that."

"Then how about we take our friends' van?" Mikey says, dangling a set of keys from his finger.

"Where did you get those?" I ask.

"Off that guy I punched. Figured we didn't want them following us if they managed to scrape themselves up off the floor."

I take the keys from Mikey, smiling at Thomas. "See? Already earning his keep."

Thomas grunts.

Mikey and I head toward the van, but Thomas stays behind in the cruiser. I double back and see that his head is ducked low, practically under the dashboard.

"What are you doing now?" I ask him.

"We're leaving the car but taking the laptop," he says, unbolting the computer from its mount on the dashboard.

Just as we're about to get into the van, Thomas stops and looks at me. Well, specifically at my chest.

"There's a bullet hole in your shirt," he says.

I realize the officer's name tag must have fallen off at some point while I was climbing up to the church steeple. Or back down from it.

"Why is there a bullet hole in your shirt?" Thomas asks, a false calm settling over him.

Mikey shakes his head like this is the dumbest question ever. "Because people shot at us? And at the cops we were with?"

"Whoa, whoa, whoa. Someone shot at you?" Thomas says.

"Yeah. Guess I forgot about that part too," I say. "They were in a van just like this one, actually, and probably working with your kidnappers. Trying to keep me from finding you, I guess."

"Angel, your standards for what's worth mentioning need some serious adjustment," Thomas says.

"I will for sure let you know next time someone shoots at us."

I open the van's back doors, thinking I'll hop in the back and let Mikey drive, but Thomas jumps in ahead of me and says, "Mikey, come here a minute. I want to show you something."

Mikey gets in and follows Thomas. Thomas kneels, sets the laptop down, and points to something on the floor. "Huh. What do you think that is?"

There's some kind of ring welded into the floor, maybe something you'd use to secure a rope. Mikey looks down at it and as he does, Thomas slaps half a pair of handcuffs onto his wrist. He snaps the other side onto the mysterious floor ring.

"Hey! What are you doing?" Mikey shouts. "Get this thing off me!"

"Just a little precaution for now. Behave and I'll set you free." Thomas picks up the laptop and heads to the front of the van, ignoring a now-struggling Mikey. I look down and notice that the handcuffs Thomas took were from my belt. His sleight-of-hand game is strong as ever.

"Angel!" Thomas calls. "You gonna drive this thing or what?"

Once we're all inside the van and back on the street, I start missing the police car right away. The car was hard enough to handle. This feels like a double-decker bus.

Thomas starts busily tapping away on the laptop like a very purposeful beaver.

"What are you doing?" I ask him.

"I'm going to run the license plate for this van on the cops' database. We'll see where they rented it from and then search for any bowling alleys nearby."

"Hey, that's pretty smart," Mikey says.

If he's offended that Thomas has handcuffed him to the floor of the vehicle, Mikey doesn't show it. He just sits cross-legged, takes his police hat off and begins buffing the silver badge above the brim with his cuff.

There's almost no traffic at this time of night. Just a few taxi-cabs cruising along with their "On Duty" lights turned off. I feel a little calmer about driving now that there aren't as many cars on the street. With the windows down, the rushing air brings a little much-needed calm, and I'm trying to read something hopeful into the silence.

"So we're looking for a bowling alley," I say, far too cheer-fully. "Easy, right? How many bowling alleys can there possibly be in New York City? I mean, who bowls anymore? Other than Mikey, apparently."

"Even if there are only a few," Thomas says, "that's still a lot of lockers to go through in twenty-four hours."

I hit the brakes hard. "Twenty-four hours? Why twenty-four hours?"

Thomas winces. "Uh, yeah. That's how much time he said I had to give them what they want, otherwise—" He points to the crook of his arm. "Whatever's going to happen to me will happen."

"You didn't think to mention that until now?"

"I've been distracted."

"You've been distracted? We've all been distracted, Thomas. Some of us have even been distracted by bullets. But considering that getting that antidote is our top priority right now, we kind of need to have all the relevant information on the table."

"And not to put an even bigger damper on things," Mikey calls from the back, "but that antidote could be even harder to find than you think. I mean, how do we know this bowling alley locker is even in New York?"

Thomas rolls his eyes. "If they're giving me one day to come up with the info they want in exchange for the antidote, I assume the locker is somewhere in this city and not Tokyo."

"Unless they were lying," Mikey says.

"Yeah, Mikey. I don't need to be reminded that guys kidnapping me and blackmailing me are also potentially liars, okay? They also probably don't floss or recycle either. Now shut it so I can concentrate."

A few minutes later, Thomas pumps his fist in front of the screen. "Our Czech friends rented their van from a place in Coney Island, and guess what's three blocks away from that rental place? A bowling alley."

"Excellent."

"Coney Island," Mikey says in this dreamy, wistful sort of voice. "I feel like maybe I've been there."

I glance over my shoulder at him, and the expression on his face makes me think he's more confused than ever. I understand that feeling all too well. Pulling a memory free from all the jagged bits of chaos surrounding it is hard enough. And if you do finally manage to remember something, chances are good it's going to hurt like crazy.

I'm so distracted by this train of thought that I nearly clip the back of a slow-moving off-duty bus. I straighten us out, oversteer toward a fire hydrant, and then swerve back to the center.

"Careful, Angel. We don't want to get pulled over for reckless driving."

"If we were still driving that police car," Mikey grumbles, "we wouldn't need to worry about getting pulled over by a police car."

Thomas ignores him. "By the way, how did you find me? Did you follow those guys who nabbed me?"

"No. We used the police computer to trace the signal from your anklet."

"Brilliant," Thomas says. His brow furrows. "But problematic. I need to get this thing off my ankle right now. No doubt my parents have noticed that I'm missing, and it won't be long before they go to the Feds and tell them I've done a runner." He scowls down at the anklet. "I know it's tamper resistant because, believe me, I've tampered with it. Maybe if I look in the security company's database, I can find the code to unlock it."

"Use the transmitter's serial number," I say. "That's how we found it."

Thomas immediately gets to work. I'm about to mention that his name wasn't in the database when we looked for it, but Thomas suddenly looks so intensely focused that I'm not sure he'd even hear me.

He types like he's playing the piano, his fingers dancing and then, a moment later, pounding as if the tempo had changed.

At last he looks up and says triumphantly, "Thar she blows."

"We supposed to know what that means?" asks Mikey.

"It's, you know, a whaling term."

"A whaling term?" In the rearview mirror I see Mikey shake his head at me. "This is the guy you date?"

"Shut up back there," Thomas says just as the ankle transmitter gives three long beeps and releases. He pulls it off. "Ahhh, I'll miss you, Nessie." He lowers his window a little more, but just as he's about to toss the monitor out, he pauses. "Hold on! Pull over right there."

"Why? What's the matter?"

"I just got a better idea about how to dispose of dear old Nessie."

Thomas jumps out of the car and runs up the sidewalk to the only restaurant that seems to be open at this time of night. He attaches the transmitter to the seat post of a delivery bike parked in front of a Chinese take-out place and then runs back to the car.

"That ought to keep them busy if they come looking for me. You've heard of a wild goose chase? This will be a Peking Duck chase. Let's go. We've got a bowling alley to infiltrate."

Fifteen minutes later I'm caught in the middle of the World War III of arguments about which route to take to Coney Island. Thomas says to take the FDR Drive down the east side of Manhattan, and Mikey is insisting on the Williamsburg Bridge to the Brooklyn-Queens Expressway.

"I'm telling you, the FDR is the totally wrong way to go," Mikey says. "We'll be stuck there for hours."

"And I'm telling you, I'm not taking driving directions from a guy who has no memory," Thomas says.

"Guys! Just plug the address into the computer, and we'll take whatever route it suggests."

When the computer's directions match Thomas's suggestion, the van quiets down, aside from Mikey grumbling, "We'll be in trouble if there's night construction . . ."

Sure enough, as we approach the on-ramp, we can see that it's already backed up. There are orange traffic cones and a flag man funneling all the cars onto the shoulder.

"Fine. I'll just find another way," Thomas concedes. He types and types and then lets out a frustrated growl.

"Just tell me where I'm supposed to turn!" I say.

Through clenched teeth Thomas says, "Take the Manhattan Bridge to the BQE."

The tires squeal as I abruptly do a U-turn to avoid hitting the lane divider, but we make it.

Once we're on the other side of the river, we head south, paralleling the East River. We can now see the Manhattan skyline. I've always thought the city is twice as beautiful at night even if it is a whole lot more dangerous.

The quiet inside the van lasts all of two more minutes before Mikey clears his throat and says, "You know, I been thinking . . ."

"Have you now?" Thomas says.

Undeterred, Mikey aims his question at me. "That guy you recognized, the one who took a shot at us? He's the one who drove you to that party, right?"

"Yeah," I say.

"And if he's working with these guys who took Big Red here—"

"Never call me that again," Thomas says.

Mikey ignores him. "I mean, here he's got the two of you in the backseat, right? Why not plug you both in the head right then and be done with it?"

"They couldn't just kill Thomas if they want something and need him to find it," I point out.

"Okay, so that makes sense of why they didn't shoot him, but what about you?"

"I don't know, Mikey. Maybe they wanted to put pressure on Thomas by threatening me?"

"I don't think so. They hurled you into a river, and then they tried to shoot you. Both looked like straight-up attempts to bump you off, if you ask me. It'd be one thing if your boy was standing there and watching the whole thing, but it's not like he even knew what was happening."

"Stop distracting Angel while she's driving," says Thomas. "I didn't come all this way to die just because she can't stay in her lane."

It's true that this highway demands my complete attention. Why are these lanes so narrow? Why is everyone driving so fast? If I hold onto this steering wheel any tighter, I'm going to cut off all blood flow to my fingers. I'd rather be climbing cranes. I'd feel a lot safer.

In the distance, I can now see the lights of the Verrazano Bridge stretching from Brooklyn to Staten Island. The river is just an indistinguishable smudge of black against the night.

Mikey only manages to stay silent for a couple seconds. "And on top of everything else, there's the Fitzgerald lady . . ."

That gets Thomas's attention. "How does Mikey know about Mrs. Fitzgerald?" he asks me.

I explain that Mikey was able to track me down in the first place because the guy who tried to kill him had my address in his phone—and that Mrs. Fitzgerald had sent him that address.

Thomas slams his palm on the dashboard. "I told you she was a black hat! But noooo, you wouldn't believe me."

"Because until now there was no evidence that I should suspect her of anything—"

"I. TOLD. YOU."

"No need to rub it in."

I take the on-ramp onto the Belt Parkway and realize at the last moment that I'm about to turn the wrong way on a one-way street. I have to swerve. Thomas braces himself, sticking his hands out onto the dashboard.

Mikey is thrown around in the back of the van. "Geez! Careful!"

"I never asked to be the driver!" I shout. "I hate driving!"

Thomas smiles for the first time since the party. I'm not pleased that it's at my expense, though. "Don't you dare laugh at me!"

"My tough chica who climbs tower cranes is afraid to drive? That's adorable."

"Have you ever driven in New York City?"

"Nope. Seems utterly terrifying, but you're doing great. Just proves that the only way to handle fear is to focus on what needs to be done. I learned that from watching you."

I feel like I used to feel when I reached the top of every building, of every crane. It's a thrill so deep and resonant, I'm momentarily invincible.

"I'd be tempted to kiss you now," he says, "but given your bad driving skills, I don't want you to crash. I'm imagining kissing you, though, and we're really enjoying it."

I smile, but something nags at me. His name. His name wasn't in the system.

Why?

This one little detail shouldn't be bothering me so much.

There could be a perfectly good explanation for why his name wasn't listed. Why do I assume he's holding something back, and if he is, why does it bother me so much?

I trust him completely.

Don't I?

"You guys," says Mikey, "I'm not feeling so great all of a sudden . . ."

I ignore him and focus on Thomas. "Thomas, what is going on?"

"I don't know yet."

"But you have a theory."

"I might have half a theory."

Suddenly Mikey starts yanking hard on the handcuffs, so hard I'm worried he's going to pull his arm out of its socket. "Get me out of here! I feel like I'm in a cell!"

"Just chill, dude," Thomas says.

But I can see the panic in Mikey's eyes. "Thomas, I don't think he's messing around. Maybe something's coming back to him. Some traumatic memory."

Mikey is now going berserk. He kicks the back doors of the van and manages to get the latch on the door open with his foot. One more kick and the doors are going to fly open.

"Let me out!" Mikey shouts. "Let me out right now! I have to get out of this van!"

I abruptly pull over onto the narrow shoulder. Thomas runs

around and opens both back doors just in time for Mikey to lean out and throw up onto the bumper.

I get out and stand with Thomas, looking down at Mikey as his body convulses repeatedly. I'm trying to get near him to unlock the handcuffs but he keeps shaking his head back and forth like a wet dog.

After another minute, he starts to calm down, and I'm able to get the cuffs off him. He climbs out of the van and puts his hands on the highway guardrail, taking deep breaths.

"Are you all right?" I ask.

He turns and watches the cars rushing past and then, with no warning, bolts out into the oncoming traffic.

Cars honk and swerve wildly to avoid him. He just stands in the middle of the road, staring straight at the headlights bearing down on him.

Thomas swears loudly. "What's his deal?"

"I have no idea! I've known him for all of three hours!"

Mikey wipes his mouth with the back of his hand. He's still standing, oblivious to the danger he's in.

As soon as there's an opening for me, I run into the road and yank him by the arm back to the car. "Are you trying to kill yourself?"

"Kill myself?" he repeats.

I can't tell if he finds the idea frightening or attractive. His closes his eyes and rubs a spot behind his ear.

"I'm okay," he says. "Just need to clear my head a little, you know? I get these headaches when I remember stuff. I get this pain right here."

He again massages behind his left ear. Then he starts

scratching so hard, I'm worried he's going to draw blood. I take his hand away from his head. "What did you remember a minute ago?"

He glances into the back of the van. His face looks like he's suddenly slammed into a brick wall.

"I remembered being in the backseat of a van once before. Kind of freaked me out for a second. It was like I was back there again, but part of me knew I couldn't be, because I'm here with you guys. It was like I was having a nightmare and trying to wake up but I couldn't."

"When you say you felt like you were 'back there' . . . back where, exactly?" I ask as gently as I can.

"I don't know," he says, now looking at the underside of the nearby bridge. He watches the water flowing around the support beams that disappear into the deep currents below it. After a moment he turns his face toward the bay. "But I feel like we're headed in the right direction."

I glance at Thomas, then back at Mikey. "Can I just look at something on your scalp for a second?"

Mikey tips his head forward. I touch the place behind his ear where he was just pointing and he winces. Underneath his hair, I feel a hard bump. I take out the small flashlight attached to my belt and look more closely. There's something round, about the size of a dime, underneath the skin. I hand the flashlight to Thomas so I can run my fingers around the crown of Mikey's head. Thomas knows exactly what I'm looking for and holds the flashlight up for me. In a moment, I count up five small lumps. There's a stitch still poking up through one of them. When I touch it, Mikey jumps.

I motion for Thomas to shine the flashlight toward Mikey's face. Mikey's pupils instantly contract to pinpoints as the light shines in his eyes. I push his hair back away from his forehead and see two incision scars similar to my own, where the halo inserts once were. I hadn't noticed them among the other cuts on Mikey's face.

"I don't understand what's going on," Mikey says in whisper.

Thomas helps Mikey into the front seat, returns his stolen police hat to him, and claps him on the shoulder. "Let's hope it's nothing a little bowling won't cure."

CHAPTER 10

We arrive in Coney Island twenty minutes later, and we know we've found the right place because the twenty-foot-tall sign in the shape of two bowling pins salsa dancing is visible from three blocks away.

"Stop right here," Thomas says suddenly.

I pull over and Thomas hops out and runs up the block. He stops in front of a guy with a sidewalk cart who's closing up shop for the night. Five minutes later, Thomas returns with two huge hoodies that say CONEY ISLAND in sequined letters across the front. He gets back into the van and hands one to me and one to Mikey.

"I'm sorry, but you two would look more like cops if you weren't actually dressed as cops. That's how unconvincing you are in those uniforms."

"I'm not changing," Mikey says, tossing the hoodie back into the front seat.

"Fine," Thomas says, throwing the hoodie back at him and

hitting him in the face with it. "Then you'll stay in the van when we go into the bowling alley."

"I don't have to listen to you."

"You do if you want our—Angel's—help."

Mikey looks at me hopefully, and I say, "I'm with Thomas on this one, Mikey."

I pull the hoodie on over my stolen uniform shirt and ditch my hat. A quick look in the rearview mirror has me appreciating the staying power of the waterproof mascara the stylist at Blake & Mikels used on me.

The bowling alley is just a few blocks farther up, across the street from Luna Park, home of the oldest roller coaster in New York—the Cyclone—which it seems very proud about. As if age is a big selling point for amusement park rides.

As we roll past the bowling alley entrance, we notice a man sitting on a bar stool near the front door. His muscled arms are crossed over an even more muscled chest, and he's got a scowl that would scare off a pack of wild dogs.

"How are we going to get past him?" I ask.

"We'll figure something out," Thomas says.

I look over at Mikey. His face is relaxed and hopeful as he looks at the lights from all the signs in and around Luna Park. We hear people laughing and whooping as the Cyclone starts climbing up and then, all at once, shrieking as it plunges down the track.

"You recognize this place, Mikey?" I say.

"Maybe. I don't know. It feels like . . . yeah, I think I've been here before. Like a long time ago. When I was little. I went on that one." Mikey points toward a tall tower called the Banshee. It must have shut down for the night because its lights are turned off. It looks like one of those free-fall rides where they strap you into the seat and then drop you a couple stories before putting the brakes on. As someone who's actually fallen from great heights, I don't get the appeal.

"Forget the Cyclone," he goes on. "The Banshee was the scariest. We went on it five times in a row."

"Who's 'we'?" I ask.

"That part I'm not sure about. Might have been a friend. Or a cousin. I think I'd remember if it was a brother. I don't think I had a brother."

Thomas's eyebrows go up at this comment, but I'm not sure why. He starts typing on the laptop again.

"I could go for some food," Mikey adds. "I'm starving."

I suddenly wonder how Mikey has been getting along the last few weeks. How he's been eating, where he's been sleeping.

"You sure you should eat?" Thomas says. "You puked barely half an hour ago."

"Exactly. My stomach is now empty, which is why I'm hungry."

"Yeah, well, first we have to find the locker that goes with this key," Thomas says.

By now I'm several blocks away from the bowling alley. I circle back around and pull over to the side of the road next to an alley blocked off with a post and chain.

"So are we going in or what?" I ask.

"I've got a better idea," Thomas says. He spins around and shoots Mikey a get lost sort of look. "Why doesn't Mikey see if there's a back door or delivery entrance or something? Some way for us to slip inside unnoticed."

"Ah, gotcha, dude," says Mikey, slapping Thomas on the shoulder. "Three's a crowd. You two enjoy some alone time. I got this."

"Put the hoodie on first," Thomas says. "Judging by the clientele going in and out of this place, the shadier you look, the more you'll fit in."

"But if they think I'm a cop, maybe—"

I cut him off. "The idea is not to draw attention to ourselves, Mikey." He sighs, takes off his hat, and puts the hoodie on.

I get out and open the side door to let Mikey out. As he heads up the street, I lean against the van, watching him. Thomas gets out and joins me. He lets out a long breath, clearly relieved to be rid of Mikey's company.

"So what did you want to talk to me about?" I ask him.

"First off, you know that ride that Mikey mentioned going on?"

I glance at the tower in the back corner of the park, near the boardwalk. "Yeah. The Banshee. What about it?"

"I looked it up on the cops' computer just now. The Banshee is only six months old. He couldn't have ridden that as a kid. He's lying."

I suddenly feel as if I've dropped a few floors on the Banshee myself. "Maybe he just got mixed up."

"Or maybe he doesn't realize he's lying."

"Meaning what?"

"Well, what if he's not recovering real memories?"

"What's he remembering then?" I say. "Someone else's life?"

My whole body tenses at the thought.

"It's possible."

"No, it's not. When Dr. Wilson's team operated on me, they might have subtracted memories from my mind but they didn't substitute new ones."

"Maybe Mikey's treatment was different. I really don't think it's a good idea to keep him around, Angel. We just don't know what's been done to him."

"But if he isn't even aware of what's been done to him, how does it matter? He's still blindly flailing around, trying to figure himself out. I remember that feeling all too well."

I rub my eyes, not sure how and when I made myself Mikey's keeper.

"I get it," says Thomas. "You want to help him. But you should understand that you might not be able to do anything for him. Somebody might have stuffed his head so full of lies it's possible he's got no memories left to recover."

I take the handcuffs off my belt and start playing with them, pushing the metal bands around and around and making the ratchet click so fast it sounds like it's buzzing. "Speaking of lying without intending to lie . . ."

"I knew we were gonna come back to that."

"Be straight with me," I say. "Is there even a small chance that 8-Bit kept any information about Velocius?"

Thomas exhales slowly. I can tell from the weight of the sigh that he's been thinking about this for a long time, a lot longer than I have—probably ever since the Feds started interrogating him.

He kicks the back tire of the van as he looks up into the sky. "If 8-Bit had something, I have no idea how, and that's saying something, seeing as I knew all the ins and outs of the family hacking business. They literally blew up the hospital mainframe with all of Larry's backup files. Anyway, none of that matters right now. I told you, these guys who kidnapped me are after something else."

"So you told me."

Mikey suddenly reappears, peeling off his hoodie and holding it at his side as he heads up the sidewalk. Before he reaches us, though, he veers into the middle of the nearby intersection.

"He's not gonna try to roadkill himself again, is he?" groans Thomas. "I'm not invested enough in his survival to keep saving his life."

"No, I think . . ." This time Mikey doesn't seem distressed. Instead he cheerfully starts directing traffic going past the amusement park.

"For cripes sake, who gave him a whistle?" Thomas says.

I pull one out of a small leather pouch attached to my belt. "Seems to be standard issue along with the handcuffs." I smile slightly at the way Mikey is directing traffic. It's like he's dancing out there in the middle of the intersection. "He definitely seems to enjoy being a fake cop."

"Yeah, it's real charming."

As the light changes, Mikey approaches a random guy who's pursuing two women across the street. I didn't catch what the guy was saying to the ladies, but it must've rubbed Mikey the wrong way. "You think that's a nice way to talk to a woman? Do you, jerkwad?" Mikey shouts, giving the guy a little shove. "Why don't you show a little respect?"

The guy's clearly not sure what to do. If Mikey wasn't dressed as a cop, he probably would've thrown a punch already. The next thing we know, Mikey grabs the front of the guy's shirt and is screaming into his face. Something about learning to be a gentleman. The guy puts his hands up and says, "All right, all right. Sorry, officer."

Mikey lets go and the guy walks quickly back the way he came. One of the women turns back, teetering in her high heels, and blows him a kiss. "Thank you, officer!"

Mikey salutes. "My pleasure, ladies. You have a safe night."

I'm caught somewhere between dismay and laughter, but mostly I'm just wondering who the heck he thinks he is.

"Will you get Officer Mikey's attention so we can get on with our evening—and before he causes a riot?" Thomas says.

I wave at Mikey. He half-waves, half-salutes back. I motion him over, and he finally seems to get the message. As he jogs back across the street toward us, I say to Thomas, "Well, whatever sort of messed up he might be, he seems to have an urge to help people."

"Maybe there's some part of his mind that's trying to make up for whatever he did to land him in that hospital to begin with," Thomas says.

"Or maybe he was like me. Maybe he didn't do anything wrong at all."

"Doubt that."

I shoot him a scathing look, which he refuses to be scathed by.

"Look, I know you empathize with him. But Mikey and you? Not the same. If you're in doubt, watch and learn."

The moment Mikey reaches the van, Thomas demands, "Did you find a back entrance?"

"Uh, no. There's a door, but it's locked up tight."

"You know, Angel, I think it might be a better idea if I go into the bowling alley by myself," Thomas says to me, though his eyes remain locked on Mikey's face. He then reaches over and sticks his hand in the front breast pocket of Mikey's uniform. "Which means I'll be needing this back."

Thomas holds up the locker key in front of Mikey's face before shoving it into his own pocket. Mikey looks down into his empty shirt pocket, looking genuinely surprised, like Thomas has just magically pulled the locker key from his ear.

"Heh," Mikey says. "Forgot I had that on me."

"I don't recall giving it to you in the first place."

"I just took it in case I was able to get in through the back—figured I might be able to find the locker and save you some time. Just trying to help is all."

"That was sweet of you."

Mikey's face turns thoughtful. "Hey, smart guy. Have you ever heard of a group called the Radical Pacifists?"

"No."

"Me neither," Mikey says.

"Then why are you bringing it up?" Thomas demands.

"I don't know. Just a name that popped into my head. I don't know how I heard about them or what they do, but I thought I should mention it."

"Sounds like the name of a band," says Thomas, clearly unimpressed.

Mikey turns to me. "Seriously, though. Maybe you should look into this group. I mean, it might be a lead about where I came from. And I just have a feeling . . . that you should know about them."

"We'll see what we can figure out," I say noncommittally. "But we need to find this locker first."

Thomas takes out his wallet and hands Mikey a fifty dollar bill. "Officer, why don't you run along and get yourself an ice cream while I go inside, okay?"

"You're thinking you're going in there by yourself?" I say. "That's cute, Thomas. I'm coming, too."

"Angel, I can handle it on my own. You wait here with the car. I'll be right back."

I'll be right back.

Everything's going to be okay.

Small reassurances that can easily become last words.

And yet even though I'm worried about what might happen to him, I'm also worried for a completely different reason. I feel like he wants to get away from me, and I wish I knew why.

I start walking toward the front door of the bowling alley.

"I can handle this alone, Angel."

"I'm sure you can. But you shouldn't. Let's go."

CHAPTER 11

It turns out the bouncer very much enjoys cash, and a hundred bucks hastily stuffed into his hand turns his scowl into a warm, welcoming smile.

He even says, "You have a lovely evening, folks," as he lifts the rope and lets us in.

The inside of the bowling alley is just about as dark and icky as I expected it to be, given the half burned-out sign and large, cracked front window kept together with duct tape. The whole place smells like the inside of a rental shoe. It's also really loud. And a lot bigger than it looks from the outside. There must be fifteen lanes on each side of the room and nearly all of them are in deafening use. At the far end of the room, two lanes are partitioned off from the rest with floor-to-ceiling lattice screens. In the doorway to reach these lanes, there's a velvet rope—an honest-to-goodness velvet rope. Evidently those two lanes, plus an adjacent lounge and private bar, are the VIP section. It's almost laughable in its seediness.

Since I'd have to shout to be heard over the noise, I don't say anything to Thomas. I just nudge him and then nod toward the far left wall, where there's a row of orange and red lockers. The red is the same color as the barrel attached to the locker key.

Thomas follows my gaze, then leans close to talk in my ear. "Stay here while I go find the locker."

"No thanks. Stop trying to protect me."

"I'm not. I want you to stay clear in the event someone jumps me and I need you to come to my aid. Keep your eyes on me the whole time."

I use two fingers to point at my eyes and then at him. "Like a hawk."

"A very sexy hawk."

He gives me a quick peck on the cheek and then heads toward the lockers, dodging rowdy patrons and waitresses with trays full of beer and fries.

I find a bench next to a rack of fluorescent loaner balls, sit down, and watch Thomas from across the room. Turns out I'm not the only person watching Thomas because the moment he finds the right locker and opens it up, two guys emerge from the VIP section. They take long, purposeful strides toward Thomas.

Before I can make my way over to them, they're escorting Thomas away from the lockers, back toward the VIP area.

Thomas does not look my way. I take that as a sign that he doesn't want to draw attention to my presence or have me get involved. I also take it as a sign that he doesn't know me very well.

They lead Thomas into the roped-off area and force him to sit down between two huge guys whose thin hair, hulking arms, and spotty skin say "steroids."

I march over, unhook the rope, and barge into the VIP section. "Hello."

Everyone—Thomas included—looks up at me in irritated surprise.

"Hey, honey. These nice gentlemen have invited me to bowl with them," Thomas says.

I scan the group surrounding Thomas. There are eight guys—some young, some old—all similarly slouched into a U-shaped booth next to the VIP lanes. These "nice gentlemen" certainly don't look happy to see me. The ball return spits out a couple of balls, one of which says THE ENFORCER.

"Guys, this is my girlfriend," Thomas says and then fake whispers while rolling his eyes. "She keeps me on a short leash, you know?"

I cross my arms. Of all the ruses he might have chosen, "possessive girlfriend" is what I have to work with now?

Okay then. Here goes.

"Where have you been? You said you were going out with your friends! Who even are these guys? What's going on?"

"Sit down and have some cheese fries, honey," Thomas says. "This will just take a few minutes to sort out."

As I sit down, the guy closest to Thomas, who smells like a barrel of cologne, pulls an empty syringe out of his pocket.

Crap. We've gone to all this trouble just to retrieve an empty syringe? I try not to show my disappointment and confusion.

"So," Cologne Guy says to Thomas, "you're the third guy tonight we saw messing with that same locker. You buying or selling?"

Thomas does a good job of pretending to look both guilty and flustered. "You guys aren't undercover cops or something, right?"

The guys all titter in a manly, menacing way. "No worries there, son."

"Okay, then fine. I'm buying. Guy told me on the phone where to come to make the pickup. That's all I know."

"Good for you. 'Cause if you were selling then we were going to have a problem."

I put my hand to my heart, near the point of fainting. "Thomas! How could you?"

"Take it easy, baby," says Thomas. He looks back at his new buddies. "So . . . we're cool?"

"Yeah, no harm, no foul. When we saw you go for that locker, we thought you were one of those idiots—Jimmy, what are their names again?"

Jimmy answers with a very communicative shrug.

Another guy blurts the answer out like he's on a game show. "Radical Pacifists!"

"Yeah. That's it. They hang out here a lot lately. They said they were all about their political cause, but I guess they're thinking about moving in on our territory. Bunch of losers and rotten bowlers on top of that."

Thomas gives a laugh and urges me to do the same by elbowing me in the ribs. I manage one "ha!" before the mood changes, and Cologne Guy again puts his arm around Thomas's shoulders.

"Nice suit," he says to Thomas as he touches the silk edge of Thomas's lapel.

"Thanks."

"Looks like you got some money to spend."

Thomas shrugs.

Cologne Guy rolls the syringe between his fingers like it's a cigar. "If you're looking for some fun, you'll need to deal with us. Those other jokers will be taking their business elsewhere. We're gonna have a little talk with them next time they're here. Right, Jimmy?"

Jimmy makes a face that makes me think he will gladly rise to the occasion of teaching someone a lesson.

"Hold on," I say. "You just said these Radical Pacifist guys claim to be focused on a political cause, not on—um—whatever your business is. Are they some kind of," I whisper the words, "terrorist group?"

Cologne Guy responds with a patronizing chuckle. "Who knows what their deal is? We don't like getting involved in politics, you know?" Cologne Guy turns back to Thomas. "How much you pay for this empty syringe?"

Thomas runs his hand through his hair. "Fifty bucks."

"Shame. You paid good money and they cheated you, but that's what happens when you're dealing with clowns rather than professionals. Next time, buy from people you trust. You got it?"

"Absolutely, sir."

"Can I hook you up with anything? What you in the mood for tonight?"

I sense it's time to end this conversation. "Ugh!" I burst out, flipping back into character. "Take me home right this minute."

Thomas stands up. "You know, actually this whole experience has made me see the error of my ways. I think I'll just, you know, stay away from that stuff from now on."

"Good luck," the guy says, clapping Thomas on the shoulder as he nods toward me. "And if you talk to those Pacifist guys again, you tell them we need to have a chat."

"I will. Sorry for the, uh, mix-up."

"No problem." Cologne Guy winks at him and then cracks his knuckles. "This time."

Thomas puts his arm around my waist, and I let him whisk me past the velvet rope out the front door. I want to stop once we're outside, but Thomas keeps walking up the block until we're back at the van. Then he starts shaking his head.

"So much for getting the upper hand," he says. "Somebody got to the locker before we did and emptied the syringe. Whoever's behind this—they must have hustled over here as soon as they realized I'd escaped with the key."

"But how could they have known you'd actually be able to find this place?"

"Obviously they have great faith in my intelligence. Justifiably so."

"You seem awfully cheerful about this."

"At least we've got a lead now."

I nod. "The Radical Pacifists. Your kidnappers. And the same group Mikey mentioned earlier."

"That doesn't mean he's trustworthy," Thomas warns.

"Not necessarily," I agree. "But it does mean he's somehow connected to what's going on, even if we don't know how. And that could be useful to us."

Thomas jumps into the passenger side of the van and starts pecking the keys of the laptop. "I'm still putting more faith in the Internet than in Mikey. Time to get in touch with these guys. Push comes to shove, I can fake some data to upload in exchange for the antidote."

"And how are you going to figure out how to contact them?"

He shrugs. "These guys, they're all the same. I can find them."

I say casually, "Sure. It's easy to find anonymous bad guys on the Internet. How silly of me."

"You just have to know where to go. Which I do. Tracing these kinds of people is like placing a personal ad bulletin board where only a very small group of people will see, and they'll know that it's you and your beautiful green eyes they saw last week on the F train."

"This isn't funny, Thomas."

"I'm not trying to be funny. I'm trying to figure out what we're going to do."

"Yeah, I'm drawing a blank on that too. Even if you figure out how to reach them, you don't even know what data they want, so how can you fake it?"

The sheepish look he gives me tells me all I need to know.

"They are after the Velocius information, aren't they?"

His gaze drops away, which is an admission as loud and clear as if he'd just shouted "I've been holding out on you, Angel." I try not to show how outraged I am. There's not much point in losing my temper now. But this sucks. Not being able to trust the one person who's ever completely earned my trust completely sucks.

"Angel . . ."

"What's your real last name?" I ask abruptly.

He gives me a blank look. "You know what my last name is."

"I thought I did. But we tried to look up your name when we were tracking the ankle transmitter. There was no one listed by that name."

"So you think I lied to you? Seriously? Why would I even do that?"

"You tell me."

"Angel, you can do any basic Internet search for my parents and confirm their surname."

He's right, of course. I can just feel how paranoid I must sound. "Then why wasn't your name in the security company's system?"

"I have no idea. Maybe because I'm a minor? Or maybe . . ."

Before Thomas can say more, I hear panicked shouts coming from the direction of the amusement park.

Someone nearby yells, "Look! The Banshee tower!"

A moment later, several other people are screaming and pointing and I'm hearing, "Call 9-1-1!" interspersed with, "He's gonna jump!"

My eyes dart to the top of the ride. I see a figure at the very top—hardly more than a human-shaped shadow, only slightly darker than the night. But I know who it is.

I immediately start toward the park entrance. Thomas takes me by my arm. "Angel, hold up. You're not really a cop, you know. You don't have to respond."

"Yes, I do! That's Mikey up there!"

CHAPTER 12

I run up the block, Thomas trailing behind me, and push through the crowd of agitated people milling around, not sure if they want to watch or look away. Thomas and I take advantage of everyone's distraction to jump the turnstiles and get inside. The Banshee is right next to the fence, right across from the Cyclone. There's a piece of clothing lying on the ground nearby. I grab it and see the silver name tag face up: V. ABRAMS.

I can see exactly how Mikey got up on the tower. Sure, there's a gate. Yes, there's a fence—a good one, too, with that kind of top that angles inward. That type of fence is supposed to be extra hard to get over.

It's not.

I search for a few handholds where I can balance a moment to pull myself up and over. Once I glance at these kinds of barriers, all I see are ways to get myself past them. I must have done these calculations hundreds of times.

I climb and pull and strain my way up. Two climbs tonight.

My hands are raw. Worse, I'm feeling another surge of memory take over my body. Damn.

What I'm remembering doesn't even make sense. This memory is so . . . sweet?

"Come over here, honey, I want to give you a hug."

That voice belonged to Mrs. Claymore—Sarah Claymore, my grandmother, though I didn't know it at the time. I'd gone to the nursing home where she was living, hoping to find a chink in the Claymore armor, anything I could use against Erskine Claymore. Instead I'd found this kind old lady. She doesn't know what's going on right now, but she sure seems to remember things from long ago like they were yesterday.

I take a step back. I really don't want a hug. From her or anyone else. I'm pretty sure my hugging days are over.

"You're so kind," she says.

"It's no big deal. I just, you know, saw them and thought you might like them."

Is that the truth?

Yeah, I think it really is that simple. I sought Mrs. Claymore out because I thought she was someone who could give me answers, but by now I know she can't tell me anything useful that I could use against her husband. And yet I still come. And there's something about her that won't allow me to be anything but respectful and gentle.

I feel sorry for her.

Imagine that. After all I've lost, here I am feeling sorry for Sarah Claymore. She has to be one of the richest women in the country. Maybe even the world.

And here she is, so ecstatic over such a small gift. I brought her a lousy box of cheap chocolates. I bought them because they came in this box that was shaped like a house, yellow with a red door. Mrs. Claymore had described her childhood home to me, and I was just walking down the street and happened to notice this box of chocolates in a store window and was like, Wow, that box looks a lot like what she described. I bought them on impulse, just because I was struck by the coincidence.

And now she's thanking me like I've actually brought her the house itself. Like I've given her something no one else could.

"Funny how the small things make you remember the big things," she says. Her voice is sad and somehow a little angry. "Do you ever wish you could get a fresh start?"

"I don't know. Maybe."

"There are so many things I would do over, my dear. So many. Don't let it happen to you."

And then she starts crying and I don't know what to say or do. I don't even know how to handle my own tears when they ambush me—how am I supposed to comfort this rich lady?

This rich lady I feel so sorry for.

We cry for the things we've lost in exactly the same way.

I want to scream. I feel like I'm remembering important moments, but I have no idea what makes them meaningful. It's almost like I'm hitting the outer rings of a target but never the bull's-eye. Last time I climbed, I thought of a person whose name and face I can't recall but who I know had something to do with my arrest, and now— now I get Sarah Claymore, who's still locked away in some luxury nursing home, somewhere in Manhattan. And no doubt the keys to her prison are still dangling from Erskine Claymore's keychain.

Fortunately, even though these memories have overtaken my mind, my body has just carried on out of habit, climbing and climbing, finding a way up. Now I'm at the top of the ride. With Mikey. This Banshee is just like the tower cranes I used to climb. It sways with every gust of wind. I feel like I'm on a boat, trying not to lose my balance.

Mikey leans forward and back again, holding onto the bars on either side of him. He looks almost as if he's swinging between the opposing points of a pendulum—only those two points are Live and Die. The way his arms and shoulders are tensing each time he pushes himself forward, I have the impression that he's fighting with himself, like he's testing which urge inside him is stronger.

I'm not happy to be up here with him, and I don't know why life keeps asking of me what I don't want to give. But maybe that's what it does with everyone and I shouldn't take it so personally.

"Mikey," I say gently.

"You shouldn't be up here."

"Neither should you. Come on back down with me."

"I don't know if that's a good idea. For you or for me."

"You don't really want to be up here at all," I say.

"What do you know about me?" He turns his head and makes eye contact. This is good. I'm going to use that eye contact like it's a lifeline. I'm going to pull him back with it.

"There was a time I didn't think I wanted to live anymore either," I say, inching closer to him. "They did something to you in that hospital, and maybe now you get these thoughts that scare you or make you think you deserve what happened, but the way you're looking at me right now, this is the guy I think you are deep down. And I think that guy deserves another chance. I think that guy deserves to live."

I can almost touch him, but if I make a quick grab for his shirt, I might startle him. I've got to keep him talking.

"You don't understand. I don't want to be up here right now. Something's making me . . . I can't stop myself."

His face tells me he's bewildered and terrified. Maybe that's a good sign. He understands what he's doing, and he doesn't want to succumb to what his brain is telling him.

"That's why I'm here. I know what it's like for your mind to turn against you. But we're going to figure it out, okay? Come on." I hold my hand out to him. "Come with me, okay?"

He nods.

There it is. I've got him. I simultaneously grab his hand and his belt, which is probably stupid of me because if he jumps now, I'm going down with him. But then I feel him lean toward me a little. He slides one foot away from the edge, then the other. I think he's beaten it now, whatever pulled him up here, but I don't want to spook him by rushing him to move back.

"Good job," I say. "Keep coming."

I let go of his hand for a moment so I can put my arms around his chest and pull him the rest of the way. He's shaking now, tremors racking his whole body.

I make him climb down the ladder first and I follow. I don't want him changing his mind and bolting back for the top of the tower. As we slowly make our way down, I can see that his hands are now practically curled into claws and he's having trouble gripping the ladder rungs. I keep telling him he's doing great, but I know he's not. His jaw is tightening as if he's trying to swallow back vomit and his neck muscles are taut. He makes a strange noise as his feet touch the ground.

Right away Thomas can see there's still something really wrong with Mikey. "Is he having a seizure or something?"

"I don't know. Let's just get him out of here."

We walk on either side of Mikey, holding him upright as his boots drag on the ground, pushing through the crowd of onlookers at the base of the ride. In the distance, a couple police cars pull up. We sneak out toward the boardwalk and then make our way back to the van parked up the street, taking a detour through a side street to avoid being seen by the arriving ambulance. As we help Mikey into the van, his face contracts a moment. He squeezes his eyes shut and runs his hand over the spot behind his ear, like he's trying to massage the pain away. "I think we should take him to a hospital," I say.

"Hold on a second." Thomas reaches down and unbuttons one of the cuffs of Mikey's uniform shirt.

"What are you doing?"

"Just a hunch," he says.

He pushes up Mikey's sleeve and reveals several needle marks in Mikey's veins, a few slightly scabbed over. There's a small halo of bruising around one of the injection sites. Thomas rolls up his sleeve and compares the two. Identical.

"Okay," Thomas says. "I'm ready to tell you what I think is going on."

I drive fast, too fast, but I feel like I'm now racing against not just one clock but several. I check on Mikey in the rearview mirror every few seconds. His eyes are closed and his head is leaning back on the seat. The tension in his body seems to have lessened but he's still shaking.

Thomas has the laptop open and pulls up directions to the nearest hospital. "Turn left up there. And by the way, I adore you but you truly are a horrific driver."

"You're still alive, aren't you?"

"For now," he says, smiling. "Here's hoping your driving does me in long before this stuff they shot me up with."

I feel like screaming at him for trying to make light of what's going on. "Stop joking and start giving me answers."

I'm not afraid of what he's going to say. No truth is worse than not knowing. Not knowing is a chasm of black, the potential for every worst-case scenario thrown together.

He faces forward again and sighs. "First of all, I haven't been holding back because I don't trust you. I was just trying to get a better handle on the situation before I said anything."

"Do you have a handle now?"

"Not really, but I'll just tell you what I know." I slow down for a red light. Thomas clears his throat.

"Here's the thing," he says. "The government program that you were part of—it might just be the tip of the iceberg. There was always the possibility that there might be others. Other patients, other places where they did research."

I'm not surprised. Not even a little bit. When the Feds told me that they shut the hospital down, I wasn't fully convinced. But everyone told me relax, don't worry, you're safe. They said it so much that I started to think maybe—just maybe—I could accept it as fact. Now I feel like a sucker for letting my handlers talk me out of listening to my own gut. They used my desire to put the past behind me as a weapon against me.

"Thomas, if you've always suspected that there were other

places they conducted research—other people who they experimented on—why didn't you ever mention that to me?"

"I was hoping it wasn't true. Because if it is—if there are ongoing projects, any information about the Velocius project could still be relevant, useful, to other research that's happening right now."

I think about Thomas's response to his kidnapping tonight— how he insisted that whatever his kidnappers wanted had nothing to do with Velocius or with me. He was lying. Straight-up lying. More of that insulting "protection" that I never asked for.

I take one hand off the wheel and momentarily pinch the bridge of my nose. "Okay, but we've already established that there isn't any surviving Velocius data."

"Hold on. I'm not done explaining."

"Go ahead. Until this light turns green, I have nowhere else to be."

"A couple weeks ago, the Feds started asking me stuff about you."

"Me?"

"Yeah, it was sort of out of the blue. Up until that point, all we discussed was 8-Bit and all the stuff he'd been doing the past few years. And I'd told them everything I knew about that. Like, everything."

"What did they ask you about me?"

"They wanted to know if you've ever said anything about more research data for the Velocius project. They seemed to think there might be more info out there and that you might have some idea about where it was."

"Me? I don't know anything."

"That's what I told them. But then I thought . . ." Thomas scrubs his hair with his fingertips. "What if you do, Angel?"

"I don't understand."

"Have you had any new memories recently?"

"No," I say right away, but I realize that's not quite true. "Well, actually I had a couple tonight, but both are from long ago. Before I was in the hospital."

"What were they about?"

"One was from that night at the police station. The night that Hodges—"

His biological mother's name makes him wince.

"The night I got arrested and she told me about what she did to my mother. I couldn't really get hold of the whole memory, though. There was some other piece to it, something about a friend of mine, a girl from my old neighborhood maybe—someone who betrayed me. And the other memory was about Sarah Claymore. You know, Erskine's wife. My grandmother. I visited her in her nursing home at some point. I had tracked her down and I was trying to dig up some dirt that could help me expose Claymore's shadiness."

"And did you?"

"No. She didn't know anything. And obviously neither of those memories has anything to do with secret locations of research data."

Behind us, Mikey starts making a strange, low noise, like an agonized animal caught in a trap. He grabs at the hair on either side of his head but it's too short for him to get a grip. Even Thomas is looking at him now like he's feeling sorry for the guy. "Good thing he doesn't have much hair because it looks like he's trying to pull it all out."

That's when something hits me.

"His hair," I say.

"What about it?"

"It took months for mine to grow back after they took me off the chemo regimen, and it didn't all grow at the same rate. If Mikey was in the hospital until a couple weeks ago . . . look at his hair. It's short, but even all over. Like it's just been shaved."

"Like someone was just trying to make it look like two or three weeks' worth of hair growth?"

"Exactly."

"Then the story he told you is definitely not real. Or not complete. Could be the result of whatever he's got in his system." As he says this, he bends his arm and rubs the inside of his arm where they injected him. He glances back at Mikey and then at me. "Maybe I'm looking at my future."

I'm not sure how I'm keeping the van on the right side of the road. My mind is too full of worry.

He glances at his laptop again. "Take your second right up ahead there."

Then he says, "I have another theory. Is there anything only you and Larry would know about?"

"Larry? I don't think so. Why?"

Larry. The doctor who saved me back at the research hospital. The man who defied his bosses, the doctors who were running the experiments, for my sake. I think of him fairly often, sometimes wondering why he did it and sometimes just grateful that he did. His actions gave me a way out, but he's as much of a puzzle as my memories once were. I don't know much about him. Although maybe I knew the best part of him and that's what matters.

"The way you described to me what Larry did at the hospital," Thomas says. "He planted information in your head, gave you the tools you needed to save yourself. He found a way to tell you your mother's name without you or any of his colleagues realizing it. I think he might have done something more. A clue to help you find hidden data about Velocius—something to lead you to a digital storage site or something."

I try to recall some of what I discussed with Larry during procedures. All of it seems far away and indistinct. Disconnected words and phrases, momentary flashes of images, surges of emotion—all of it is clouded by the drowsy fog that lay over my heavily medicated brain. And I'm sure my memory of those times is even more pockmarked and incomplete because subconsciously, I'd rather not remember any of what happened.

Thomas isn't the first person to ask me this question about Larry. After I got back to New York, my handlers asked me as well.

Had Larry ever mentioned anything unusual about my case?

Had he ever said something strange to me that might have had another meaning?

I told them that everything Larry said to me was odd. Every topic he introduced was out of left field. After a while the Feds stopped asking.

The light changes and I hit the gas too hard. We hit a pothole that pitches Mikey across the floor.

"You okay back there?" Thomas asks.

Mikey nods once, but his eyes roll back in his head.

Now I think about the morning of my last operation—about how strange Larry was acting, with his cryptic quotes from

Hamlet. Of course, his behavior made sense later, but maybe there was more that I was supposed to unpack from his words.

Maybe he seeded something else in my mind—the location of the very information that the Radical Pacifists want Thomas to deliver. Larry to the rescue once again.

"Do a search on 'Larry and Polonius' and see if you get any hits," I say.

I look in the rearview mirror at Mikey again. He's completely still, though his face is pinched in pain. I wonder if he's fallen asleep like that.

Thomas types and then says, "Huh. Well, that's something."

"What?"

"I've just found something called Larry's Elizabethan Fan Site. It's pretty bare bones. Just a list of quotes from Hamlet. That's quite a coincidence, don't you think?"

"Or else," I say, "it's a message."

CHAPTER 13

Thomas points at the front entrance of King's Borough Hospital. "I picked this place because they're noted for having an especially serene and secure psych ward," Thomas says.

I pull up in front of the Emergency Room doors. Thomas and I get out and open up the back of the van.

Mikey can't keep his feet under him, so we sling each of his arms around the backs of our necks and drag him toward the doors.

"Sure you don't want to just leave him here with a note pinned to his shirt?" asks Thomas as the doors slide open for us.

"Thomas, come on. We owe it to him to at least take him inside."

The waiting room is standing room only. People are moaning and calling out, kids are crying, phones are ringing but going unanswered.

"Let's just find a nice quiet corner and put him down and then get the heck out of here," Thomas says.

We lower Mikey into an empty wheelchair parked next to a wall of pamphlets about infectious diseases, and just as we turn to leave, we hear a voice behind us. A not-to-be-trifled-with kind of voice. The only people who have voices like that are nurses and guards in maximum-security prisons—and I should know.

"Nuh-uh-uh," the woman says, checking Mikey's pupils with the kind of mini flashlight that nurses used to poke into my eyes on a daily basis. "The only place you can drop and go is the morgue." She shoves a clipboard at me and adds, "Fill this out. I'll let you know what's wrong with your friend when I can. You can wait in the cafeteria if you want."

Thomas opens his mouth to protest, but I hook my arm around his, coupling us together like two train cars. As soon as the nurse turns away, I ditch the clipboard on an empty chair and pull Thomas toward the signs for the cafeteria, dodging the flow of patients and nurses and doctors, all of whom seem to be having the worst night of their lives.

"Let's just take a few minutes to rest and process everything before we decide where to go from here," I say.

"Fine," grumbles Thomas. "Guess we can get a closer look at Larry's little fan site while we catch our breath."

"But we don't have the laptop—"

Thomas produces a smartphone from his tuxedo pocket.

"Where did you get that?"

"From someone at the amusement park who wasn't paying close enough attention to his back pocket."

"Seriously? Mikey was about to leap to his death and you took the time to pickpocket somebody?"

"You have your skill set, I have mine."

We follow the signs to the cafeteria one floor up. They seem to have closed down except for one small display case of granola bars, candy, and a bowl of bruised fruit. Most school lunchrooms have more panache than this place.

Thomas puts the phone in my hand. "Sit down and have a look at that Larry and Polonius site while I get us some coffee and something to eat."

I look down at the screen and read. Within two minutes, I'm blinking fiercely, fighting to focus. Reading lines from Shakespeare plays is not exactly the best way to stay alert in the middle of the night.

Then is doomsday near: but your news is not true.
Let me question more in particular: what have you,
my good friends, deserved at the hands of fortune,
that she sends you to prison hither?

I can hear Larry's voice reciting these words to me. When did this happen? Am I just imagining it?

Each memory modification procedure was the same. I would talk to Larry, the hours would pass and the drill would bore deeper into my brain, and then it would be over and I'd be returned to my room to spend a couple days under mild sedation, strapped to my bed so I wouldn't accidentally pull out any of the tubes or wires. I hated that feeling of being paralyzed, lost in a twilight of confusion while people would come and go. Nurses would take my vitals and then leave the room without saying a word. It was almost like being dead.

The moments, the days all blended together, nothing distinct. Weeks would pass and then it would be time for another session. And now I've got to put myself back there again and relive it.

Larry's voice is suddenly vibrant in my mind as I read the words on the screen.

Though this be madness, yet there is method in 't.

I can hear the sound of the drill in the background. I can smell the Betadine antiseptic and feel the straps around my chest. Larry's voice has weight to it, each word penetrating my mind like the needles sinking deep into my brain tissue.

—to thine own self be true.
And it must follow, as the night the day,
Thou canst not then be false to any man.
Act 40, scene 46.08, line 73.59

A none-too-gentle tap on my shoulder startles me.

I straighten up fast, gripping the sides of the table. Standing in front of me is a very concerned-looking Thomas with a tray in his hand.

"You had me worried. I said your name a couple times and you didn't respond."

"I was just thinking. Or sleeping. Or something in between. I feel like there's something teasing me about these quotes, but I can't figure it out."

"Ah, Larry. Man of a thousand mysteries." He sets a tray down in front of me. "I brought you coffee and some sort of . . . old-people food. It's pudding. I think. Or it used to be."

I recognize the substance in the little glass dish. "It's rice pudding! I ate a lot of it at the hospital."

More concern bleeds into his expression. "Maybe this was a bad choice then. I didn't mean to bring those ugly memories back—more than we have to, anyway."

"No, it's okay. It's not a bad memory at all." I take a spoonful and eat it. "I think rice pudding might be the least threatening substance on earth."

He exhales with relief. "Only the best for my lovely lady on our first dinner out together."

I smile and push the tray toward him. "You should eat too. We both need to keep up our strength if we intend to unravel the mysteries of Larry."

He's about to take a bite and then puts his spoon down. "Angel, if I told you that you'd be better off getting up from this table, right now, and walking out and disappearing, would you do it?"

"Of course not. I don't run out on people I care about."

"Right now you should."

"I believe I once told you to do the same thing, and you wouldn't leave. I hope you're not suggesting you're nobler than I am."

"Then you should understand why I'm saying this. Look, you're the person I care about most in the world and I want to protect you, and maybe the way to do it is to let you go."

"I don't want you to protect me," I say. "I want you to have faith in my ability to protect myself. I'd also like to have some say in any 'letting go' you might be doing, especially if it's supposedly for my own good."

I reach across the table and take his hand, but his mood is all wrong. The Thomas I know would crack wise while plummeting to earth with a parachute that won't open. This Thomas—it's like he's already given up.

"When you showed up at the church tonight, ready to save me from my kidnappers, do you know what I thought? I thought, 'Oh, no. I failed her.' All I want is to keep you out of danger, and I failed."

Thomas gets up from the table and comes around to my side. He slides into the booth next to me and takes my hand in his.

He kisses me so lightly, I almost don't even feel it.

"If they threaten you," he says, "if they tell me that they'll hurt you if I don't give them what they want—I will give it to them. Whatever it is. I will give it to them."

"But you don't have anything to give them!"

"I'll make something up. And they will eventually figure out that I made something up, and that will anger them, and that will end badly for everybody. So we'll all be better off if you go somewhere safe, where they can't reach you, where they can't use you as leverage against me."

"Counterproposal: I help you find the actual data on Velocius, and then you trade it for the antidote and—"

He kisses me again.

"Kissing me doesn't make an interruption any less rude, you know?"

But he won't let anything get in the way of what he's trying to tell me. His brown eyes are swallowing me up.

"Think of it this way. Someone's already tried to kill you twice in the past twenty-four hours. We don't know who or why. All we know is that the people who should be protecting you can't be trusted. Whatever's going on with me, whatever these Radical Pacifists are up to, it's nothing compared to whatever you're up against. Angel, I'm scared for you. What if what's coming for you is bigger and badder than anything before? You should walk out right now and never look back. Just disappear. Virgil could help you."

"Virgil can't help me unless Mrs. Fitzgerald helps him," I say. "He's totally dependent on her. And we know now that she can't be trusted. Besides, what would happen to you if I just left? You know how much you need me."

I smile at him, but he doesn't smile back.

"Please go, Angel."

"I won't. And do not ever ask me this again. Do you know something? You're doing just what they tried to do to me at the hospital. Trying to protect me by not letting me know the truth, by not letting me make my own choices. You're doing just what your mother—" I stop myself, but it's too late.

He flinches, like I've actually stabbed him with my stupid, impulsive words.

"I'm sorry. I didn't . . . I know you're not anything like her."

He looks at me in resignation. "I'm—sorry if I've made you feel like that. It's just a hard instinct to overcome. The desire to protect someone you love. You never know how you'll react until you're in the same position."

"What I'd like a lot more than your 'protection' is your trust. Your belief that we're going to get through this together."

He reaches for my hand and looks down at our fingers intertwining. "I wish I could believe that. But I can't say I'm liking our odds right now."

"Bravery isn't for times when you know everything is going to turn out all right," I say.

"Who said that?"

"I did, just now."

He shakes his head. "That's a great quote, but brave people still die, Angel. All the time. I don't want you to be one of them."

I slap my hand to my forehead and try to stand up, banging my hip against the table as I do. "The quote!"

"Huh?"

"On Larry's blog. The citations for those Hamlet quotes! They're all correct except this one." I fumble with the phone as I rush to show him the quote on the screen. "The last two sentences Polonius speaks after his famous line, 'to thine own self be true.' Look. This one makes no sense. There's no act 40 in Hamlet. There's no act 40 in any play. So what do you think those numbers could be?"

Thomas's eyes go round. He grabs the phone and plugs the numbers into the search bar. "Let's see what we get."

A few seconds later we have our answer.

GPS coordinates.

CHAPTER 14

Thomas types quickly and then holds the phone up in front of my face. I see a building, seemingly forged from one continuous piece of silver, polished to a mirror finish. The top of the tower is shaped like a sword.

"Claymore Tower," I say. The flagship of Claymore's real estate holdings. One hundred fourteen floors of luxurious condos and offices and, on the lower levels, the most expensive retail stores in Manhattan.

Thomas slumps down in his chair.

"What's the matter?" I say. "We just figured out a huge piece of the puzzle!"

"Yeah, but so what? The information is useless. Larry might as well have sent us to the Pentagon. What are we supposed to do now? Go up to the penthouse apartment and knock on all the doors? 'Why, hello there! You ever heard of Dr. Larry Ladner? If so, you got any secrets you'd like to share with a couple random strangers?'"

"Hey, that's a brilliant plan. Let's go with that."

I take his hand but he immediately pulls it away. Not in time to hide what I've just discovered, though.

"Thomas. How long have your hands been shaking like that?"

"Off and on for the last half an hour."

"Is it the drug or are you just scared?" I ask.

"I think it's both."

Without saying so out loud, we both decide that leaving Mikey behind is the best move right now. We're about to pass through the sliding doors and exit the ER when I notice the television screen in the upper corner of the waiting room. *Reports of Gunfire near South Street Seaport* flashes across the bottom of the screen.

"Oh, no." I stop in my tracks. Thomas plows into the back of me.

"What?" Thomas asks.

I point to the television. We move closer to get a better look.

A reporter stands near the dock, and behind him, the nose of a yacht is visible. The volume is turned off but the closed captioning reads: "Several people reported hearing shots fired and two witnesses claim to have seen police exchange gunfire with an assailant in a white van. Yet there has been no official police response following the alleged incident . . ."

Thomas looks at me, his eyes widening slightly. "We need to get out of here now."

I'm already two steps ahead of him.

We rush back out to the van. I slide behind the wheel, and Thomas gets into the passenger side and opens up the laptop right away. "Let me see if I can—"

A croaky voice rises from the back, echoing through the empty van. "How you guys doing?"

I nearly bang my head on the inside of the roof when I jump in surprise.

Mikey is sitting against the back wall of the van. "Sorry. Didn't mean to startle you."

He's looking a little better. At least there's color in his face again, and he's no longer writhing in pain.

"He's back," Thomas says. "Like a psychotic bad penny."

"Some stuff came back to me while I was in there," Mikey says.

"That's great, but we're in a bit of a hurry . . ."

"I know what they gave you," Mikey says, looking at Thomas. "The shot?"

"Yeah. It's this stuff called Snowball."

An ambulance is pulling into the ER bay. We need to get out of here before we're boxed in by emergency vehicles. I put the van in drive and Thomas pulls up directions back into Manhattan.

"So this Snowball stuff—what does it do?" I ask Mikey once we're on the road.

Mikey scrunches up his face like remembering is hard physical work and he's not sure he can lift such a heavy load. "They give you the first injection," he says, rubbing the crook of his arm. "Then they give you a second one sometime later. Could be hours or days, but anything that happens between those two injections, you don't remember."

A shudder runs through me. Now there's some precise way to wipe out tiny pieces of your memory as soon as you've created them? There's no risk of post-traumatic stress disorder with this method. You could put test subjects through all kinds of horrors, force them to do just about anything, and they wouldn't remember any of it afterward. It's a much more refined—more advanced—version of what Dr. Wilson's team did to me.

I almost don't want to know but I have to ask. "So why is it called Snowball?"

Mikey looks at Thomas with a sympathetic, brace yourself for bad news sort of expression. "Because if you don't get that second shot . . . the drug just keeps going, it keeps wiping stuff out. It's like a snowball rolling downhill. It eats up more and more of your memory. Until there's nothing left. Until there's nothing left of you."

I can feel the blood surging into my face. It's not fair of me, but I feel like this is somehow Mikey's fault, like he brought this into Thomas's life. I know he's probably a victim too, but at this moment, I can't help seeing him as the carrier of some virus.

And now Thomas has been infected.

"Well, I guess that proves the Radical Pacifists aren't working alone," says Thomas, sounding unbelievably calm. "You can't exactly get memory modification serum at your local pharmacy. They must be connected to some pretty high-powered people. I mean, the guys who nabbed me were losers, but if they know about Velocius *and* they have access to a top-secret drug, they must be working for a bigger entity . . ."

"Great. We were already outnumbered, and now there might be even more bad guys to fight?"

By now we're back on the Brooklyn-Queens Expressway, the skyline rising up in front of us as if it were an impenetrable fortress. When I've calmed down a little and can fight back the irrational anger I feel at Mikey, I ask, "What happened up there on the tower? Why did you try to jump? Was that another side effect of Snowball?"

"I don't think so. Not exactly, anyway. If I veer from the plan, I get these urges."

"Plan?" I echo.

"Whatever I'm supposed to be doing, I'm not doing it right, I guess. I—I don't think I'm supposed to be on your side. That time I ran onto the highway, and then when I almost jumped off that tower—I think that was my punishment for helping you."

"You mean because you pulled me out of the river?" I ask.

"No. Not that."

I rack my brain for other ways that Mikey's helped us. Knocking out Thomas's captors, getting the keys to the van, figuring out that we needed to find a bowling alley . . . "You told us about the Radical Pacifists."

He nods once, like it hurts to move his head. "Apparently that wasn't something they wanted you to know about. I must've endangered their mission somehow."

"And what's their mission?" I push.

Thomas crosses his arms. "More to the point, who's 'they'?"

"I don't know. All I know is that some of the things I've been doing—it's like they've been programmed into me. I didn't want to take the—" Mikey clams up and glances toward Thomas, and something clicks into place in my head. Something's finally making sense, at least in one small corner of this bigger puzzle.

"The syringe," I say. "You're the one who emptied it."

"What?" Thomas says.

I'm still glaring at Mikey in the rearview mirror. "When you went around to the back of the bowling alley to check if there was another way in. There was a door, wasn't there, Mikey? You got inside, you used the key to get into the locker before we did, and you emptied the syringe."

I turn to Thomas. "That's why that guy at the bowling alley said there'd been three guys messing with that locker. The guy who put the syringe there in the first place, then Mikey, and then you."

Mikey doesn't say anything. Possibly because Thomas doesn't give him a chance. "GET OUT OF THE CAR. RIGHT NOW."

Thomas jumps out of his seat and tries to get into the back of the van, but I grab his tux jacket. "Thomas!"

"Angel, he sabotaged us! He ruined our chance to get the antidote! We were right there, the antidote was in reach, and he—"

"I know! But you have to calm down!"

"Pull over and dump him out."

"I can't! There's nowhere to stop. I'm nearly on the bridge!"

Thomas sits back down, mostly because the van is swerving back and forth as I struggle to hold onto him.

"I don't get you, man. I don't care what stuff they shot into your veins. You're the one who told us to look for a bowling alley in the first place. Why bother, if you were just going to screw us over? What kind of master plan is that?"

Mikey kicks the back of the seat. "I don't know!" He looks down at his arm as if it belongs to someone else. "You shouldn't trust me."

Thomas and I look at each other: *Yeah, obviously.*

"His behavior's clearly being guided by someone or something outside his control," I say.

"Which means he could be even more dangerous than we realized."

As we cross the bridge and head back into the city, Mikey says quietly, "I still want to help you."

"Yeah, you want to help us so I'll help you," I say. "That's what you said. Unless that was a lie too?"

"No. I mean, I guess I don't actually know, but . . . I do need your help. It's not like I asked for any of this."

"You're breaking my heart, Mikey," Thomas says. "Slow down, Angel, and I'll push him out. I just hope we don't get busted for littering."

"But I know where the antidote is!" Mikey blurts out.

I almost turn around and stare at him before I remember to watch the road. "Are you serious?"

"I mean . . . I remember the inside of the building where it's kept. The layout. The room where they store the meds. I just don't know where the building itself is."

Thomas throws his hands in the air and then lets them drop into his lap. "Well, that's super helpful. You got anything actually useful to share with us? Because if not, you're nothing but a continuing liability." As we roll to a stop at the first traffic light on the other side of the bridge, he says, "Oh, look! Here's a lovely gutter filled with broken glass and taco wrappers. A perfect place to ditch this loser!"

"Hold on," I say. "If he has even a vague idea of where the antidote is kept, we need to keep all options open. So for now, I think we're stuck with him."

Thomas leans against the side of the car and squeezes his head with his hands. Sort of how I used to do. I need to check that my head is still here sometimes. It's not a look I'm used to seeing on Thomas, and it unsettles me. Plus his hands are shaking more than ever.

"Thomas, are you all right?"

"This stuff they put in me. It's . . . I can't think anymore. My brain isn't working right."

"You're just tired." But I know it's more than that. His symptoms are getting worse.

"Lack of sleep usually doesn't even put a dent in my brilliance."

"Yeesh," Mikey says. "Big ego much?"

"It's going to be okay," I assure Thomas. "For now we'll just follow Larry's clues over to Claymore Tower. But first . . . give me that phone, will you? I'm going to call home."

"What?! Are you out of your mind? Mrs. Fitzgerald sold you out."

"We don't actually know that. We only have Mikey's word for it, and we agree that's not reliable. And if we're wrong, if it turns out she hasn't betrayed me, then maybe she can help us. So I'm going to call her and test her. Tell her this kid found me and I'm in trouble. We'll see how she reacts, what she suggests. I won't tell her where I am, I'll just feel her out."

"Okay, but make it quick. Don't stay on the line long enough for the call to get traced." Thomas hands over the stolen phone and after I dial Mrs. Fitzgerald's number, he leans close so we can both listen in.

The phone rings once.

A woman's voice greets me right away, wide awake even though it's the wee hours of the morning.

"Hello, darling! Why didn't you call earlier?"

Already I know something's weird. First of all, Mrs. Fitzgerald never answers the phone so cheerily. Second, I'm calling from an unfamiliar number, and yet she knows it's me.

"Mrs. Fitzgerald, I—"

"It's fine, Sarah. I know you're staying at your friend's house tonight. Don't forget, though, that you've got a dental appointment with Dr. Nickles at 1:30 tomorrow. Virgil is worried that you forgot. Oh, and his phone isn't working properly. In case you tried to reach him earlier."

Thomas mouths, "What is she talking about?"

I ignore him and say into the phone, "Don't worry, I'll be there on time, no problem. Tell Virgil not to worry."

I hang up.

"You call her at three o'clock in the morning and she's reminding you about a dental appointment?"

"The bit about Dr. Nickles is our code for something unexpected happening. I think she's trying to tell me something."

I look down at the black watch I'm wearing. "I'm supposed to hit this panic button if anything goes wrong, and we have an emergency protocol—a safe spot that I'm supposed to go to. I think her question 'Why didn't you call earlier?' was a reference to that. She probably doesn't understand why I didn't follow the emergency plan. And telling me that Virgil's phone isn't working—I think she was warning me not to try to contact Virgil."

"In case Virgil might actually be able to help you," Thomas grumbles darkly.

"Or," I say, "in case the Feds are monitoring calls to Virgil's phone. Calling him might give them a chance to trace my location. Anyway, she didn't sound like someone who'd just betrayed me."

"I guess. But she also isn't helping you find your way out of this mess, is she?"

Maybe not. Even if she wants to, it doesn't seem like she's in a position to do much. Still, it's a relief to know that she doesn't seem to want me dead. At this point, that's no small thing.

CHAPTER 15

We're back in the car again and the sky is starting to grow lighter, but dawn breaking is not good news. The cover of night has given us a small measure of safety, and that's about to end. Not to mention that Thomas's window of opportunity is narrowing by the minute. I'm not even going to look at the clock right now, because I don't need any more pressure than I'm already feeling.

"So we're going to Claymore Tower?" Mikey says.

"No, Angel and I are going to Claymore Tower," Thomas says.

"I said I want to help."

"I believe you, Mikey," I say. "But the last time you helped us, you almost jumped to your death."

"Plus we have no guarantee that you won't screw us over again," adds Thomas. "Considering that you're clearly somebody's puppet, we can't afford to trust you even this much." He holds his thumb and forefinger pinched together.

"I get it! But I want to know what's going on just as much as you do. I just want to find out who I am."

Thomas and I exchange looks and for the first time, his face softens. He knows that I understand that feeling Mikey is describing. The curiosity that won't go away, the unnameable longing, the promise of that missing piece of your identity.

Mikey slides forward until his upper body is practically in the front seat. "Hey, I got an idea. What if you put me in handcuffs?" He holds up his fists, with wrists touching. "Better yet, put the cuffs on me with my hands behind my back. Even if I'm hardwired to hurt you, what am I gonna do while I'm cuffed?"

"That's not a bad idea," I say. "Would that make you feel better about bringing him along, Thomas?"

"Maybe. Could we put a bag over his face too?"

"What for?"

"So I don't have to look at his ugly mug."

"Nice," Mikey says. "Kick me while I'm down, why don't you?"

I glance over at Thomas. He's still scowling, arms crossed over his chest.

I know the whole idea of this Snowball stuff is freaking him out. If there's one thing he's afraid of losing, it's his brain.

We need to get him that antidote.

Between the buildings, I see the first flush of an orangey sunrise. Time is growing short and our immediate options seem to be narrowed to one. I take our final turn onto Central Park South. Claymore Tower is straight ahead at Columbus Circle.

I take the handcuffs off my utility belt and hand them to Mikey. "Put those on yourself. We're going to see what Larry wanted me to find."

• • •

As soon as we pull up in front of Claymore Tower, there's a skittering feeling inside my ribs, like something with small, sharp claws is hiding there. I've avoided coming here since I returned home. Being anywhere near this building triggers the same creepy feeling as a graveyard or a too-quiet alley in the middle of the night. I'm not sure if that's because of the structure itself, or if it's just that this is the place I most closely associate with Erskine Claymore—a man I hated so much that I risked my life just to bring him down. I have to say, I haven't changed my opinion of him since then.

"Okay, so we're here," Mikey says. "Now what?"

"We wait and see if Angel remembers anything important."

We sit still for a few minutes as I try to let my mind relax. That was always Larry's first instruction to me. Let my thoughts become weightless. Let them wander.

I close my eyes and try to find that peaceful, meandering mental state, but the pressure on me to find something inside my own memory is so great, Thomas and Mikey's hopes and expectations might as well be sitting in my lap.

"Staring at me doesn't help," I say, without opening my eyes.

"Don't stare at her," Thomas says to Mikey.

"You were staring at her, too!"

"How about, you both keep your eyes to yourselves and shut up?"

I press my fingers to my temples.

We wait some more.

"There's nothing," I say after a frustrating five minutes. "I'm sorry but nothing's coming to me. Other than irritation that Larry made this so hard."

"Maybe you're supposed to go up," Mikey says.

I turn around and look at Mikey. "Are you crazy? You think I'm going to climb up that building?"

"Not climb up the side, just go to the top. Look." He points to a queueing area with poles and chains. "Observation deck. Big tourist attraction."

"Oh, right. What time is it?"

"Just before six," Thomas says, checking the website for Claymore Tower's visiting hours. "First tour is at 8:30. I guess we're going to have to kill some time before then. Who's up for a delicious barrel of coffee?"

I'm about to start the van up again when Thomas touches my arm.

"What?"

His face is frozen. He points. "Look."

At the next intersection, the front grills of two police cruisers are just visible from behind the parked cars on either side of the street, sort of like two pinchers about to snap shut. "And now look in the rearview mirror."

Two large black SUVs—both unmarked—have blocked off the street twenty yards back. They look just like the vehicles my FBI security detail uses. Probably because this is my FBI security detail.

Only I have a feeling they're not here to protect me.

"How did they know how to find us?" I ask.

Thomas shoots a quick glance my way and taps a spot on his head, just above his ear. The same place where Mikey had that hard bump under his scalp.

There's no way Mikey is a puppet of the FBI. But if someone planted a tracking device on him—and the FBI used that to trace us—that's practically proof that the Feds are not working on my behalf. They must've teamed up with someone just as sinister as the creators of the Velocius project.

And it's definitely time to part ways with Mikey.

I do a quick sweep of the immediate area to assess possible escape routes. "Okay," I say. "When I say go, we all bail out and run in different directions. I'll go downtown. Thomas, you head up Central Park West. Mikey, you get the whole park to yourself."

Thomas grabs both my hands. "If you get caught, you demand a court-appointed lawyer, and you make sure they put you in the city lockup. Do not let them hand you over to the Feds."

"Deal." I glance back at Mikey. He's crouching by the back doors. "You ready?"

"I'm ready," he says.

I keep my eyes on the mirror. The SUVs aren't moving yet. But I don't expect them to be content with just watching us for much longer.

"We meet back at Claymore Tower at eight thirty," I add.

Thomas leans over and gives me a kiss that for a moment nearly blots out all the terror I'm feeling. Nearly. I pull back. "Okay—go."

We run.

CHAPTER 16

I bolt out into the street and into the oncoming lane. I run a jag-ged pattern around the few cars coming at me, honking their horns, and stopping in the street as one of the police vehicles tries to turn around and pursue me.

When I glance over my shoulder, I see four police cruisers closing in behind me, lights and sirens at full blast. I'm moving at full speed, which is pretty fast but not fast enough to outrun a car. There's no hope for me if I don't find a place to hide.

I need some help. My eyes search frantically as I keep running. Then I see it.

Up ahead, a huge construction project runs the length of a city block. Thanks to the scaffolding over the sidewalk and the tall plywood walls to keep pedestrians back, it will be my salvation. I'm up the scaffolding and onto the roof of the overhang before I have a second to dwell on it. I'm not sure if my Velocius abilities are helping me or if it's pure reflex from the old days, but I know if I scoot to the far side of the scaffolding roof and just lie flat, no one will be able to see me from the street.

Just in time. I hear the police cruiser come by and give a squawk as it slides past. The car goes around the corner. I peek over the top of the wall just long enough to catch the eye of the middle-aged street vendor standing a few feet from where I climbed up.

I know he must have seen me but he turns away nonchalantly. He refills the napkin dispenser and straightens a few displays of chips and gum as another police car slowly inches by. It comes to a stop. I think my heart has moved into my throat. I'm nearly choking on it.

They're asking him if he saw me.

They describe what I look like.

I wait.

"Nope, officer, 'fraid I didn't see a thing," he says.

I don't know who you are but I love you!

I lie still, trying to silently catch my breath. Staring up into the sky, I can just make out the very top of Claymore Tower, reaching up into the milky blue morning sky like a sword.

"Sarah, are you ready to talk?"

No. Not today.

I'm not my usual self.

Larry's question irritates me, because I was enjoying the feeling of floating along like a twig in a stream and he interrupted that. But I can't ignore him or he'll think there's something wrong. So I clear my dry throat and force my lips to move. I have to think very hard to get the words to travel from my brain to my mouth. The effort is exhausting.

"Yes. I'm ready. What are we talking about today?"

"Fears."

"Fears?"

"It's a vocabulary test. I'm going to give you the name of a phobia and you're going to break the word down into its constituent parts and figure out what it means."

Last night, while I was trying to prepare myself for my latest injection procedure, I was thinking a lot about fears. Like the fear of someone drilling into your skull. If there isn't a word for that, there should be. They could name it after me in my honor.

Usually the odd topics Larry brings up during the surgeries help calm me. This particular topic, not so much.

"Easy one to start: hemophobia."

"This is an easy one? For who?"

"Like I said, break the word down. Think about it."

"Well, I hear you guys talking about hematocrit levels all the time and I know that has something to do with blood. So I'll say hemophobia is the fear of blood?"

"Correct. Next one: nostophobia."

It's so hard to think when I'm pinned in this halo, with my mind trying to flow away on a beautiful bubbling brook.

"Can I ask a question?" I say.

"Sorry. No."

"Then can you use it in a sentence?"

"This isn't a spelling bee."

"I'm in the middle of brain surgery here. You can spot me one question," I say.

When Larry replies, I hear a smile in his voice. "Okay. Here's your sentence: 'Sarah should not have nostophobia.'"

"Are you kidding? That's not helpful at all."

"You asked for a sentence, I gave you one."

I puff my cheeks up with air and then let it out slowly. "Fine, then I'll figure it out on my own. I'll say, nosto- sounds like, I don't know, nostalgia maybe?"

"Hmmm."

"You're supposed to say warmer when I'm getting close to the right answer."

"Then you're getting warmer."

"Okay. Then I'm going to guess that nostophobia is the fear of the past, or remembering the past, or something like that?"

"Correct."

If I didn't know better, I'd say Larry sounds proud of me right now. But I realize something.

"Wait. But you said I shouldn't have nostophobia?"

"You shouldn't."

"But I'm here," I say.

I mean, the entire point of being here is that I should be afraid of remembering the past.

Larry doesn't respond. I hear the sounds of metal instruments being dropped onto a metal tray and the quiet whirring of gears as the robotic arm takes up a new position, possibly readying itself to plunge into the next drill site. I brace myself and listen, but the room remains quiet except for my breathing and the dozen blipping machines monitoring my life signs.

"Last one, Sarah. You should get this one, easy."

Emphasis on you. Meaning it's something personal?

"Acrophobia."

Well, he was wrong about this word. I got nothing. "Fear of acrobats?"

"Seriously? Who's afraid of acrobats?" he asks.

"I'll bet someone is."

"Possibly, but no, try again," he says. His voice suddenly sounds like he's determined for me. He wants to make sure I get this last one correct. "You can figure this out. What do acrobats do?"

"I don't know. I'm not allowed to go to the circus this week on account of my skull is full of holes and I'd scare the clowns."

"Come on, Sarah. Reason it out."

"I don't know. Acrobats do flips and stuff."

"Where?"

"At the circus. I just said that."

"No, I mean, where at the circus? Here's the only hint I'm going to give you."

The robotic arm suddenly swings around the side of my head and positions itself directly in front of my face. The drill attachment on the end moves like a finger until it's pointing toward the ceiling.

"Up? On a high wire maybe?"

"Good. So you couldn't be an acrobat if you were afraid of what?"

"Heights?"

"Bingo."

"Why was that supposed to be an easy one?"

"No reason. I doubt you suffer from acrophobia, that's all."

I think about my times at the gym, climbing to the highest point I could reach, not even sure why but knowing that I just had to get to the top. It was like all the answers, the peace I craved, the something I needed . . . it was always at the top. No, I definitely don't have acrophobia. Acrophilia, maybe.

"So I do not have acrophobia and I should not have nostophobia," I say.

"You're getting warmer."

Warmer? Does he mean I'm getting closer to the right answer? But wait. What was the question again?

• • •

I'm lying on the scaffolding, looking up at the sky above New York City, and I realize that even back then, Larry was trying to tell me something.

And right now Claymore Tower is like the needle of a compass pointing me in the right direction.

CHAPTER 17

I lie still for a few more minutes, listening to the sounds of the city getting louder and letting the noise chase away that memory of Larry talking to me. I really don't like remembering those times in the halo because I don't just remember them. I'm not sure what remembering feels like for most people, but for me, it's like I'm there again. It's as if I disappear for a moment, only to reappear, and when it's over, I need a moment to reorient myself.

I need to get off this scaffolding. But I don't want to call attention to myself by climbing back down the way I came, in full view of anyone on the street. So I scoot over to the other side. But a quick look over the edge of the plywood wall tells me it's a straight drop, maybe sixty feet into a mound of gravel inside the construction zone. I can either lie up here all day or climb back down on the street side.

By now, one of the SUVs has circled back and is trawling up the block slowly. I wait while it does two more slow circuits around the block. And suddenly my prayers are answered in the form of a double-decker, open-top tour bus.

Either this one hasn't started its run for the day or no one wants to take a tour through Manhattan at eight o'clock in the morning. In any event, the top level of the bus is empty. I leap to my feet and run the length of the block along the top of the scaffolding, hoping I can overtake the bus when it stops at the intersection. Up ahead, the light turns yellow and then red. The bus cruises to a halt, giving me the precious seconds I need to catch up to it. The top of the bus is almost level with the scaffolding. It's barely a jump at all and I land lightly in the center aisle. I turn around to see if anyone's noticed, and I can see the street vendor waving at me. I give him a salute before squatting low next to one of the seats.

A moment later, the bus rounds the corner. Fortunately it's heading back toward Central Park, and when it stops for some people in the crosswalk a few blocks later, I grab the safety railing along the bus top, leap over, and hang as far down as I can before letting myself fall the rest of the way into the road. Not a pleasant sensation for my feet as I hit the pavement, but I've experienced way worse.

I jog up the street, back in the direction I came from near the southwest corner of Central Park. I try to stay out of view, walking between parked cars and running next to vans and buses to shield me from view whenever I can. I've lost track of the time until I pass a jeweler's window and see a few diamond-studded Rolex watches all set to 8:20 a.m.

In front of Claymore Tower there's no sign of the SUVs, but I stay out of sight and keep my eyes peeled for Thomas. A tour bus comes to a stop at the curb, and within a minute, the sidewalk is filled with tourists.

This is my chance. Time to blend in.

I cross the street and mill about with the people who've just come off the bus. Okay, so blending in might be easier if these folks weren't Japanese.

Suddenly there's an arm around my waist and a voice in my ear. "Excuse me, could you take a picture of me and my girlfriend?"

I turn to face Thomas and pull him into a hug. Then I step back to get a better look at him.

"You left two hours ago in a tuxedo and now you're wearing a completely different set of clothes?"

"I'm resourceful."

"You're a thief. Not that I'm judging."

"I appreciate your moral flexibility during these times of stress." He reaches over and pulls the hood on my Coney Island hoodie over the top of my head. "Better keep your head down. Who knows what advanced capabilities Claymore's security cameras have, and the police might have facial recognition software that can peg you from here."

I look down and pull the strings of the hoodie so that it nearly cinches closed on my nose.

"Alternatively, to hide your face from view, we could just make out constantly all the way up to the observation deck," Thomas says.

"I don't think so."

"You never want to go with the make-out option, Angel. What is up with that?"

A security guard unlocks the front doors and begins directing the people at the front of the line to the set of three elevator cars dedicated to the observation deck tour. We follow the surge of chatting, laughing tourists. When it's our turn to file into the next available elevator, we try to put plenty of people between us and the security camera in the upper corner of the elevator car.

The car rises and with it, my hopes. Can there be something useful here? Some clue, some tool, that Larry intended for me to find? Or am I being used again for something I don't understand and didn't agree to?

When the observation deck doors open, we spill out onto a magnificent, nearly 360 degree view of upper Manhattan, thanks to the clear Lucite walls and thin silver cords designed to make sure the view is as unobstructed as possible.

Seeing the city below—and the seeming lack of protective barriers along the edge of the roof—several people immediately freeze and then turn around. Apparently this reaction happens frequently because another elevator car is waiting to receive all the tourists with cases of cold feet. Even Thomas seems a bit queasy when someone bumps into him and jostles him closer to the edge.

"You just walk around and think," Thomas says. "I'll be over here trying not to look too shady or terrified."

I step toward the roof's edge. Around me, people are taking little steps, battling the sensation that they're close to falling. Some of them lunge for the clear wall as if pretending to leap off. Thomas is quickly drafted into taking photo after photo of tourists posing against the skyline background. Then they pull him into their group and want to take pictures with him. Looking at him, I'm struck by the way he can ease himself into just about any situation. I have to force myself to stop staring at him, because my admiration quickly segues into worry.

We have to get him that next injection.

Which means I have to remember something useful.

I put my hands on the nearly invisible railing and look out over Central Park. Then I look north toward my old neighborhood. Out of nowhere, all these feelings hit me like a series of punches, one after the other.

Dread.

Exhaustion.

Sadness.

Longing.

I'm back in the chair, listening to that drill biting down into my skull. This time, it hurts. Not the drill, but the memory it's seeking out . . .

"What's your favorite food?" Larry asks.

I can feel the vibration of the drill in my jaw as I try to speak. I'm aware of each breath I take, like I have to remember to keep breathing or else I'll stop. Maybe this is it, finally it. They've hit the wrong part of my brain. The "good-bye, so long, farewell" part.

"Sarah? You with me?"

"Yeah." I think of caramel-flavored ice cream. Spicy beef empanadas. Coconut shaved ice. Jerk chicken. Chocolate birthday cake made from a boxed mix with vanilla frosting right from the can, the kind my mother thinks tastes terrible.

"I don't know," I say. "I have lots of favorite foods."

"Pick one."

"I don't want to."

"Come on, Sarah, this isn't a life-or-death choice."

"I have one, I just don't want to tell you what it is."

"Why not? It's a harmless question."

But that's not true. There are no harmless questions. Everything he asks, he asks for a reason. Every memory is a trail of bread crumbs to another memory. I've given them enough. They've taken too much of me already. What will happen when they finally have it all? Will my skull cave in once all the contents are emptied out?

"If I tell you, you're going to take it away from me," I say.

"What do you mean?"

"I know how this works. I say something, and those electrodes show you those bursts of electrical activity. You see all the lights inside my mind. Then you drill into my head and one by one you put the lights out."

For a few seconds, I hear nothing but a dull hum of a live mic capturing the dead air between us. Dead air filled with lies.

"No, Sarah," Larry says, and for the first time ever, his voice is choked with emotion. "Today is different. I promise."

I'm trying to fight off the sleepy, careless feeling that the drugs bring on. They seem to make it harder to look on the bright side. To believe in the promise of this treatment. It's like a shot of liquid "I don't care" straight into my veins. But today, Larry's words go deep into me, as though they bypass my awareness and instead lodge just below the surface, waiting.

Larry might be able to look into my head but he can't know, can't see what I'm feeling. My thoughts are more than just small, colorful electrical storms on a monitor.

I was right.

There really are no harmless questions.

I feel a hand slide across my back and I flinch.

"You all right?" Thomas says.

"Yeah."

"Did you remember something?"

"Yeah."

I turn and look out over the park again. Gradually I turn myself north, like my whole body is a divining rod. My old neighborhood. I've walked those streets several times since my return, disappointed that I felt like a stranger there. But now . . . now something is different.

Thomas takes me by the shoulders and pulls me into a hug. "Hey, come on. Tell me what's going on."

"I could really go for some Thai food," I say into his ear.

He releases me and gives me a squinty look of confusion. "Um . . . what?"

"I know it sounds strange, but I have this incredible craving for Thai food." I try to remember ever having it or seeing a Thai restaurant in my old neighborhood. I don't recall one, not that that means anything, but why would I crave it like this, so specifically, as if I'm starving for it?

I pull Thomas by the arm, pushing our way through the crowd toward the elevators. "It's a clue. I know it is. I can't explain it but . . . this means something."

"You're jonesing for some pad thai at nine o'clock in the morning and we're just gonna run with that?"

"I remembered . . . in the hospital. Larry asked me about my favorite food. And there was something else we talked about that day. Something important. I think that's why he linked the two things in my mind. Anyway, I think we have to go to my old neighborhood . . ." I look at him and suddenly stop speaking, because his expression as he looks down at his phone is broadcasting distress in every language, at full volume. "What's the matter?"

He turns his stolen phone toward me. "There's a live street-view cam set up at Columbus Circle. This is a shot of the street in front of the building about ten minutes ago. Right after we went inside."

There must be ten police cars parked at the curb, and several cops are re-directing traffic around the circle and setting up a blockade with yellow sawhorses. They seem to be asking the tourists to move away from the waiting line. All of them are in riot gear.

"Oh, wow. That's quite the party going on down there."

"It gets worse," he says. "Here's a video of the street right now."

The police cars are moving off, and in their place, several unmarked black SUVs have shown up.

"I don't get it. Where did all the police go?"

"I don't know, but I'd rather deal with city cops than whoever those guys are."

"If they were able to clear away the police, that means . . ."

"Yeah. Only a federal agency would be able to just come in and claim jurisdiction."

Considering how much help I've gotten from federal agencies in the past twenty-four hours, this doesn't seem like a promising development. "Come on, let's go."

He nudges me into an open elevator car, cutting directly in front of a group of people waiting to get on. "Sorry, folks! My girlfriend gets queasy from heights, and oddly she had chili for breakfast. Might want to wait for the next car."

People scramble to step back, and the doors close a moment later.

"Thomas! Why are we going down there if we know they're waiting for us?"

"The observation deck is the only thing open to the public, and this elevator bypasses all the floors with offices or private apartments. Except if there's an emergency."

"So what are we going to do?"

"Obviously we're going to create an emergency."

CHAPTER 18

Thomas pulls out a Swiss Army knife and unfolds it. There's a grim glint in his eye, like he's a military doctor about to engage in a battlefield amputation. He uses the knife to pry off the console cover surrounding the buttons. A bunch of wires spill out, all of which look very complicated and fragile and not like anything someone should be indiscriminately yanking on. Like Thomas is doing right now.

"Do you know what you're doing?" I ask.

"Not at all."

He starts cutting wires one at a time. We keep descending. Finally he puts his whole hand in, grabs a fistful of wires, and yanks them out.

The elevator seems to wobble and shimmy. There's a weird squealing noise and the lights go out. We're now in a blacked-out box but we're still descending. Thomas takes out his phone and uses it like a flashlight. "This is not working out the way I envisioned," he says. "Let's try this."

He kicks the console over and over until the elevator car seems to bounce and then drop a few feet, then bounce again. Then after a moment, the car begins to rise very slowly, maybe inches at a time.

"Why are we going back up?" I say.

"It must have a designated floor that it automatically goes to if there's a problem."

The doors open with a muffled *whoosh* and we step out. We're greeted by an empty hallway. It's hushed and still and extremely cold. Not temperature-wise, just the decor. The floors are white stone and the walls are covered in some kind of shiny plastic tiles. Sunlight streams in from a large window opposite the elevator bank and the brightness of it all is almost blinding.

"Where to?" I ask.

Thomas is looking down at his phone. He's got what looks like a map on the screen.

"Hold on . . . okay, according to the real estate listing for the luxury apartment for sale on the ninety-fourth floor, there's a set of elevators just for residents to use that take you down to the shopping plaza below the building. There's a subway station down there too."

"Perfect. Now if we can just find those elevators . . ."

"Over there."

We rush over. No sooner does Thomas hit the call button than a woman in a black and pink track suit comes trotting up with a dog tucked under her arm. We all step in once the elevator arrives. Thomas presses the button for the lower level shopping concourse and we wait, holding our breath as the woman with the dog decides where she's heading, ultimately pushing the button for the lobby.

I immediately push the cancel button. "I'm sorry but you're not going to the lobby."

Her face seizes up in terror. "Oh my God! Are you mugging me?"

"No, we're just in a hurr—"

The woman hastily pushes her purse at me. "Just please don't hurt us," she says, pulling her trembling long-haired Chihuahua close to her chest.

I can't help being sort of insulted. "Wait. Why did you give me your purse?"

"We don't want your money," says Thomas. "Besides, what sort of idiot robs someone on an elevator? How would we get away?"

The woman is hyperventilating now. I try to push the purse back into her hands, but she backs herself into the corner of the elevator. She squeezes her dog so hard, it yelps.

"Just take it! Don't hurt me!"

The doors open. We've reached the underground level. Thomas yanks me out of the elevator car before I have a chance to offload the purse.

"Now who's the thief?" Thomas says as we jog down the nearby escalator. "Why did you have to mug that nice lady, you thuggish Latina, you."

"I didn't mug her, she mugged herself!"

I stuff the purse into the pouch of my hoodie as we run toward the entrance to the subway. I keep looking back and around me to see if we're being followed. Thomas produces two fare cards just as we approach the turnstiles to enter.

"Stolen?"

"From here on, I'd just advise you not to ask about the origins of our assets."

Once we're inside the subway and standing on the platform, I have a fleeting feeling that we've made it to safety, which I don't trust.

It doesn't last long. Because now I see them coming. Men in black suits, each with an earpiece and a hand on the weapon at his side. Closing in on us from both sides.

They haven't spotted us yet. We're standing in a fairly tight knot of commuters waiting for the next train. But it won't take them long to pick us out of the crowd.

And that's when it turns on.

This power.

At first I only want it to give me the focus I need to quickly map out an escape route, but I get a bonus—the courage to try something very dangerous, something that could easily go wrong but might also save us.

"Get down," I hiss into Thomas's ear. Thomas drops to his knees and I crouch down next to him. "There are four guys with guns coming toward us. Stay down until the train comes. Then get on. Meet me at the top of the park."

"Angel, I don't think we should separate right—"

"It's all right. This is what I do best." I see the lights on the rails and then feel the blast of hot breath from the incoming train. "Oh, and I'm sorry about this."

"Sorry about wha—"

I stand up, step onto Thomas's back and, from there, leap up onto the top of the subway car. There's just enough room for me to squeeze between the top of the train and all the pipes and wires crusted with black brake dust along the ceiling. I'm up and over before anyone fully realizes what's happening.

This stop at Columbus Circle has a weird center platform running between the track for the commuter train and the track for the express train. I land on this platform, successfully putting a high-speed railcar between me and the guys with the guns. Along with the adrenaline rush, I feel a memory returning . . .

The beeping, always the beeping. Sometimes I can tune it out, but sometimes it's all I hear.

"What do all these machines do, anyway?" I say.

"They keep you alive," he says.

"Why so many?"

"This is just how many it takes."

If it were possible to communicate a shrug through the microphone, that's what I'd be hearing right now from Larry.

"It's weird, isn't it?" I say. "It's like, if one thing inside you breaks, you need ten machines to keep you going and two people to run each one."

"That's the moral of the story, then. Never put yourself at risk unless you have ten machines and twenty people to operate them."

"Nobody has that kind of support," I say.

I sure don't. I never did. And now I have only me, and maybe for not much longer. I'm becoming more of a stranger to myself every day.

I bite my lower lip hard.

"Something's upsetting you," Larry says.

"It's all upsetting, isn't it? Remembering. Making yourself relive it."

Larry waits for me to say more. He knows I can't resist talking when I'm in the halo. It all comes spilling out eventually. I have no secrets anymore.

"She was my friend," I say. "I trusted her."

"What did she do, this friend of yours?"

"She called the cops and told them where to find me. She's the only one who knew where I was going to be that day. It had to be her."

That memory has cost me. I was lost for a moment and in those brief seconds, I'm caught off guard. The train departs, leaving me with a clear view of the platform I just escaped, but the men in the black suits are standing there, looking straight at me. We're separated by maybe ten feet. They could shoot me, but they don't for some reason. Why are they not shooting me?

Not that I'm complaining.

In fact, they've put their guns away. I see one of the men nod as he listens on his earpiece. Maybe they're still hoping they can take me in without anyone noticing.

They don't want any witnesses.

Well, I'm not going to help them in that department. If they want to keep what's happening a secret, then I'm going to put it out in the open if I have to. I lift my eyebrows, daring them to make the leap over the track.

I can see one of men is practically twitching. He's thinking about jumping onto my platform.

Behind me, on the other track, the express train is approaching. The train normally goes about forty miles an hour, and it will slow down a little as it rumbles through the station, but not much. If I get this wrong, I'll probably break something or maybe even electrocute myself on the track. And yet my brain gives me the thumbs-up. I realize that Velocius is no longer some cutting-edge technology that exists like a foreign object inside me. It is me. Me, only faster.

As the train roars behind me, I pivot, start running, and leap onto the very back of the last car as it barrels past me. I barely get a grip on one of the chains that blocks the back door, keeping my head below the glass so no one inside the last car can see me.

The train picks up speed again as soon as it's through the station. I ride along in the darkness until the train stops at the Seventy-Second Street Station. I hop off the back, hoping no one will see me. One little kid spots me stepping onto the platform. Fortunately, his mother isn't paying any attention to his urgent finger-pointing.

I run up the steps and out onto the street, then turn toward the park. I'm probably a little ahead of Thomas, since he was riding the local train. I'm jogging along the sidewalk when a taxi pulls up beside me and I hear someone whistle. I turn and see a redhead waving at me from the backseat of the cab.

"Hey, baby. Want a ride?"

I hop in. After a quick embrace and a mutual check that we're both all right, we notice the cabbie looking at us in the rearview mirror.

"Where to?" he asks, his eyes slits of suspicion.

"Morningside Avenue and 123rd Street," I say, my jaw set.

"What's there?" Thomas asks.

"I had another memory. I think Larry wanted me to remember a specific person. The person who betrayed me."

CHAPTER 19

Owing to a shoddy suspension and a too-quick tap of the brakes, the cab comes to a bouncy, screechy halt in front of a small restaurant next to a scruffy little dog park. I know right away we're simultaneously in the right and wrong place. Thomas pays the driver with money from the not-really-stolen purse. As soon as we jump out, the driver peels away like we've got trouble written all over us.

I don't blame him.

We stand in front of the restaurant.

"Café Pilar," I say, reading the sign drawn by hand with gold glitter paint.

"Is this the place you remember?" he says. "It doesn't look like a Thai place. Maybe it used to be a different restaurant?"

I shake my head. I know we're close . . .

As I stare at the reflection in the window glass, my eyes are drawn to a small dry cleaning store across the street from the café. Its lighted sign spells out Spiffy Uniform Services, though one of the f's isn't illuminated.

I spin around and point. "I was standing inside that store, looking out the window, and I saw the sign for this restaurant."

"So that dry cleaners is important?"

"Yeah."

"Let's go over there."

Just as we're about to cross the street, a bus comes around the corner and sails toward us. I stop but Thomas doesn't. He's looking down at his phone, oblivious to the danger. He steps into the street right in front of the bus, which instantly starts honking and putting on its brakes.

But it's too late. Thomas isn't going to get out of the way in time.

Everything around me seizes up and stops. It's as if I'm watching myself from above. I'm so outside my own body right now I've become my thoughts.

I grab him by the hood of his jacket and pull him back just in time. The momentum sends him sailing backward onto the sidewalk, where he rolls back so far he does a somersault. A mother with a stroller has her hand pressed to her chest, staring at me, trying to make sense of what she just witnessed.

"You saved his life!" she says.

I stand over Thomas, relieved but also furious. "What's the matter with you?"

He looks up at me, horrified.

"I'm sorry. I didn't even see it. I'm feeling so spaced out and disconnected right now—I have to work really hard to concentrate."

"No kidding."

He brushes himself off and stands up just as I realize that I really need to sit down. My legs almost collapse beneath me. I have to hold onto the small wrought iron fence that borders the dog park. I pull myself along until I come to a bench and let myself spill onto it, taking deep breaths like I've just run as far and as fast as I could.

Thomas sits down next to me as I continue to pant.

"Angel," he says quietly. There's a look in his eyes that falls somewhere in the gray zone between amazement and fear. "You do realize . . . you threw me with one hand."

I'm still trying to catch my breath. "Yeah. I . . . I've never been able to do that before. Do you think—do you think it's part of the Velocius stuff?"

"I don't know. Those abilities of yours are based on extreme stress reactions. Ordinary people do have bursts of adrenaline and endorphins that give them momentary superstrength. It's possible that Velocius intensifies those reactions for you."

"But Velocius is only supposed to speed up my thinking."

"I don't think we know all the supposed-to's when it comes to Velocius. Maybe you've got way more going on in your head than anyone wants you to know."

I wrap my arms around my middle and double over. "I'm exhausted."

"We've been up all night on the run. I could sleep for a week."

"No, it's more than that," I say. "Throwing you like that. It's drained me in a way Velocius never has before." I put my hands on my knees and push so I'm sitting up straight.

"Can you walk?"

"I'm going to have to, aren't I? Unless you'd like to carry me."

"Believe me, I would love to, but I'm not doing so hot myself." He puts his hands out in front of him. Tremors are rippling through both of his hands even as I can see that he's fighting to keep them still.

We can't afford to waste any more time.

Unfortunately, the dry cleaning store is closed. The sign on the door says it opens at 11:00 a.m.

"So we wait, I guess," I say. Thomas doesn't respond. I realize he's just standing in the middle of the sidewalk, staring off at nothing. "Are you okay?"

"I know what I need to do next."

I'm not sure if that comes as a relief or a new thing to worry about. It also bothers me that he said "I" and not "we."

Again.

CHAPTER 20

We sit in Café Pilar and wait for the dry cleaners to open. While Thomas types madly on his phone, I poke at the plate of food he insisted on ordering.

"Eat," Thomas says, glancing up from his screen. "Your superfast brain is starved for sugar."

I take a few bites of my pancake to humor him, and I have to admit, I do start to feel better. I suddenly dive in, shoving food into my mouth like I've got to eat enough to last a week. Meanwhile Thomas stares at the screen of his stolen phone.

"You should eat something too," I say, pointing at the eggs growing cold on his plate. "You're just as exhausted as I am."

"Haven't you ever heard that old adage? Feed a superpower, starve a radical memory-altering drug," he says.

"That's not funny. Are you going to tell me about this idea?"

I could count to one hundred before he finally responds.

He sets the phone down on the table. "There. Did it."

"Did what?"

He takes a swig of his black coffee. "Contacted the Radical Pacifists. Told them that I'll give them the data in person, no upload."

"But you don't have any data to give them."

"Of course I don't. That's what we criminal masterminds call a bluff."

He motions to the waitress that he wants the check, purposely avoiding looking at me.

"Thomas, what are you thinking? What are you hoping to get out of doing that?"

"I'm hoping they're going to tell me where to meet them," he says. "And maybe that will give us a new lead on where they're keeping their stash of pharmaceuticals."

I push my pancakes away, suddenly feeling sick. "What happens if they say no?"

"I don't think they will. Besides, we've got nothing to lose."

"I just wish we knew what you were walking into. I wish we knew more about these Radical Pacifist people."

Thomas picks up his phone again. "Well, while I was on the train I posted on a message board asking about them. I pretended that I was making sure they could pay me for a job." He winks at me. "Don't ask how I know about the message board, just be grateful that I have a nefarious past."

"Okay. So has anyone posted a response?"

"A charming fellow called BlackDog214 says that the Radical Pacifists should be able to pay me well. In fact I should double whatever fee I'm charging them because they are, according to him, 'flush with cash.' He says someone pumped a lot of money into their operations as recently as two weeks ago."

"Around the time Mikey says someone tried to kill him," I say.

"We don't even know if that's true, but yeah, maybe the timing is important. BlackDog also says, 'Don't know who would fund those guys. No one wants to see them succeed. Take their money if you must but don't help them. Stick a worm in their software. If they get what they want, we're all out of business.'"

"What does that mean?"

"Not sure, but when he says 'we,' he means people like me. Hackers for hire."

"Soooo, he's saying that whatever the Radical Pacifists are doing is bad for bad guys? Does that make it good?"

"I doubt it." Thomas looks down at the phone again. "Oh. Hey. Just got a brand-new message from DeepSeaSquid1227: 'I wouldn't do business with those open source zealots if I were you. I agree with BlackDog. Bad for bidness.' Interesting."

"What's an 'open source zealot'?"

"I think he means these Pacifist guys are for open source information. No secrets. Everyone has access to anything." Thomas sets the phone down and massages his forehead. "Now I can see why they'd be after what 8-Bit was working on. Velocius would be the ultimate scoop for them. A top-secret mind-altering program, exposed to the whole world."

My partially-digested pancakes churn in my stomach.

"This is why I wish you could lie low and stay out of this, Angel. If Velocius is the hot fudge sundae of secret data, you're the cherry on top."

I shake my head. "If the Radical Pacifists knew about me, wouldn't they have tried to kidnap me along with you? Instead they tried to kill me."

"You're right," he sighs. "It doesn't make sense."

I think about the disappearance of my security detail. "Then again . . . we know the Feds don't want anyone else to find out about me. I think the reason they hound me and trail me is not so much to protect me as to make sure I stay hidden."

"Given your history exposing Erskine Claymore's sketchy business dealings, that's understandable."

"True. Maybe they're afraid that I'll do to them what I did to Claymore. In fact, I bet they'd rather see me wind up dead than have me fall into the hands of a group like the Radical Pacifists. If they thought there was a good chance the Radical Pacifists could stumble across me . . ."

Thomas's voice turns grim. "They'd do anything they could to keep you out of their hands."

"Right. From their perspective, better a dead girl than an exposed secret."

I tap the side of my water glass with a spoon. It sounds like a bell going off over and over again.

Thomas nods toward the diner's front window. "Hey. Looks like we're back on the trail."

A balding man in a New York Rangers jacket stands in front of the cleaners. He pulls out a set of keys and unlocks the store. Thomas and I get up. Though our check hasn't come yet, Thomas leaves several twenties on the table, courtesy of the woman I "mugged."

As we enter the dry cleaners, I try to prepare myself for an onslaught of memories. I take a deep breath and feel Thomas's hand on my back. He's bracing me for bad news.

But as the door closes behind us, the bell attached to it tinkles and I feel . . . nothing.

Nothing at all.

I stand face to face with the man in the Rangers jacket—he's Asian, mid-fifties. The phone immediately starts to ring and as he picks it up he says to us in an unfriendly way, "Be with you in a minute."

Behind us, the bell tinkles again. A girl with long bangs hanging over half her face walks in, looking tired and miserable. She has dozens of braided cloth bracelets on each wrist. She's small and twitchy and her long, grumpy face looks very familiar.

"Tai! You're late again," the man says, covering the phone with his hand. "I'm doing your job right now. You see this?" She doesn't respond, just heads to the back room. By the time the guy hangs up the phone, she's back, without her coat and purse. "This is the last time you're late or you're done," her boss snaps. "See what these people want!"

He waves a hand at us and stalks into the back room.

The girl takes his place at the counter. "Can I help you with some—"

Our eyes meet. Recognition instantly inflates between us like an air bag.

"You," I say.

Not Thai. Tai.

I lunge across the counter at her.

"Angel! What are you doing?" Thomas manages to grab me just before I get my hands around her throat. He yanks me back and lifts me up as I kick my legs at her. She backs up into a rack of nurses' uniforms.

"Angel," she says, looking at me and then at Thomas. "Oh my God. I can't believe it. You're . . . I thought . . ."

"You thought I was dead, Tai? Is that what you were going to say?"

"Yeah, I did." She puts her hand over her mouth and her eyes fill with tears. "Where have you been all this time?"

Her boss sticks his head out of the back room and scowls at her. "This is a workplace. Not a place for hanging out with your friends."

"We're not friends," I say through clenched teeth.

Thomas still has his arms wrapped around me from behind. "Angel. We need answers. She might be able to help us."

I don't want to need anything from the person who sent me into the clutches of Evangeline Hodges.

Tai's eyes dart toward her boss, who's about to start fuming again. "It's okay, Mr. Yee. They were just going. It's fine."

After shooting us another suspicious look, he disappears again. I pull away from Thomas and head for the door. "Let's get out of here. This was a mistake."

"Come back in twenty minutes," Tai says quietly. "Mr. Yee is going on delivery. We can talk then." She shoots a nervous glance toward me and then says to Thomas, "Please."

I walk out with no intention of returning. My anger is so enormous, it's blotting out all reason, and probably the sun along with it. I hate her. I hate her for what she did, what it led to, and what I became because of her betrayal. I don't care if she knows something that could help us; I never want to see her again.

Thomas catches up to me but I pull my arm from his grip.

"Don't you want to hear what she has to say?" he says.

"No!"

"Angel, if Larry sent you to her, maybe she knows something that can help us."

"That girl is the reason I have holes in my head!" I point at the small scar above my eyebrow. "That girl is the reason I've got holes in my life!"

"Whatever she did then, she might be able to help you now."

"She turned me in," I say.

"I know. It was a crappy thing to do—beyond crappy. You have every right to be . . ." He backs up and looks me up and down. "On the verge of punching a lion in the face. But you've got to put that aside—"

"Put it aside? PUT IT ASIDE?"

"Yes. Put it aside. What's done is done, and we need whatever information she might have. Larry seeded your brain with clues that sent you back to this place, specifically to this girl. Let's just hear what she has to say. Come on."

He tries to pull me into a hug, but I push away from him and plant my feet, not wanting to move or listen or be touched at all.

"I don't want to hear her excuses," I say.

"Maybe they're good excuses."

"Good? What are you saying? That I deserved what she did to me?"

"No, but I can tell she's sorry," he says, looking back toward the storefront. "She asked us to come back. And I saw her eyes when she realized you weren't dead. She was happy to see you, but afraid too."

"How do you know?"

"I have a PhD in guilt, remember? And there's that hacking thing I do so well."

"Right. You can hack people's souls, is that it? So hack me right now. Tell me what I'm thinking."

He gives me a tired smile and puts his hands on my shoulders. "You're not thinking at all. You're just angry."

"Yes, I'm angry. She's the one who's responsible for what happened to me!"

"No, she's not. At least she's not alone in being responsible."

He rubs my cheek with his thumb but I don't look into his eyes. "If she hadn't called the police, if I hadn't ever gotten caught . . ."

"Your mother would still be gone. You'd be what? Bouncing around foster care? Out there, making life difficult for your grandfather? Same old, same old."

"At least I'd still have all my memories!"

"And you'd be living a life built on lies and not even know it. You wouldn't know the truth about who you really are, about Virgil being your father. And worse than that . . ." He gets in front of me, leans forward, and puts his mouth next to my ear. "We would never have met."

That shuts me up.

He kisses me on the cheek. I work hard to keep my anger from ebbing away completely, but his words have opened up some sort of release valve inside me.

I take a step toward him. He pulls on one of my hoodie drawstrings and puts his forehead against mine.

"See, life is good at consolation prizes. I'm the best consolation prize you could ask for, right?"

I look at him, trying very hard not to smile.

"And you're also thinking, 'Wow, he's so super hot when he's right.'" He winks and starts gently guiding me back toward the dry cleaners.

He's halfway down the block when I pause again.

Because suddenly I realize why we're here. Not because Larry wanted me to remember anything about files or possible backup data locations. Maybe there wasn't any secret agenda except this: He was trying to send me home. That's all.

All the things he told me—all the mental breadcrumbs he scattered inside my mind—it was just so I could find my way back home.

I hug myself tightly.

I should be disappointed—frustrated. We came all this way, followed all these clues, hoping it would lead us to valuable information, information that would save Thomas. And yet—I'm grateful for this. Larry saved me once. Maybe he's doing it again.

CHAPTER 21

"I'm sorry, Angel," Tai says. "You don't even know how sorry."

I look at her, trying to place her among the scattered, cloudy memories I have from my life before the hospital. It's almost like picking up a photograph that someone has crumpled and tossed onto the ground. I open the thoughts, try to smooth them flat so I can get a better look. She is familiar to me, but it isn't until she flicks her long bangs out of her eyes and bites her lower lip that I know her, remember her, as someone who was part of a life that's now gone.

"You got your nose pierced," I say.

"Yeah. It's kind of annoying when you need to blow your nose, actually. Been thinking of letting the hole close up."

She looks up, looks past me, looks anywhere but in my direction. Finally, when there's no avoiding it, she makes eye contact. Thomas is right. She is deeply sorry.

The pain in her eyes moves me to a place beyond my own anger. As soon as I imagine what it would feel like to forgive her, my own pain lessens. It shouldn't work like that, but somehow it does.

"Maybe you guys should hug or something?" Thomas says.

I shoot him an irritated look and then notice that he's got one hand clamped over the other to keep the tremors in check.

"Who is this guy, by the way?" Tai says.

"He's my . . . you know. He's Thomas."

She gives Thomas the once-over and then looks back at me. She seems to be bracing herself for my questions, so I start with the one that sits heaviest on me.

"Did you do it for the reward money?" I ask.

She gives me a blank look. "There was a reward? Seriously?"

"Yes, there was a reward! Like a huge amount of money. You didn't know that?"

"No, I didn't." She wipes her nose and makes a hiccuping noise. "It doesn't matter. It won't bring her back."

"Bring who back? My mother?"

"No, my sister," she says.

"What happened to your sister?" Thomas asks.

The phone rings and we're momentarily interrupted so she can do her actual job. After she hangs up, she goes to the front door, puts up a sign that says "Be right back!" and motions for us to follow her into the back room.

This area is filled with canvas bags full of dirty linens. Against one wall is floor to ceiling, row upon row of white medical coats and blue scrubs bagged in plastic. There are no chairs, so we sit on the floor.

"If I'd known that making that call would lead to—I didn't know. I swear."

I sigh. And soften. I was so ready to be angry at her. To unload on her for what she did. But now I can't.

"Just tell me what happened," I say. "Why did you—"

"Rat you out?" She says with an appalled laugh. "I did it because I was tired of getting used by you. I was angry about what happened to my sister. What you did to her. It was retaliation. Simple as that."

"I . . . don't really know what you mean. Did I hurt your sister?"

"Are you kidding me? I know what I did was wrong, but don't pretend what you did never happened."

Now she looks at me squarely in the face, her brown eyes boring into me, at once glinting and full of despair.

Thomas says, "Angel doesn't remember a lot of things from that period."

"Really? That's convenient," Tai scoffs. "Wish I could say the same."

"Convenient?" I say. "You have no idea what I've been through."

Thomas puts his hand on my leg and I let the tension in my body drain away. "If you could just tell us what happened, it might help her remember," he says. "Start with your sister."

Tai pushes her hair out of her eyes and then lets it fall back over her face again.

"Tam was right out of nursing school and she'd just split from her horrible, controlling boyfriend and she got this really good, well-paying job at a nursing home over on the West Side. I was so happy for her. She was able to get her own place. And she helped me out too. I found out through her that Mr. Yee needed some help here. All the nursing home's laundry comes here." She looks around at all the uniforms, clean and pressed and waiting for delivery. "Then you showed up. I let you sleep back here a few times because you had nowhere else to go. Do you remember that?"

I shake my head.

She sighs, playing with the sleeve of a medical coat. She's too young to sigh like that, like the whole world has tired her out for too long.

"Anyway, you said you needed to visit someone at that nursing home but you couldn't get in because of the high security. I guess the place was full of rich old people or something. So Tam helped you get in. I let you take one of the nurses' uniforms from here, to make it easier for you to blend in. But then Tam's boss found out there'd been a security breach, and my sister got fired. Her whole life went down the drain after that and you never even apologized. I didn't see you for weeks, in fact, and I when I told you what had happened to Tam, you just shrugged and said, 'She's better off never setting foot in that place again.'"

"I don't remember that," I say.

Tai crosses her arms. I can see that it's hard for her to keep talking about her sister.

Thomas clears his throat. "Is there anything else?"

Tai looks at me, her eyes leaking tears of pain and anger. "I didn't see you again for another couple weeks after that. Not until you needed a place to stay again. I couldn't believe you would dare ask me, but you didn't even seem to notice that I was angry at you. You just kept telling me that you had something important to do that night. I was afraid you were planning on blowing something up but you assured me it wasn't anything like that. I didn't know what to believe, though. After the way you acted about Tam's job—the way you were so numb about it—I figured you were capable of anything. You were obsessed with that Claymore guy."

"That much I remember," I say. "The obsession part."

"I finally got you to tell me where you were going. But when I asked you what you were planning to do there, you said, 'You'll find out tomorrow when everyone else in the city does.'"

Part of me doesn't want to believe I could treat someone like that. Someone who'd helped me, someone who'd suffered because of me. But based on what I remember from that period of my life, I was single-minded in my pursuit of revenge against Claymore. I don't doubt that I tossed our friendship aside. It was all justified in my mind.

Even now, it's tempting to make excuses for myself. But looking at Tai, I just feel an overwhelming sense of shame. That I let myself become so hardened, so blinded. Was I so different from my grandfather after all?

"Tai, I don't remember any of that, but if I could go back in time and act differently, I would. I'm so sorry."

"And I'm sorry I called the cops that night. I swear I just figured you'd get in trouble. That's all. And then when you just vanished—God, Angel, I thought you were dead. I thought somebody killed you."

"They almost did," I say, suddenly aware that I'm rubbing the top of my head. "I hope your sister is okay now," I add.

Tai's jaw clenches. The tears are back.

"Two weeks after you disappeared, my sister disappeared too," she says, fighting to get the words out. "Ten days later, they found her body in a Dumpster. Shot in the head. Everyone thinks her ex did it. They picked him up for questioning, but there was nothing to tie him to it. As much as I hated that guy, I don't think it was him. I think she found something out about what was going on in that nursing home. Or at least someone thought she did—someone tied her to you and figured you two were working together. I asked about the ballistics tests and the other evidence they had and the cops told me all of it was inconclusive."

No evidence. No answers. No justice. It's disgusting what people get away with. It's like someone cut Tai's heart out and then shrugged.

"That's horrible, Tai. I don't even know what else to say other than I'm so, so sorry."

Thomas and I share that helpless, lonely feeling you get when you wish you could make someone feel better but know that you can't do anything at all to ease their pain.

Tai just shakes her head. The load she's been carrying is so big, it somehow makes her look even smaller than she already is. Like all the hurt she's feeling has compressed her. "That's when I knew—I knew you were dead too. You had to be because it turned out you were right. What you'd told me about that nursing home was true."

"What did I tell you?"

"You said that there was something going on in that building. Some really screwed up research. It wasn't a nursing home at all, it was some kind of laboratory. I thought you were crazy."

"But now you don't?" I ask.

"Well, I don't think you were lying. Not after what happened to Tam. But Angel, where have you been? Were you hiding out?"

I tell her briefly about some of the things that happened to me in the hospital. Not all of it—nothing about Hodges and Thomas's connection to her. But I do tell her about the secret project called Velocius. I'm not supposed to—I swore an oath I wouldn't disclose what had happened to me at the hospital—but considering all the ways the Feds have screwed me over in the past twenty-four hours, I figure all bets are off. Spilling their secrets gives me a grim sense of satisfaction.

Tai doesn't interrupt me. She just listens—her eyes occasionally going wide and her face intermittently registering complete disbelief—until I'm done. Then, finally, she says, "Soooo, they wiped your memories out?"

"Yeah. Most of them."

"Well, you do seem different."

"How?"

"You're a little . . . not as spiky maybe?"

"Wow," Thomas says. "Hard to imagine Angel being spikier than she is now."

I give him a swat.

"Yeah," Tai says. "She was tough. She didn't let anything get in her way. I admired her right up until she used me."

"I would've felt the same way if I'd been in your position," I say.

She's back to pondering the state of my brain. "And now this veloci-whatever ability—"

"Velocius," Thomas says.

"Yeah. I don't get it. They did this thing to your brain and now it, like, takes longer for you to die?"

I nod. Granted, it also shortens my overall lifespan, but everything has a flip side.

"And that's supposed to be a good thing?"

I shrug. "Longer to die gives you more of a chance to live, right?"

"Now I know you've changed," she says. "That's almost optimistic, Angel."

A sad smile flashes across her lips and is gone a moment later. I reach out and take her hand and say again, "I'm really sorry about your sister."

She makes a fist and knocks me lightly on the top of the head. "Thanks. And I'm sorry about whatever they did to your brain."

Our brief moment of reconciliation is interrupted by the buzz of an incoming text message on Thomas's phone. He takes the phone out of his pocket and looks down at the screen. I watch his face but his expression doesn't change. Once again he looks like he's not fully registering what he's seeing. That makes me uneasy. If there's one thing I've taken for granted about Thomas all this time, it's his ability to instantly understand the implications of things.

For a split second, I try to talk myself out of it. Maybe he's just tired, maybe he's just thinking deeply. But this is not like his usual intense look of concentration. And I know I'm not imagining it—the blankness in his eyes. He's trying to figure something out and he can't.

The phone trembles in his hand. He switches hands but that's not much better. In a forced, falsely confident tone, he says, "Uh, Tai? Just out of curiosity. What's the address for that nursing home where your sister worked?"

"I don't know the actual street address," she says. "I could look it up. I know how to get there."

He holds up his phone and displays the map on his screen. "Is it on Riverside Drive?"

She takes a closer look and nods. "Yeah. That's it."

"How did you know?" I ask him.

"This is the address for the nursing home where Sarah Claymore lives. And this," he points to the screen, to a dot just half a block away, "is where the Radical Pacifists just told me to deliver my data at ten o'clock tonight. What are the chances those two things are unrelated?"

CHAPTER 22

The bell above the door chimes, and Tai gets up. "I gotta go out front. Angel, if you need to, you can hang out here 'til closing. On Saturdays, Mr. Yee usually makes his deliveries and then just heads home. Just try not to make much noise, or the customers might get suspicious."

"Thanks," I say.

She nods and closes the door behind her as she leaves.

In hushed voices, Thomas and I discuss our next move, and suddenly I'm fighting against a rising tide of Thomas's doubts.

"The problem is, we have no real data so we have no real leverage," he says. "These Radical Pacifist guys might be dopes, but they're gonna figure out real quick that the 'data' I'm giving them is stuff I just randomly cut and pasted from a 1994 study about the effects of hallucinogenic mushrooms on mice."

"You don't need to give them anything. All we need to do is get you that antidote. And since there's a pretty good chance it's stored at the nursing home, all we have to do is get there and find it before you're supposed to meet with the Radical Paficists."

"Angel . . ."

I cut him off.

"Do not even start with the 'I should go alone, and you should skip away unharmed' business. I am not having it, young man."

He sighs. "Angel, I don't want to argue."

"I don't want to argue either. So let's not."

He suddenly looks so forlorn and scared that it pains my heart. I put my arm around his slumping shoulders. "I know you're worried that you can't figure all this out, but you don't have to. Two brains are better than one and all that, right?"

"I'm not sure my brain is going to be worth much of anything when all this is over."

"Don't say that."

He looks down at his phone, staring at the map as if he's hoping something will become clearer. "What if this stuff they put in me is doing damage, not just to my memory but to how I think? Real, long-term damage?"

I take the phone out of his hand. "I came through the memory drug without any damage to my cognitive abilities. At least that's what they told me when I had all my follow-up exams, and I think it's true."

"Yeah, but you've got that Velocius thing going on. I don't."

"Well, we're going to get the antidote for you, so don't worry." I shift into planning mode. "Since the Radical Pacifists won't be expecting you to show up until ten, we should have plenty of time to infiltrate the nursing home, get the antidote, and run for the hills."

"Are there hills in Manhattan?"

"You know what I mean. Look, by the time they realize you're not going to show up with their data, we'll be long gone and your brain will be as good as new. Sound good?"

"Yeah. Sure." Thomas shoves his hands in his pockets. "It's a good thing you've got a handle on this because I don't. My handle has just about fallen off."

I can see how exhausted he is. I'm exhausted too, and I'm not even fighting off mind-altering gunk. We both need to recharge if we're going to pull off a heist without dozing off in the middle of it.

Time for a nap.

I steer him across the room, and he lets himself be led along. "Probably best to wait until dark before we try to sneak in. Meanwhile let's just get some rest if we can. Even your brilliant mind can't function without sleep."

I push a few laundry bundles around and we both sink onto them like we're sitting in big, lumpy beanbags. Our heads tipping back, we look up at the ceiling, which is full of water stains and crisscrossed by ugly air conditioning ducts.

I listen to Thomas's breathing slow and deepen, like every breath he takes is thoughtful, intentional, and cleansing. Though I would never say this out loud, I can't help thinking that it wouldn't be so bad for him to forget this day. To forget the way he withheld information from me, strained my trust in him, tried to push me away. I'll make sure he doesn't forget, though. I'll say, "Remember that time you were all misguided and thought you were protecting me? Wasn't that funny?"

It'll be a big joke between us.

Someday.

Gradually we both fade into sleep.

Beside me, Thomas is still asleep. I want him to stay that way for as long as he needs.

I get up and open the door to the front of the store. I find Tai sitting on a stool behind the counter, her hands cupped around a ceramic mug that says World's Best Golfer.

"You get some rest?" she asks.

"Yeah. What time is it?"

"About three o'clock."

I pull up a stool next to her and sit. "Can you tell me about . . . back then? Before I disappeared. What do you know about how I was living back then and what I was doing? And be totally honest."

"How honest are we talking?" she asks.

"Honest like you're talking about me behind my back. I want to know everything, no matter how bad it sounds."

So she does. And it's hard to hear, but it's also good. All the fears I had back in the hospital, about how I might have done terrible things—I believed I was a criminal, a murderer even, and this is probably why. Even though I was desperate, I knew I was hurting innocent people. Not Claymore. He deserved what he got. But I used other people, dragged them into my revenge plot.

As she tells me about my past self—how I used to manipulate people, how I lied and hid and said whatever I had to say to get what I needed—I get this weird sensation of things becoming clearer, almost as if someone is rinsing away a greasy film over my eyes. Or over my mind, really.

I can't believe I'm even thinking this, but if there was any benefit to my memory modification surgery, it was that it gave me a chance to be someone a little less ruthless. Someone who doesn't believe the end justifies the means. Because I lived those awful means.

So what do I do about the fact that I need help now? I'm not going to make the same mistakes I used to make. I guess I just have to ask and, if the answer is no, accept that.

"Tai, I cannot believe I'm going to ask you for a favor after everything I've put you through, but . . ."

She smiles.

"Why are you smiling?"

"Because at least you're asking instead of just using me."

"Don't say yes until you know what you'd be getting yourself into."

"Okay. What do you need?"

"I need help finding a way into that hospital."

The smile doesn't falter. She nods. "I think I can do that. I feel like Tam would want me to help you somehow."

"Thank you, Tai." I give her a hug until she starts squirming and telling me I'm crushing her.

"I should go see if Thomas is awake."

Just as I reach the door to the back room, Tai says, "Uh, Angel?"

She's looking down at her phone now. "Didn't you say you went to that fancy party last night? The Met thing?"

"Yeah. Why?"

She's scrolling through something on her phone, her eyes getting wider by the second. My heart stops. No, it doesn't just stop. It vacates my chest and runs out the back door.

She hands her phone to me. "Check it out."

There's a paused video and it's kind of blurry, but I recognize the girl in the yellow dress. Cassidy Something. I hit Play and watch as Cassidy flicks her hand back in the direction of the yacht.

"I knew who she was the moment I saw that tattoo. I mean, who else could it be? People have been looking all over for her, thinking she's dead or whatever, and apparently she's just been hanging around, going to fancy parties. . . ."

We play a bunch of related clips, including a television news interview with a man dressed in a black suit, who's identified only as a "limousine driver to the rich and famous." He's pointing wildly toward the street where Mikey and I had our run-in with the white van and where we ended up hijacking the police cruiser.

I click on another video, and I recognize the reporter Thomas and I saw on the television in the hospital waiting room.

"This new information, coming to light just in the last few hours, raises the question of whether the disturbance near Claymore Tower this morning and the earlier incident near the Met Gala are somehow related. Police claim that there is no apparent link between these two incidents, and given the lack of physical evidence, they currently have no plan to investigate them as such. . . ."

"This day keeps getting weirder," says Tai.

"Yeah," Thomas says, suddenly appearing from the back room. "That's how it is when you hang with Angel. All weird, all the time." He gives me a kiss on the head.

"Thanks, baby," I say.

He's now fully awake but he doesn't look at all rested. In fact, he looks worse. He's pale and hollow-eyed.

"I just had a terrifying dream about Mikey and me going to a fancy party together."

I almost laugh, but I can't quite pull it off. "I wonder what happened to him. I hope he's all right." Even after the problems he's caused us, I can't help pitying him—wishing we could've helped him.

"Somebody must have picked him up," Thomas says. "Otherwise he would've tracked us down by now. He was pretty intent on keeping tabs on you."

"Who's Mikey?" Tai asks.

"Let's see if he turned up on any of these news clips." Thomas scrolls down through all the videos until he comes to one, dated just an hour ago, that's titled "Angel Lives?"

I let out a disgusted noise. "Oh, great. This is just what I need."

Thomas plays the video. The "reporter" who's talking into the microphone and standing near the party yacht looks like he's just shooting this "interview" on his phone. Watching the shaky video gives me an instant headache, so I just close my eyes and listen instead. The opening sentences skim over the surface of my brain. Nothing sticks until . . .

"Witnesses say there was a girl at the party in a white dress with wing tattoos on her back. And at one point, do you know who she was hanging out with? Erskine Claymore. If this is the Angel who once targeted Claymore's building projects, maybe she hasn't been missing at all. Maybe she's now getting cozy with Claymore and his money. Can you say 'sell out'?"

"Man, I miss the days when people used to pretend that there were still two or three journalism ethics standards left in the world," Thomas says.

I shake my head slowly, my jaw set.

The reporter continues, "Now we're hearing news that two police officers were left in a downtown warehouse with their hands and feet tied, and their cruiser was recovered uptown. The police are denying that anything has happened and insist that the gunfire reported near the Met Gala and the lockdown near Claymore Tower earlier today are not linked in any way. But right now, the media manhunt is on for the truth."

"Yeah, I'd like to go on a manhunt for the truth myself," Thomas says, closing the browser window.

The video vanishes, but I can still see that ghostly image of the girl on the screen and the image of me from last night, shaking hands with Erskine Claymore.

"A manhunt for some anti-Snowball medication will have to do," I say.

CHAPTER 23

The plan we come up with is terrible. It depends too heavily on good fortune and perhaps a miracle or three. Even if everything happens just as it should—not that we have any of the details worked out—we haven't got more than the slimmest chance of getting in and out again with the drug Thomas needs.

Thomas is trying not to smile as he looks at me in my blue scrubs. "What?"

"I was going to make a sexy-nurse comment, but I decided not to," he says. He gestures down at his blue scrubs. "About myself, I mean."

Tai is driving the delivery van. "Mr. Yee will kill me if he knows I took the delivery van after hours, but I owe you some help on this, Angel."

"You don't owe me anything. Which makes me even more grateful for this."

Thomas and I are sitting on a couple milk crates in the back of the van, sandwiched between laundry bags full of soiled uniforms—and that soil is blood and some other fluids that don't smell so great—and a rack of clean, pressed scrubs in individual plastic bags.

"Thomas, how much time do we have?"

"About ninety minutes until I'm supposed to show up and give them the data stick."

Except for the swishing of plastic, we drive in silence for another five minutes. Then Tai says, "That's it, there on the corner. That big townhouse."

Thomas and I get up to have a look through the windshield.

He says, "It just looks like your regular, garden-variety six-story mansion."

"Yeah," Tai says. "It's pretty amazing inside too. I've gone in a few times to drop laundry off. Never got past the first floor but everything I could see was gorgeous. Tam told me that she was only allowed to go to the floors where the nursing home patients were. I think she said fourth and fifth floors, but I'm not positive about that."

"So are you sure you can get us in there?" Thomas asks.

"I can use my ID to get into the basement parking lot," she says. "There's a big addition on the back of the building you can't see from here. I'll drive you around the block so you can get a better look."

She takes a left and we sweep past.

"This whole block is basically part of that building. See? There's a small hallway that connects the mansion house with the rest of the nursing home."

I look at the building, so focused it's like my eyes are trying to x-ray the place. I wish I felt something, remembered something. I know I've been here but nothing is coming to me.

"Does it seem familiar?" she asks.

"No."

"They put that tall fence up about six months ago, probably because of you, plus they increased their security like crazy. Mr. Yee was really annoyed. They made him submit to a background check if he wanted to keep the contract with them." She points to the entrance to the parking garage. There's a security camera pointed down at the gate. "They're going to figure out pretty quick that we don't usually deliver uniforms at 8:30 p.m. on Saturday, but I can talk my way in. I think. Don't know if I can come back and get you, though."

"Getting back out is on me," I say. "Don't worry about it. This is not your problem, and I've caused you enough trouble as it is."

Suddenly Thomas slumps over.

"Are you okay?"

I take his hand. It's shaking again.

He nods—not convincingly—but I'm instantly distracted by what I see out the window. A black SUV is pulled up to the curb, the engine idling and the lights off. It's parked right next to the small guard's booth just inside the high gate on the grounds of the nursing home. I stiffen and motion to Thomas so we can both keep an eye on the vehicle. If we just drive past at a normal speed, the driver shouldn't notice us . . .

Two men haul Mikey out of the SUV. He stumbles a little as they push him into the building. The guard shuts the gate behind them.

I swear under my breath.

Tai is keeping her eyes on the road, still not sure what we're looking at. "What?"

"We just saw our pal Mikey," Thomas says.

"He knows where the antidote is," I remind Thomas. "He knows his way around this building. If we can get to him—free him—maybe he can make this a lot easier for us."

"You're assuming it's more time-effective to rescue him than to just search on our own," he says.

"You and I are very efficient rescuers. Besides, Mikey is full of surprises." I don't say this out loud, but part of me thinks we owe Mikey at least one feeble attempt to help his messed-up self.

Thomas sighs, but I'm not sure if it's a sigh of agreement or resignation.

I look away from the window, and suddenly thoughts of Mikey vanish. "Thomas, where did that blood come from?"

"What blood?"

"The blood all over the front of your shirt?"

He looks down at the blood droplets soaked into his scrubs and then touches his nose. I notice small rings of fresh blood around each nostril. He sniffs. "I'm okay. I didn't even notice."

The fact that he didn't notice blood dripping out of his nose seems like a worse sign than the blood itself. "Tai, we need to get in there now, please."

She pulls a U-turn at the next intersection. A moment later, she's turning into the garage entrance.

"Ready?" she says.

I nod.

Just as we approach the guard booth at the entrance to the parking ramp, she picks up her phone and starts cursing at the top of her lungs, complaining about having to make such a late-night delivery. "Well, you had better pay me overtime because I have better things to do on Saturday nights than make up for your screw-ups . . ." I have no idea how the guard is taking this. Thomas and I are hiding underneath the unpleasantly scented bags of dirty uniforms.

When the van pulls forward, Thomas whispers to me, "I have to remember to try her method next time."

"Next time? Do you plan to have to bluff your way past security guards on a regular basis?"

"If you're in my life, and I hope you will be, then I need to prepare for all eventualities."

I kiss him. "Likewise."

"Here we go, guys," Tai says over her shoulder as we turn down the winding ramp to the lower level of the parking garage. "One more guard to deal with and then you're in. But this one might be a tougher sell."

After an endless series of spirals, the van comes to a halt and then we hear beeping as Tai backs up.

"Get ready," she says and then gets out of the van.

A moment later we hear her call out, "Hey, you got time to help me unload some stuff?"

"Can't," a man's voice says.

"Aw, come on. The sacks are only sixty pounds each. Could be a good workout."

We don't hear him respond, but a second later, one of the back doors opens. Tai pulls out a big white bag and slings it over her shoulder. She must be as strong as an ant because I'm sure that bag weighs as much as she does.

When she turns back around to grab the second bag, she whispers, "He just unlocked the door and walked away so he didn't have to help me. Hurry up before he gets back."

"This girl is amazing," Thomas says as we hop out of the van. "We should totally draft her into our gang."

We each take a bundle of laundry to carry like a shield. Another idea of Tai's. We can hide behind them and, worse comes to worst, throw them if we have to. Thomas has to put one knee up under his bundle to keep his grip on it. His strength is fading by the minute and we don't have time to waste. I glance over and catch him wiping more blood from his nose but pretend I don't see.

I give Tai a quick one-armed hug. "Thank you again."

She flicks her hair back and looks down at the ground. "Just . . . be careful."

"We will. And I have one more favor to ask. If we haven't made contact in one hour, call 9-1-1. Say there's been a break-in or something. Whatever it takes to get the police here."

"Got it. Good luck."

We watch forlornly as she gets into the van and pulls away. This is it. We're on our own.

"You're assuming the police will actually show up here if she calls them," Thomas says.

"You don't?"

"No. I think we're about to enter no-man's-land."

CHAPTER 24

I remember the foyer. Kind of. It has this swirly pink marble on the floors. Fresh flowers. Tall ceramic vases filled with some kind of decorative bushy grass next to the elevators and fussy old-people chairs with claw feet.

But this vague sense of familiarity is overshadowed by what I see as we enter. Two men are shoving a struggling Mikey into one of the elevators. He must've been fighting them for a while or we wouldn't have caught up to them. The elevator doors close, cutting off the sound of Mikey's yelps.

I rush over to the elevator, balancing my laundry bag on my hip. Thomas shuffles along behind me, his bag dragging on the ground. The LED sign above the elevator doors displays the floor number: 1 changes to 2, 2 changes to 3. And it stops there.

I turn to look at Thomas. He's breathing hard but trying not to show it.

"They took him to the third floor," I say. "How about we make that our first stop?"

He flashes me a thumbs-up. "Aye, captain." I push the button to summon our lift.

When we get out of the elevator at the third floor, I know we're in the right place because someone is screaming.

The hallway is so full of tension I get a prickling sensation on the back of my neck.

Three nurses and a guard are wrestling a youngish woman into one of the rooms. Fortunately, a year at a research hospital where they do experimental brain surgery has conditioned me well. That and living in New York City. I'm good at minding my own business. I hustle past the action, and now I have a clear view of the rest of the corridor.

Which means I can see Mikey's guards push him around the corner into an intersecting hallway.

I wait until the sounds of their scuffling feet die down before I follow them. I peer around the corner just in time to see a door closing.

"Um, Angel . . ."

I look back at Thomas. All of a sudden, his bloody nose seems to turn on like a spigot. He looks down like he's not sure where all this blood is coming from. Before I can figure out how to help, his face goes white. It's like someone just pulled a shade down over his eyes. He's going to faint.

He staggers to the right, his laundry bag tipping him over even farther when he tries to hold onto it. I grab him, then steer him down the empty hall. I duck into some sort of examination room, right next to the one they put Mikey in. It's hardly large enough for the bare gurney that looks as though it's been hurled into the room and forgotten. A huge window opens onto an interior courtyard below. I barely get Thomas through the doorway before he goes down face-first onto the edge of the gurney. As I try to brace him, both our laundry bags drop to the ground, and dirty laundry spills out in a silent explosion of color and unsavory smells.

I kick the door closed behind me. The only light in the room comes through the window, since it's never fully dark in Manhattan.

In the room next to us, I hear bumping and what sounds like furniture being shoved into the wall.

Thomas raises his head. "Did I just faint?"

"Yeah. A little bit."

"That is so not cool."

In the outer hallway, we hear men talking. Through the door, I can barely make out what they're saying. They're speaking fluent murmur.

"We're gonna have to wipe him again later when the doctor gets back," one voice says.

A woman's voice answers, "I'll do it, but he may be reaching the limit. He's starting to exhibit symptoms of—"

"Just keep him quiet for now, okay?"

"Yes, sir."

Thomas has turned himself onto his side.

"Stay there," I hiss.

I take two quick steps toward the window. It's got a big center window and two side panels, maybe twelve inches wide, that open like doors. It's one of those old-fashioned kinds that looks nice but is completely unsafe in this sort of setting. By which I mean a place containing people who could figure out ways to hurt either themselves or someone else. People like me.

"There is no way you're going to fit through there," Thomas says.

"Watch and learn."

I turn sideways and snake my upper body through the window, put my hand down on the ledge, and hold myself in a push-up position until I can pull my legs through slowly enough that I don't send myself down into the courtyard below. I squat on the ledge and put my face back through the window.

"It's the rule of cats," I say, giving Thomas a thumbs-up. "If you can get your shoulders through, you can get the rest of you through. Be right back."

I take a few steps along the ledge—thankful that early twentieth-century architects loved putting lots of uselessly ornate decorations on old townhouses, so I have plenty of things to hold onto. Now I'm close enough to Mikey's window to peek in. The nurse's back is to me but Mikey is looking up from the bed, where he's strapped down. His eyes grow wider when he sees me. At first he looks terrified, like maybe he thinks he's hallucinating, but then his expression turns hopeful.

I put my finger to my lips and then point to the window lock, trying to make him understand what I need him to do.

He lets his head fall back against the pillow and stops fighting with the nurse. He points to the window and I think I see him say the word "air."

She shrugs and nods.

Of course she's accommodating. He can't cause much trouble while he's strapped down to the bed, under the influence of whatever drug she just administered—probably a sedative. I take a step back on the ledge and press myself against the wall of the building so the nurse won't see me when she opens the window.

The sash swings outward. As soon as I hear the exam room's door close, I lean forward and listen. "It's safe. She's gone," Mikey says from inside.

I climb in and rush to the bed, where I automatically start undoing the straps holding him down. He's got a fat lip but otherwise seems unhurt.

"How long will she be gone, do you think?" I whisper, pulling at the straps little by little so the sound of the Velcro tearing isn't too loud.

"Probably a while. They just gave me a shot of something to calm me down."

Already his body is sort of loose and relaxed. I remember that stuff well. It doesn't knock you out, just makes you a little goofy and docile.

"Can you fight it?" I ask.

"Yeah."

He sits up as I undo the last two straps around his ankles. Once he's finally free, he swings himself off the bed and sort of stumbles into me. I'm not sure if he's hugging me or just trying to stand up.

"You came to get me," he says. "Thank you."

I can't bear to tell him the truth—that we kind of wrote him off, and that I'm only here because we're hoping he can lead us to the antidote.

Mikey's head starts to loll on his shoulders. I put my hands on either side of his face to keep him looking straight ahead. "You said you know your way around this place. Where can we get the antidote to Snowball?"

"Fourth floor." He holds his hand up and can't quite manage

to use just four fingers, so he pushes his thumb down with his other hand.

"But isn't that where the nursing home patients are?"

"Just one," he says, putting up his index finger, pleasantly surprised that his motor skills are up to this task. "One old lady."

Thomas only reluctantly agrees to be strapped down on the gurney.

"Why can't Mikey be the patient?" he says.

"I hate to break it to you, but you look sicker than Mikey does at the moment," I say.

We've dressed Mikey quickly in a pair of slightly-too-small nursing scrubs from a drawer in the examination room.

Mikey insists he knows exactly where he's going, but I feel like I'm using a drunken monkey as a guide. As we head out into the hallway, toward the elevator, he sways from side to side, points and smiles at things we can't see, and occasionally answers questions that he must have asked himself inside his own mind.

Thomas and I keep looking at each other with increasingly panicked expressions. I lean down and whisper into his ear, "Just a little while longer. It can't be much farther."

"You guys are, like, in love or something, right?" Mikey says, turning around and walking backward so that he's facing us. He slaps Thomas right on the stomach.

"Ooof!"

"You're a lucky guy. This girl . . ." Mikey puts his arm around my shoulders. "She's amazing. She's Spider-girl!"

"Mikey, focus!" I grab his hands, which he's using to mimic spiders crawling. "Just keep it together for five more minutes."

We stop in front of the elevator. Heading toward us now is a harried-looking nurse carrying a tray of little paper cups—meds cups just like the ones I remember from the research hospital. She looks up and I roll my eyes toward Mikey. She doesn't smile but she also doesn't stop us. I guess looking annoyed is the surest way to imitate medical professionals.

The elevator car arrives and we take it to the fourth floor. But when we get there, the doors don't open. Thomas raises his head. "What's the deal?"

"Can't get through without the code!" Mikey says in a sing-song way, pointing to a number pad right above the regular elevator buttons.

"Why didn't you say that before?" I practically shout at Mikey.

"Hold on a sec." Mikey slaps himself on the side of the face. "I know it! The nurses go like this . . ." He uses his finger to press buttons in the air. "Boop, boop, beep, boop."

Thomas sits up on the gurney and watches him, fighting to maintain his concentration. "Do that again."

Mikey makes the same motion and repeats the boops and beeps. Thomas watches—no, he listens—and then reaches for the pad. He types in a four-digit code.

The elevators dings, and the doors slide open. Mikey raises his fists in the air triumphantly. "Yeah!"

I pin his arms to his sides. "Quiet!"

"Mikey might just be the only person to fall into the category of 'useful idiot,'" Thomas says.

We're about to find out exactly how useful.

The fourth floor looks nothing like a hospital. It's like the elevator has opened up into the middle of someone's country estate. We're in a mirrored foyer with a chandelier. A woman wearing a pastel blue cardigan sits at a desk nearby, looking like a receptionist at a spa. Behind her is a set of French doors with heavy leaded glass that distorts the flames of a crackling fire in the room beyond.

I stare through the door. The familiarity of it calls to me. I know exactly what I'll see on the other side: a little oasis of hominess nestled inside the sterility of the hospital. But it's a deception. All the Persian rugs and oil paintings and throw pillows won't change the fact that it's just a gilded cage.

"Hello!" the nurse says cheerfully. "I think you're on the wrong floor. The operating room is one more level up . . ."

I continue walking forward, right past her desk. I reach for the French doors.

"Wait! What are you doing?" she says. She leaps up and grabs me by the arm. "You can't just go in—"

It'll be no trouble to shake her off. But before I have a chance, Mikey lays her out with one punch, knocking her off her feet.

"Jeez, Mikey!" I say, helping Thomas slide off the gurney. "Still a bit trigger happy, I see."

Without responding, Mikey picks up the nurse and straps her down onto the gurney. Meanwhile I start opening desk drawers until I find some duct tape. Mikey grabs the roll from me and starts layering pieces over the unconscious receptionist's mouth.

"Angel, what's going on?" Thomas says.

"I need to get in there."

"This isn't where they keep the meds," Mikey points out.

"I just need to look around a moment."

"For what?"

"Not for what . . . for who." Thomas and Mikey leave the gurney and follow me. They close the doors behind me.

We're standing in a beautiful room filled with luxurious furniture, paintings, silk curtains, and bouquets of fresh flowers. There's a real fireplace built into one wall and a flat-screen TV on the opposite wall. As far as prisons go, it's top of the line.

She's sitting by the fire, her slight body dwarfed by the large armchair she's in. She's so still, it's almost as if she's a wild animal trying to blend in with her surroundings.

"Mrs. Claymore," I say.

She turns, startled, but as soon as she sees me, her face lights up. Her eyes are deep blue. She has a cute bobbed hairstyle, dyed platinum blonde like she wore it when she was young. She once told me she hadn't seen her natural hair color in more than fifty years.

"Angel! How lovely to see you! It's been so long." She extends both hands for me to take. "And what is this 'Mrs. Claymore' business? It's Sarah, of course!"

Her skin is smooth and cool and she holds on very tight.

"Tell me where you've been all this time. I've missed you."

"I've missed you too."

Even if I didn't realize it.

Mikey heads straight for the sofa and curls himself up on it like a cat. Thomas begins to pace, scrubbing his hair as he walks. I know we're wasting precious time. At the moment, Thomas has regained enough strength to walk, but at any second he could keel over again. If we don't get him the antidote within the next hour, something unthinkable could happen to him.

But how can I walk away from my . . . grandmother?

This is my grandmother. My family. How strange for a stranger to be your family.

I clear my throat and look down at her small hands. "Um, Sarah, I—"

"Angel," she cuts me off. "I know who you are."

"You do?"

I feel simultaneously elated and alarmed that my disguise has been stripped away.

"Yes. But I wasn't sure that you knew."

"How did you figure it out?" I ask.

"Your eyes, of course. Though I had no real proof until Grace Fitzgerald told me for sure. She's a lovely woman. She's been sneaking in here for years to keep me apprised of what's going on."

"Mrs. Fitzgerald," I say. "You trust her?"

"Of course I do!"

Thomas cuts in. "Angel, I don't mean to interrupt the family reunion, but I really think we need to go. Before security or someone worse shows up."

"Yeah. I know." I turn to Mrs. Claymore. "I'm so sorry. I can't stay right now. I'll come back, though."

Will I?

I jump up from the chair and kneel in front of Mikey, who's fallen into a blissful sleep on the sofa.

"Hey!" I give him a series of increasingly hard pokes. Then I slap his cheeks. No reaction. Our tour guide appears to be down for the count.

"Great!" says Thomas. "Now what are we going to do?"

"It's okay. We'll find the meds on our own." I stand up, already regretting this little detour. It's cost us time. I just hope it doesn't cost us more than that. "Mrs. Claymore—Sarah—we're not supposed to be in here right now. And we're also trying to—well, I'll be straight with you. We need to find a certain medication as soon as possible."

Mrs. Claymore uses her four-pronged cane to push herself up from her cushy chair. "Does this have anything to do with that zombie juice they use on people to make them forget things?"

"How do you know about that?" Thomas asks, looking as taken aback as I am.

She moves slowly over to a wheelchair that's sitting against the back wall. "You'd be surprised what you can find out when nobody thinks you're right in the head," she says, tapping her temple. "Come with me. I'll show you where you need to go."

Mrs. Claymore is remarkably unfazed by the nurse strapped to the gurney in the reception area. She just sniffs and says, "Never liked her anyway, talks to me like I'm enfeebled. Of course, in her defense, I do an awfully good job of faking it. Even my darling husband doesn't have a clue . . ."

I push her wheelchair while Thomas limps along beside us. If anyone asks, we're supposed to say Mrs. Claymore demanded we walk her around. This is apparently a fairly frequent occurrence.

"I've been up and down their 'secret' laboratory halls countless times. I whistle and hum and ask if they've seen my pet baby elephant, Amanda. The poor thing is always getting lost. They pay me no attention at all. Actually, some of them claim to have spotted her and send me off on an imaginary elephant hunt."

I lean down and kiss the top of her head. "You are brilliant."

"And my granddaughter takes after me. Go left when we get to the end of this hallway."

We pass two people in lab coats, one of whom looks at me, then at Mrs. Claymore, and smirks sympathetically.

I'm worried about Thomas. He's fighting to walk again, dragging his feet along as if they've gone numb. He stumbles a few times and then gives me an irritated "I'm fine" when I look at him. I'm torn between wanting to push the wheelchair more quickly, to get us where we're going as soon as possible, and worrying that Thomas won't be able to keep up if I go any faster.

"Here we are," says Mrs. Claymore when we reach an unmarked door. "I'll wheel myself back up the hallway and give a shout if I see anyone coming this way. Now hurry, and get out of here as soon as you have what you need."

I kiss her cheek by way of saying thanks.

Thomas and I push the door open. It's an examination room with gray subway tiles on the walls, a steel table in the middle, and a drain in the center of the floor. On the other side of the room I see a familiar item: a stainless steel chair with a dome like a birdcage above it.

"The halo," I say, unable to keep the loathing out of my voice.

Thomas puts his hand on my shoulder. At first I think he's reaching out to me in sympathy, but he's holding on a little too tight, putting too much of his weight on me. He needs me as a crutch.

There are a dozen cabinets to go through. They all have glass doors and are lit from within. I realize that they're all small refrigerators. I guess these drugs need to be kept cool. Some of the refrigerator doors have labels, but other than a few basics like saline, sucrose, heparin—things I remember hearing about in the hospital—it's all gibberish to me.

"I have no idea what we're even looking for," I say miserably.

"That makes two of us," Thomas says, opening doors and picking up individual vials to examine. "I can't believe I'm saying this, but I wish Mikey was here."

At that moment the door opens. Mikey rushes in.

"Speak of the devil," I say.

I don't notice the gun in Mikey's hand until it's pointing right at me.

CHAPTER 25

"I'm sorry, Angel," Mikey says. "I can't help it."

There's real self-recrimination in his tone, for all that's worth.

"I really don't want to hear it."

"You don't understand." He grabs my arm with his free hand. In his other hand, the gun doesn't waver. "I'm not trying to make excuses. But what I'm doing, it's not some choice I'm making."

"That's very comforting." I pull away from him and try to help Thomas to his feet. "So who are you working for? The Radical Pacifists?"

"You're about to meet my boss. Come on."

Just then Thomas's body spasms like he's just been hit between the shoulder blades by a javelin. Clutching his head and groaning in pain, he slips to the floor. I'm not fast enough to stop him from falling, but I catch him a little so his head doesn't hit the tile.

Mikey moves toward us but I shove him back. "Don't touch him! I don't need any more of your help."

Thomas pushes himself up onto his hands and knees and then manages to stand again.

"Can you walk?" I ask Thomas.

He nods.

Mikey leads us back down the hallway. I need to keep an arm around Thomas so he can lean on me to keep his balance.

"I retract my gratitude toward you for saving my life," I say. "Oh, wait. You probably didn't really save me at all, right? It was just supposed to look like you had. Then you give me the lost-dog routine, and I feel sorry for you and take you into my confidence."

"Seriously, Angel, I really want to help you. Like in my conscious brain. But I guess . . ."

"It was all a setup. Was the stunt with those guys in the van shooting at me—shooting at those cops—the same deal?"

"I guess. But it didn't feel that way to me at the time."

His shoulders drop and if he had a tail, I'm sure it would be between his legs.

But I can't work up much sympathy for his plight anymore. We've suspected all along that he was someone's puppet, but now that it's confirmed beyond doubt, all I feel is disgust.

As we turn a corner and enter the elevator lobby, I see two armed men waiting for us. One is our limo driver from last night. Was it really only last night? He looks pretty pissed off, which is probably why he immediately aims his pistol directly at my head.

I glance around. Where did Mrs. Claymore go? Is she safely back in her room?

Behind our welcoming committee, the "UP" arrow above an elevator door lights up. Someone else is heading to the fourth floor.

The limo driver nods to the guy with him. "Cuff 'em." Mikey steps aside, letting the gun fall to his side, while the goon puts handcuffs on Thomas and me. "Make sure hers are extra tight," adds the limo driver. "She's a tricky one."

"Thanks for noticing," I say, sneering at him.

But that sneer leaves my face as soon as I see the man who exits the elevator. He's dressed in loose-fitting jeans, shiny loafers, and a V-neck sweater. He looks like he's about to go golfing. His smile is so warm, so charming, that I almost believe him when he says, "The infamous Angel. At last we meet. This is quite an honor."

Erskine Claymore himself.

"Technically, we've met before," I say icily.

"Ah, yes. You were at the party," he says. "But of course, I didn't recognize you then. You were all dressed up, not in your usual sloppy attire." Claymore's green eyes meet mine, and perhaps I imagine it, but for just a moment—just the briefest fraction of a second—he seems to register the similarity.

I think about blurting it out, right now, right here. The truth about who I am. Not just a thorn in his side, but his only grandchild. But even if he believed me, would it make any difference? I see my connection to him as an unclaimed piece of my history, not my future, and it's something I can walk away from. Just as Virgil did.

Now Claymore turns to the limo driver. "This way. I might as well kill several birds with one stone and take this opportunity to visit my wife."

He leads the way to Mrs. Claymore's room, with the limo driver dragging Thomas, Mikey steering me, and one nameless goon bringing up the rear. As we pass the receptionist's desk, Claymore glances at the struggling nurse strapped to the gurney. "Mr. Deeks, please liberate this poor woman, will you? And bring that gurney in here when you're finished."

He sweeps past her into his wife's room, where Mrs. Claymore is sitting next to the fireplace, once again staring into oblivion.

"Darling!" Claymore calls out, his tone rich with what sounds like genuine tenderness. "Are you having a nice evening?"

She turns her head and smiles blankly.

Claymore leans down to give her a kiss on the cheek. "We have some young guests."

"That's nice," she says as her unfocused eyes drift toward us. "Have they seen Amanda?"

"No, I'm afraid not," Claymore answers. "But I've got our best people searching for her right now."

She looks back to the fire. "You're so good to me. Thank you."

She seems only dimly aware that we're here. Did they drug her or is this all an act? I can't tell. If she's faking it, she's doing a very good job. I also have to admit that there's a possibility her dementia act isn't an act at all, even if she did seem totally lucid only minutes ago.

Claymore sits in a wingback chair opposite to the one Mrs. Claymore is sitting in. He reaches over and pats his wife's knee. Turning to us, he points to the sofa. "Both of you, sit. Make yourselves comfortable."

When I don't immediately comply, I'm coaxed onto the sofa with the help of Mikey's pistol pressed against the base of my skull. Thomas gets the same VIP treatment. Right now I desperately wish there were some obvious switch I could flip to use that superstrength I had earlier, but I've never been able to access my Velocius abilities at will. I just have to wait for instinct to kick in.

I try to reach over and take Thomas's hand but Claymore doesn't like this. He gestures to his goons, who move us to opposite ends of the sofa.

Claymore clasps his hands and smiles, like this is all just a big misunderstanding between us, like all this mayhem and pain will get wrapped up with a heart-to-heart just like some half-hour sitcom. "Let's just open up the lines of communication between us, Angel. It was very frustrating for me not to be able to find out more about you since your triumphant return to New York. It's not easy to hide things from me, and yet . . . you've been hidden very well. The FBI has done an exemplary job at shielding you from me."

"Then why did they turn on me?" I demand.

"They didn't turn on you so much as turn a blind eye," Claymore says. "With a lot of persuasion from me."

"So they just walked away and let your people have a crack at me." I shoot a glare at the limo driver. He gives me a two-finger salute across his brow, and I really, really want to return it with a one-finger salute of my own.

"Essentially, yes."

Maybe if I can keep Claymore talking, something will trigger my Velocius abilities and I'll be able to get us out of here. At the very least, if I stall long enough, Tai will realize we're in trouble. "I have to admit, I am curious about how you got my federal shadows to ditch me. Even you can't be rich enough to bribe a federal agency."

He shrugs. "I convinced them that I could dispose of a looming threat to our society. To every society."

"If I'm such a huge threat, why didn't they just kill me themselves? That's easier than outsourcing the job, isn't it?"

Another shrug. "For various pesky legal reasons and the ever-present threat of scandal, governments like ours don't directly participate in that kind of cleanup operation. But fortunately, the world is full of people who do the hands-on dirty work that allows others to carry on blithely, even guiltlessly. Thomas knows. He used to work with one of the best. He might well have become one of the best if things had turned out differently. If you hadn't happened."

I know he's trying to get a rise out of me, so I just smile. "You're giving me a lot of credit. I've singlehandedly ruined Thomas's life *and* I'm a looming threat to society?"

"Don't be so modest. The Feds have known all along that you're a force to be reckoned with. And you'd be capable of causing much more trouble if you fell under the influence of certain people. People who would love to expose some of the government's best-kept secrets to the whole world."

"The Radical Pacifists," I say.

Thomas manages a feeble scoff. "I can't believe the Feds thought those jokers were something to be afraid of."

"Oh, as a matter of fact, it didn't take much to convince their threat assessment experts. The Radical Pacifists are a very scary bunch. It's almost as if they were tailor-made to strike fear in the hearts of secretive government entities."

Even without a Velocius brain boost, I realize what his smirk means. "Wait. Are you saying—you manufactured them?" I say.

"Not wholly. Let's say I 'discovered' them and gave them an infusion of professional help. That was enough to put them on the government's radar." I remember Thomas's message board intel: flush with cash.

"I suppose these guys are their perfect nightmare," Thomas says.

"Absolutely. The Radical Pacifists have made it their mission to expose the military and tradecraft secrets of every country on earth. Not just who's spying on whom, but all the cutting-edge research and development that countries hope will protect them in the future. They want to dump everything onto the Internet for anyone to see. They believe that if this information is made available to everyone, it will mean everyone is on a level playing field, and there will be peace through equality. No one will have the weaponry advantage."

Claymore shakes his head pityingly, as if this group is merely a misguided child needing a firm hand.

"So you used them to scare the Feds," I say. "You made it look like I might be the Radical Pacifists' next big story."

"Exactly. From my perspective, it was an incredible bargain. Very little invested to yield maximum results. The funny thing is, the Feds are the ones who gave me the idea in the first place. After that—unfortunate—situation at your hospital, Angel, the Feds found something on the body of one of our key researchers. You might remember him—his name was Dr. Larry Ladner."

I fight to keep my face neutral.

"When the Feds retrieved his body from the rubble, they found a piece of paper in his pocket—some sort of list of a dozen or so words. What were they? The Feds didn't know, but they were worried. They'd been briefed on how Ladner had manipulated your treatment under our collective nose, how the whole Velocius project had veered into murky moral waters, how Ladner had had second thoughts about it. That's why he'd tried to help you escape, after all."

I try to keep my composure. I try to quiet my racing, raging thoughts. But it's so hard. Larry, how could you be stupid enough to write down a bunch of secret passwords and carry them around with you? And what were those passwords for?

"But here was the big question: What if Dr. Ladner didn't just want to help you, Angel? What if he wanted the whole world to know what had been going on in that hospital?"

Claymore puts his hand to his chin as if perplexed.

"What if you were his weapon?"

"I am not a weapon."

"All right then. Let's say 'emissary' instead. What if you were meant to go out into the world and expose the truth to everyone? All this is hypothetical, of course, but the funny thing is, even the hypothetical can be threatening. You haven't exactly been cooperative with the Feds, have you? It's not too hard for them to imagine that you'd want their secrets known. Maybe because of your own anger about being experimented upon or because of some foolish idea that the public had the right to know what had happened or maybe . . . maybe because of some unconscious urge Dr. Ladner has placed inside your mind? For any of those reasons, you might try to expose Velocius to the whole world."

"The Feds have been watching me like hawks," I say, rolling my eyes. "They know I haven't done anything."

"Yes, but as much as they watched you and listened to you, they couldn't know what was in your mind or what your intentions were. Sometimes mere suspicion, paired with the means to do something, is all the evidence they need to act. They became convinced that you must be silenced simply because of the chance you might betray Velocius. And in their defense, you do have a history of setting up elaborate revenge scenarios, do you not?"

I make a noise that doesn't even begin to express my disgust. Those green eyes keep boring into mine.

"That's the fear that I exploited in them. That's when I reached out to our Radical Pacifist friends and made them my allies, paying them to find what David Perry—better known by his nickname, 8-Bit—had uploaded the day of his death."

"But he didn't upload anything," I say coldly. "There is no data."

Claymore seems to find this mildly interesting, but not surprising or upsetting. "I see. Well, that's good to know. I wasn't sure, which is why I've let you run around the city for the last twenty-four hours instead of simply snatching you immediately. I certainly would've been happy to have that data, if it did turn out to exist. But I'm sure I can persuade the Radical Pacifists to get over their disappointment. And I, of course, have other resources at my disposal."

I clench my fists and try to keep my voice level. I can't afford to lose my temper. Not yet. "So you think Larry had some stash of research data? And you think he told me how to find it? And the government is so grateful that you're willing to take care of this 'potential' security threat that they'll just let you do whatever you want to me."

"Grateful? No, they're not grateful. They're smart. Did you honestly think they're more interested in your well-being than the world's? Surely you're not still that idealistic."

I suck my teeth and refuse to look Claymore in the eye. Which he doesn't like. He steps to the side and then bends over slightly until I'm forced to look directly at him.

"Angel, I know people imagine you to be some sort of redemptive figure, but I'll bet once they discover that you disappeared because I paid you off—yes, that will be the story that the press will hear from 'anonymous source close to me'—they'll feel much less inclined to mythologize you." He stands up and walks around to the back of the chair, putting his hands on the top. He reaches down and fluffs up the throw pillow, putting it back in the center of the cushion. Maybe I inherit some of my restlessness from him. The idea of even the smallest similarity between us nauseates me.

"Angel, as a point of respect—yes, I do respect your abilities—this is now a negotiation. I'm going to deal with you as I would anyone else I was making a business deal with. So for starters, I need to know the points on which you're willing to negotiate."

Claymore walks over to the end of the sofa and puts his hand on Thomas's shoulder. Thomas tries to move but he gets a pistol pushed into his jaw for his trouble.

"I know you want to get away," he says. "To achieve that, would you be willing to sacrifice Thomas here, for example?"

Thomas tries to turn toward me but his guard raps him on the cheek with his gun.

"Of course not," I say.

"I'm not surprised to hear that. I know you two are very close, but the plain fact of the matter is, you are not good for him. You must see that."

"Ignore him," Thomas says. "He's just trying to get under your skin."

Thomas's guard, the limo driver, grabs him by the hair and jerks his head back so far, it looks like he plans to slit Thomas's throat.

Claymore steeples his fingers. "So, if Thomas's safety is, for you, not negotiable, here's something to consider. What if giving him up is the only way to save him? What if I offered to treat him in the most merciful way possible, in exchange for your cooperation?"

"Whatever he asks for, don't do it, Angel," Thomas says.

"What do you mean by 'in the most merciful way possible'?" I ask.

"Let me put it another way. I can give you a demonstration of what won't happen to him if you cooperate." He nods at the limo driver.

The guy strikes Thomas across the face with the gun, sending him toward the center of the sofa, toward me. I try to reach over and touch his hair but my own guard pulls me back. The pistol against my skull presses down harder.

Thomas's attacker raises his gun again.

"Stop!"

My shriek does nothing to stop the second blow.

I look down helplessly. Thomas's nose and mouth are bleeding freely onto the cushion. His groans are sad, almost like weeping.

"What do you want!?" I scream at Claymore.

Claymore looks at me, incredulous. "What did you want when you climbed up all those cranes and hung your banners and got people sent to jail? You wanted to make a point. That's what I'm doing right now."

"You've made your point! I'll do what you want!"

"That was never in doubt, Angel. It's more the speed and the completeness of your surrender that are at issue."

Now our green eyes are trained on each other. There it is again. That curiosity. He looks at me like he's going to reach into the tunnel of my pupils, pull whatever he finds interesting, and toss the rest. Like I'm garbage.

"I'm glad we've reached an understanding now." His eyes flick toward Thomas. "Young man, don't worry. You're going to get medical attention of the highest quality. When the time is right."

"You mean when enough time has passed for Snowball to erase my memories," Thomas chokes out, wiping the blood from his mouth with his cuffed hands.

"Very clever. I probably shouldn't be surprised you figured that out. Your mother did tell me how smart you are."

"Evangeline Hodges is not my mother."

"Don't say that. You should take pride in the connection. I'd even go so far as to say you get the lion's share of your intelligence from her."

"Stop baiting him!" I snap. "If you want his brilliant mind to stay intact, he needs that second Snowball injection now!"

"As I said," Claymore says evenly, "we'll give it to him when the time is right. As soon as enough time has passed for the last year to be erased from his memory, the antidote will be administered. Thomas won't remember a thing about being on house arrest or running off with his father. More to the point, he won't remember you. You are the chief danger in his life right now. Without you, without knowing and caring about you, he would be perfectly safe."

I can't bear to look at Thomas anymore. Claymore's no fool. He might be cruel, but he's logical as math. As long as Thomas is with me, he's in the line of fire. People like Claymore, people like the Feds, can use him to hurt me. If I subtracted myself from Thomas's life . . . the equation would work in his favor. He would be safe. I hate it but it's true.

Claymore walks over to Mikey, who is short by comparison, and claps a hand on Mikey's shoulder like he's a proud dad. Again he gives that high-wattage, unbearably smug smile.

"We've used Snowball on Mikey perhaps seven or eight times. Most people are only good for two, maybe three times. Then they start to break down. Some people are only good for one time. The injection just disagrees with them, like with Thomas here. I don't have any research findings to back this up, of course, it's more anecdotal, but I think that Mikey has been so successful because he's a far simpler mechanism. Of course, that's part of his charm."

He flicks his hand dismissively just as the doors open and Claymore's other goon wheels the gurney in.

Claymore beams. "Excellent timing!"

He turns to the limo driver. "Take the young man downstairs to the car," he says, motioning toward Thomas.

The limo driver and the other henchman roll Thomas off the couch and lift him onto the gurney.

"Where are you taking him?" I shout.

"A secure location," Claymore says smoothly.

What the hell is Velocius waiting for? I couldn't be more in need of my lightning-fast reflexes right now and there's so much adrenaline coursing through me, I could surf on it. Yet I still can't find that elusive *on* switch.

They push Thomas toward the door. I'm running out of time. Need to stall them . . .

"That's why his name wasn't in the probation registry!" I blurt.

Claymore's head jerks back slightly. The corners of his mouth turn down. He's impressed.

"So you figured that out too. I suppose I shouldn't be surprised. Only someone bright could've been such a persistent thorn in my side. Yes, as soon as we began our operation to bring you in last night, we got a start on changing Thomas's identity. In several weeks, after an exhaustive search, his parents will be notified that his body was found in Paris. No doubt they will be saddened but not surprised, given his history of running off with his birth father."

"You said you weren't going to hurt him!"

"This is the story his parents will be told. In reality, he'll be in a sort of witness protection program. My version of it, anyway. Don't worry, he'll be well taken care of. Part of my deal with the Feds involves leniency for Thomas's mother."

Hodges. The woman who killed my mother and went to incredible lengths to have me killed too. The woman Thomas has vowed he wants nothing to do with. Thomas tries to raise his hand but can only wiggle his fingers.

"Yes," Claymore says. "Once the Feds are convinced you're dead, Evangeline Hodges will be released from federal prison. Just in time to get her son back with no memory of you, or her."

It makes a sort of perverse sense. Claymore is strangely trying to do right by the person who served him so loyally. Hodges's reward for taking the fall for the whole Velocius thing is this: getting out of jail and getting her claws into Thomas in the only way it could ever be possible. The stories they'll tell him—they all come to me in one sickening flash of images. Hodges explaining herself, her motives. A tearful reunion in which she tells him that she never gave up hoping she'd see him again.

"The Feds are letting you just take me away like this?" Thomas bursts out.

"Of course. They've given me carte blanche. Do you know what that means, Angel?"

I just clench my teeth in response. I'm done playing along with this showboating villain monologue. I've let him talk long enough, and all the time it's bought me hasn't done me any good. I need Velocius.

I fist my hands and kick the coffee table over, causing Claymore to step back to get out of the way. He gives me a disapproving look. Like I have no manners at all. Mikey quickly sets the table upright again without taking his sights off me.

"It's a French term," Claymore goes on, ignoring the interruption. "It literally translates to 'white or blank paper.' It means that there are no written rules about what I can do, and hence, no limits. It means that in exchange for neutralizing a threat on the government's behalf, I can do whatever I want. With you as well as with Thomas. Though I believe they're under the impression I'm simply going to kill you."

"Yeah, well, that's a pretty logical assumption on their part. Why aren't you going to kill me?"

"Because you're far more valuable to me alive."

I try to stand up, but Mikey shoves me back down onto the sofa before I can even lock my knees. "You think we know where Larry's data is? You think you can get me to lead you to it? Well, we don't."

Claymore just smiles. I don't know what it means. I can't tell if he's being condescending or if he's genuinely amused.

"You're the prize we've been after," he says. "I own what's inside your mind. I paid for it. I'm excited to see where our next step leads once we read Dr. Ladner's list of words to you. I wonder what else you can do or what else you'll tell us."

I start to shake. I'd thought the mental clues Larry left me were just meant to lead me home, but what if Thomas was right—what if there really is something out there that I'm supposed to find? Something buried in those words Larry wrote down.

Not passwords. Trigger words. Just like my mother's name once was.

Claymore thinks that he can read these words to me, and that it will unlock some memory and I'll lead him to his treasure like I'm some sort of hound on a leash, finding an invisible scent trail.

"It doesn't matter," I say. "You can read those words to me and maybe I'll remember something that Larry wanted me to know, but you can't compel me to tell you anything. I'm never going to tell you where those backup data files are. Thomas wouldn't want me to tell you either."

"You still aren't getting it," Claymore says, looking up at the ceiling now, a look of exasperation on his face. "I don't care if there are no computer files, no research notes, no instructions for the pharmaceutical compounds that turned you into what you are today. If all of that really did go up in flames back at the hospital, that's a shame. But I didn't spend a billion dollars on research projects to let my only living success walk around Manhattan, cowed by federal authorities into remaining a lowly, unremarkable peasant. No, we don't want you to lead us to any data. My dear, you are the data."

CHAPTER 26

I wish I could smack the look of false pity right off Erskine Claymore's face, but I can't. Not with my hands cuffed together.

He wants me as a test subject?

There's no way I'm going to let that happen.

"Just remember, Angel—your cooperation guarantees Thomas's safety."

I look over at Thomas. By now he's strapped down on the gurney, and Claymore's men are pushing him toward the double doors. It's like Claymore is undoing all the connections that we worked to build, that we earned with our pain and courage and patience these last few months. We tried to do everything right. We listened, we played by their rules, we did what they asked of us. And this is what we get for it?

Thomas is whisked out of the room. I watch through the glass doors as the guards ease him past the reception desk. A moment later, the elevator doors open.

Claymore's project once took away my past. Now he's taking away my future.

I twist around to look at Mikey, willing him to find a way to help us—a way to fight the instructions coded into his brain. Claymore catches me, though.

"I wouldn't bother appealing to Mikey. Even if he wanted to help you, you shouldn't ask him to. You hold his fate in your hands as well."

"What are you talking about?" I say sharply.

"Before his injection, he was briefed on his mission and the expectations we had for him. His job was to make certain you didn't contact my son or his caregiver, or approach any local authorities—and to ensure that you didn't make any other unwise decisions, such as, say, trying to make a run for the Canadian border. So right now, if he were to assist you in escaping, or hinder our plans in any other way, he would be overcome by the desire to harm himself. And you've got to ask yourself, Angel, do you want to be responsible for that? I realize he's not as special to you as Thomas, but I think you do harbor some fondness for him. Would you really let this boy kill himself so you can go free?"

Mikey's eyes are filled with confused, desperate shame that I know all too well. I know it's not his fault, but I can't help being angry that he was the lure that helped steer me into this trap. And I can't help but notice that however bad he feels, he doesn't lower his pistol even one inch.

"Ah, Angel! I can see you're not happy with him about this. I hope you won't take this the wrong way, but you're very judgmental. And yet I'd imagine you've left a string of disgruntled people in your wake yourself, haven't you? People who didn't appreciate the way you used them."

He can see, in the rush of blood to my face, that he's scored a hit.

"Consider that, before you're so quick to condemn us. And now, perhaps you'll learn what making a sacrifice—a true sacrifice that hurts every single day after you make it—is all about." Claymore glances at his wife—I'm not sure why.

"I want to make it clear to you that there is an alternative," he goes on. "We're about to embark on an amazing new phase of this project, and it's our hope that you'll work with us instead of against us. Working against us would have grave consequences, of course. For both you and Thomas."

Claymore waves his hand, as if trying to rise above such unpleasant things.

"I believe—my whole research team believes—that you're capable of amazing things. Perhaps you've even stumbled on a few of them already, even if your federal handlers have discouraged you from using your abilities."

Claymore goes over to stand behind his wife, putting his hands on her shoulders. She keeps her glassy-eyed stare toward the window. I think I sense a small shiver of revulsion at his touch but he doesn't seem to notice.

"We have an opportunity, Angel. The Feds wanted you eliminated. Dead. That's what they thought would solve their security concerns." He shakes his head. "Such a waste. I'm giving you a second chance. I think we should discover your potential together."

He looks down at his watch and sighs. Perhaps he's realizing he's let himself talk for too long. He's let himself say too much.

"I really need to get home to change into my tuxedo soon. I

have yet another social engagement tonight. It never ends now, does it, Sarah?"

He takes and kisses her hand, then places it gently back on the arm of the chair. As he moves away from her—toward me—she gets up and hobbles over to the window.

"One last thing before we head down to the parking garage, Angel. I know—of course I know—how difficult you are to kill. But I will make you this promise: if you even attempt to get away, Thomas will die."

He throws his hands out and shrugs, as if these consequences are all beyond his control.

My eyes drift to Mrs. Claymore—my grandmother. She's still staring out the window. She presses her fingertips to the glass, lightly at first, and then harder, like she's testing the bars of a cage.

That's when we hear multiple sirens accompanied by the deep bass of a fire truck honking. All of it seems to be converging nearby. "Erskine, darling, what's going on outside?" asks Mrs. Claymore innocently.

Claymore crosses the room with the energy of a man half his age. Whatever he sees down on the street below triggers a look of searing irritation. This is not part of his plan.

It's part of mine.

An internal security alarm starts going off. Ironically, that seems to help Claymore recover his composure. "Everything will be fine," he says to his wife. "Don't you worry."

He walks toward the door in no particular hurry, and he says quietly to Mikey, "Let me see if I can do some damage control and send these folks on their way. Keep that pistol pressed to the back of her head. I'll call you when we're ready to move her."

As soon as Claymore makes his exit, Mikey walks around from behind the sofa.

"I'm sorry," he says. "I know you don't want to hear it, but it's true." He sounds like a little boy. I sigh.

"Mikey. I get it. I know what it's like to have no control over your own brain."

He puts the gun down on the coffee table in front of me but has troubling taking his hand off it. After a few seconds, he grits his teeth and jerks his hand away.

"What are you doing?" I ask.

"I'm not going to be their puppet anymore. I'm going to let you go."

"But you heard what Claymore said. If you help me, you'll . . ."

"Whatever's going to happen to me, will happen," he says. "I know what I'm doing. I remember what it was like when I climbed up that tower at Coney Island. If the only thing I have control over is this choice, then I'll make it."

He's crouching down and fumbling at something around his ankle. "Good thing I kept this in my sock, huh? I wanted a souvenir from my day-and-a-half as one of the good guys."

He holds up a handcuff key.

Even as he unlocks my handcuffs, tension spreads through his body. When the cuffs drop to the floor, he makes two fists at his sides as if he's readying himself for a fight. His eyes drift back to the pistol.

"That's a nice gesture, son, but it will do no one any good," Mrs. Claymore says.

Her voice is steady and certain. We both turn to her. The

bright light behind her eyes has turned her gaze steely. "Even if you're willing to sacrifice yourself, you'd be handing that other boy a death sentence."

Mikey shakes his head and backs away from the gun on the table, even as his fingers twitch and he leans forward. He's resisting the pull, but how long will he last?

"First of all, Mikey, pick the gun back up," I say. "Just hold it, okay?"

Mikey reluctantly trains the pistol on me again.

"On the bright side," says Mrs. Claymore, "Angel may not need your help to get out of this predicament, young man. The whole street is filled with police cars and fire trucks."

She smiles.

"That's going to be very vexing to my dear husband."

What's going on outside is this: Tai made good on her promise.

And then some.

She hadn't heard from us so she called the police. And the fire department. And apparently every news organization imaginable. Outside this nursing home—hospital, prison, secret lab, take your pick—is what I believe is known as a "media circus." The whole street is jam-packed with news vans, their satellite dishes already deployed, their reporters already jockeying for position on the sidewalk so they can cover the unfolding story. Someone is now talking into a bullhorn, telling the reporters and other onlookers to stay back behind the police lines.

"Erskine will definitely not be happy about all this media attention," Mrs. Claymore says, clucking her tongue. "But it might be just what you need."

We turn on the television. Every local channel is covering the breaking news.

"Angel lives."

"Despite vehement denials from local authorities, we have sources confirming that the infamous 'Angel'—who was spotted late last night at the Metropolitan Museum Gala, an event attended by some of the wealthiest people in New York—is possibly behind the abduction and shooting of two NYPD officers. And the story only gets stranger from there. An anonymous source tipped police off to Angel's attempt to break in here, a nursing home where Erskine Claymore's wife currently resides. What Angel's intentions are, we don't know, but it may indicate that she's taking her vendetta against the Claymore family to a new level. Perhaps by taking Mrs. Sarah Claymore hostage? Back to you in the studio, Ron. . . ."

"You have got to be kidding me," I say to the screen. "He just made that up out of thin air!"

"Oh, I doubt the reporter made it up on his own," Mrs. Claymore says. "I'm sure he was fed that information moments ago by another anonymous tip."

I mutter, "I hate anonymous tipsters."

This hostage story is a new hurdle I've got to figure out how to clear. Not only does the idea that I'd threaten some innocent little old lady succeed in widely vilifying me and putting a target on my back with the police, but it also allows Claymore to bypass the local police force and bring in the same people who've helped him thus far: the Feds.

I keep listening to the coverage, even though it sickens me. Piece by piece, minute by minute, the hostage theory gets repeated enough to become the accepted truth, and soon the wildfire Claymore started spreads even further. With their cameras trained on the narrow roof of the nursing home, one reporter after another claims that I'll soon be surrendering and that authorities will be taking me away via helicopter. Because the situation is so volatile, they've also been warned that police can't come through the doors because I've set up booby traps at every entrance. If the NYPD tries to bust in, they risk being blown up.

How I did all this doesn't matter. The story is so juicy, everyone is salivating for it. Claymore has succeeded in painting me as a menace to society, and they're willing to believe me capable of anything.

"I'm never watching the news again," I say. "They have no idea what they're talking about."

Mikey's whipping his head back and forth, alternating between looking out the window and watching the newscast. He stays hidden behind the drapes as he peers out the window. A searchlight strafes the building, flashing momentarily into the room before moving on toward other floors.

"Wow. They've got sharpshooters on the roof over there," Mikey mutters. "SWAT teams, a couple armored vehicles. It's pretty impressive, Angel. You should come take a look."

As Mikey continues to inventory all the firepower being amassed outside, Mrs. Claymore says to me, "I have to give my husband credit. He's doing his best to turn this to his advantage. And he'll succeed unless you act quickly."

"But Thomas," I say. "Like you said, I can't escape if I want to keep him safe. And if Mikey helps me, he'll suddenly have the urge to impale himself on the nearest sharp object. I'm stuck."

"Perhaps there's another way." She lowers her voice to a whisper. "One of my talents these last few years has been pretending to exist within a sort of living death. My mind, they believe, is gone. I pose no threat, so I'm allowed to carry on, drifting around these halls like a ghost. Sometimes the only way to survive is to make others believe there's nothing left of you to kill."

She meets my eyes and I understand what she's saying and that she must not say it out loud. Not in front of Mikey.

Erskine Claymore is very good at boxing people into corners, marching them toward whatever end he allows them to have. But there is one place I can hide where he can't pursue me or control me, no matter how many billions he's invested in me.

He assumes that I won't go there, but I will. I've been close before. A thousand times I've reached out and touched that dark, ferocious beast. I've stroked its fur and looked into its ravenous eyes.

I'm not afraid to die.

CHAPTER 27

peek out the window for the twentieth time. I'm no expert on estimating crowds, but there must be hundreds of people down there now, so many the police keep using their bullhorns, angrily telling them to stay back or risk being arrested.

I look down at my big, ugly black watch. There have been so many lies flying around me the last twenty-four hours that I'm not sure what to believe anymore. So I'm going to have to trust my instincts. Mrs. Fitzgerald might not like me, but if she wanted me dead, she could have killed me a dozen times over by now.

Besides, it is not possible to be in more trouble than I am at the moment, so if there's a chance that Mrs. Fitzgerald is still on my side, I'm going to grab at it.

I press down on the watch crystal and hold it for ten seconds.

Mikey checks his phone, as if it's possible he might have missed a call. He's been holding it in one hand continuously since Claymore left, his gun loosely gripped in the other.

And then a phone does ring.

But it's not the one in Mikey's hand. Mikey and I exchange baffled looks. Meanwhile, Mrs. Claymore points to a small table in the corner of the room, home to an old-fashioned touch-tone phone that looks like some old movie prop. "That phone can receive calls but doesn't allow outgoing calls. One of my husband's precautions. It hasn't rung in so long, I'd forgotten it was even here."

She shuffles over to the table and picks up the handset. "Hello. This is Sarah Claymore," she says pleasantly. "Yes. Of course." She holds the phone out to me. "It's for you."

I tentatively take the phone from her. I'm expecting it to be the police calling, asking me to surrender or demand to hear my terms. Instead . . .

"Angel, listen carefully—"

"Mrs. Fitzgerald! How did you get this number?"

"Mrs. Claymore may have mentioned the fact that I've visited her several times. I need you to listen. An FBI helicopter will be landing on the roof of the hospital in twenty minutes. That's how Claymore plans to depart, as part of a seeming hostage evacuation. Do whatever you must to avoid getting in that helicopter."

I can't exactly feel Mrs. Fitzgerald's warmth and concern radiating through the phone, but for some reason, this further convinces me that she hasn't betrayed me. She is the same as ever, and she's just given me a piece of important information.

"Got it," I say. "But once I get out of here, I'm going to need to lie low. I could use some help with that."

"Understood. Are you incapacitated or injured in any way?"

"No."

"If you survive, go to the meet-up point we've previously discussed."

She hangs up.

If I survive. How reassuring that Mrs. Fitzgerald has such full confidence in me.

And now, finally, Mikey's phone rings. Mikey answers, says, "Yes, sir," and hangs up. He looks at me.

"I'm supposed to bring both of you up to the roof."

"Okay."

"But first I'm supposed to shoot you in the shoulder."

"What?!"

"Claymore wants you visibly injured, to help explain how we were able to overpower you and convince you to give yourself up."

Mikey raises his gun and points it at me. "Where you want it, right or left?"

"Neither, thanks very much!"

"Sorry, Angel, you know I don't want to do this . . ."

With a sudden rush of movement that I didn't think she was capable of, Mrs. Claymore strikes Mikey's arm with her cane, knocking the gun out of his hand. I immediately lunge for it, but it slides across the polished wood floor and rolls under the sofa. While I dive to the floor to retrieve it, Mrs. Claymore moves between me and Mikey, brandishing her cane at him.

"You'll have to come through me, son," Mrs. Claymore says.

"Come on, Mrs. Claymore. I don't want to hit an old lady."

Mrs. Claymore juts out her chin defiantly. "That's what you're going to have to do if you take one step toward my granddaughter."

"Angel, tell her to stop this. I'm gonna be forced to hit her."

My straining fingers find the gun under the sofa. Just as I'm about to straighten up, Mikey lunges.

And then Mrs. Claymore whacks him again. Hard, right on the ear. She must have had a killer golf swing at some point because it sends him flying back.

"I don't feel as bound by civility as you seem to be," she tells him. "One of the only good things about being an old lady."

I roll over and point the gun at Mikey.

"You're not going to kill me," he says.

"Nope. But I might shoot you in both your knees. That would be just as effective." I kick the handcuffs over to him. "Put these on. For real this time. Then get in Mrs. Claymore's wheelchair."

"Are you serious?" "Should I shoot you in the right knee first or the left?"

"Fine!"

He stands up, clicks the cuffs into place, and throws himself into the chair. I use my free hand to strap him in with the Velcro restraints, around the chest and legs.

"Well done," says Mrs. Claymore approvingly.

"Couldn't have done it without you . . . Grandma."

A sad smile flashes across her face. "No one's ever called me that before. I like the sound of it."

"I . . . I have to go now." The last thing I want to do is leave her here in this prison. But bringing her with us would be a stupid move. Right now she's in no danger, and she might be in harm's way if I bring her along.

"I have the utmost confidence in you, my dear."

There's so much warmth and pride in her eyes that I feel a little ache of loss when she looks away. Now she seems to slip back into that self-protective fog she created to keep herself alive all these years. There's so much more I want to say to her, but there's no time. I've got to move.

I wheel Mikey down the hallway to the medication room.

"Okay, Mikey, I'm going to need you to fight Claymore's orders again, just for half a second. Which bottle is the Snowball antidote?"

Mikey clenches his jaw, shuts his eyes.

"Middle shelf, blue label."

"Good."

I take out two of the vials that match this description and cram one into my pocket. "How long does this stuff last without refrigeration?"

"Do I look like a doctor? I have no idea."

"Do you know the dosage?" I ask.

His body starts to tremble and he begins to thrash against the restraints.

"I think . . . you need to give me . . . the whole thing . . ."

I've certainly gotten enough injections in my life that I know how to administer one. I load the syringe and plunge it into his arm. Ideally, I would've taken the time to prep the injection site with alcohol, but time is in short supply right now. He can sue me for malpractice if he gets an infection.

Within ten seconds, Mikey's eyes start to grow dim and unfocused. While he's zoning out, I help myself to a pint of donor blood and smear some over my shoulder. That ought to fool people from a distance, even with spotlights trained on me.

As soon as Mikey looks docile enough for me to move him, I untie him and lead him down the stairwell, checking at each level to make sure no one sees us. Even though he's woozy and confused, I keep the gun on him the whole time, just for good measure.

We head all the way down to the parking garage. I steer us to a spot just outside the loading dock where Tai dropped us off. Here, I ease Mikey into a sitting position on the ground, uncuff him, and crouch down to look him in the eye.

"You're not going to remember me, Mikey, but I hope you remember this much. You deserve a chance at a good life. You should look into becoming a cop. How's that sound? I think you'd be a really good cop."

I tuck the handcuffs into the waistband of my scrubs next to the gun and slip Mikey's phone out of his pocket to make a call. The number tumbles easily from my mind like a small gift from Velocius—perfect recall.

"Hello?"

"Tai. It's Angel."

"Oh, my God! You're all right! Should I not have called the police?"

"No, you did great. In fact, I think you saved us. Some of us, anyway. Listen, I need you to make another call and tell the police that a hostage has been left in the parking garage, right where you dropped us off earlier. Can you do that?"

"Sure, but—"

"Can't talk more. Thank you! Bye."

"Angel, wait! What are you going to do?"

What am I going to do?

I rub Mikey on the top of his ridiculously irritating, mistreated, Brooklyn-born head, and say, "What people usually do in these situations—go out in a blaze of glory."

CHAPTER 28

As soon as I get back in the stairway, the power shuts off in the building. Standard operating procedure in a hostage scenario, but it's interesting that this didn't happen sooner. Must be the result of so many law enforcement cooks in the kitchen—local authorities, FBI, et cetera—losing track of what's happening and what needs to be done.

I guess they think it'll be easier to flush me out now that I can't watch television or blow-dry my hair.

I take the stairs as fast as I can. It's not like I haven't been in this situation before.

Mikey's phone rings in my pocket. At first I think Tai is calling me back, but it's a blocked number. Which means it can only be one of Claymore's men, if not Claymore himself, calling to give further instructions.

Still sprinting up the steps, I answer. "'Sup."

"What are you doing with this phone?" a male voice asks. I'm not sure who it belongs to, but I know it's not Claymore.

"Mikey had a seizure, okay? He just collapsed. I know the deal, so just tell me where you wanted him to take me and I'll be there. No games. I don't want anything to happen to Thomas."

There's a pause. The guy is probably covering the phone while he relays this information.

I'm now at the third floor.

Henchman dude speaks again. "Bring Mrs. Claymore to the roof."

Fat chance. "Why? What do you need her for?"

"That's not your concern."

"Well, she's not very keen on coming with me, so is there something I should say to convince her?"

"Tell her that her husband wants to make certain she's safe."

Sure. More likely, Claymore belatedly realized that if he just sails off in his FBI helicopter without her, people might start to suspect that he actually doesn't care what happens to her. This way he gets to play the white knight, rescuing her from her deranged would-be kidnapper and then sweeping her off to a safer location.

Well, that's not going to happen. The more distance between my grandmother and her creep of a husband, the better. Of course, henchman dude doesn't need to know that yet. "Okay, we're on our way."

"Be here in two minutes."

"Mrs. Claymore is elderly and can barely walk. I'm not going to be able to get her up three flights of stairs to the roof in two minutes. Give me more like ten."

"Four."

Before I can object to this stinginess, he hangs up.

Two floors later, I can hear the sound of a helicopter descending. The sound makes me tense. Helicopters bring mayhem and death. They can also be your salvation.

I guess I'm about to find out which it's going to be.

At the fourth floor landing, I pause to put on the cuffs I took off Mikey, careful not to push them closed all the way so that the clasp doesn't catch. They look like they're on but they're not locked. I keep heading up and up until I'm mounting the final set of stairs to the roof. Near the top of the steps, I see Claymore, his two hired guns, and a very pale, weak-looking Thomas, all waiting for me. My eyes zero in on Thomas. He can barely stand up, but he gives me the merest smile, full of admiration. He knows I'm going to try something.

"Where's Sarah?" Claymore demands sharply.

"She refused to come. I don't think she understood what was happening."

Claymore looks very annoyed, but the limo driver says, "The police will make their way in once we're gone. They'll find her and make sure she's safe."

Claymore nods, apparently placated.

Outside, up on the roof, the noise of the helicopter is deafening. It must have landed by now. I see impatience flash in Claymore's eyes. This whole night has turned into a string of contingency plans for him and, at this point, he clearly just wants to get it over with.

He gestures toward the final set of steps. "The helicopter's almost here. We're going. Now."

Claymore's men put their guns away. This all has to be staged perfectly. Once we get up there in the open, it won't look very sporting of them to shoot an unarmed, seemingly already-bleeding teenage girl. Some of the cameras are set up on rooftops almost two blocks away, but I have confidence in those telephoto lenses. Knowing how much my grandfather must hate conducting his business out in the public eye, recorded for all to see, with no filter and no opportunity to manipulate the truth, is a small consolation right now.

Claymore pushes open the door to the roof and one of his men steps out into the open with Thomas at his side. He's got to support Thomas's weight a little, but I can tell by the way he's holding Thomas's arm that he's also restraining him. To my surprise, the helicopter hasn't landed. It's still circling. I guess that makes sense. The roof of this building wasn't really designed for helicopters to land. There's not nearly enough clearance on either side for the helicopter's rotors. I'm guessing the pilot will have to lower a ladder.

Claymore takes a swipe at his hair to muss it up and even undoes the top two buttons on his shirt. This is what he believes passes for rumpled, I guess. He wants to seem like he's been roughed up. He steps out of the shelter of the stairwell onto the roof and take his place next to Thomas.

Now it's just me and my friend the limo driver, and the limo driver's gun is pressed against my back.

"Just so you know," he whispers, "they'd ideally like you to cooperate, but they told me that if I have to shoot you, not to shoot you in the head. I guess they want your brain for research." He presses the gun into my back as if he's trying to stab me with the barrel. "I promised I'd shoot you in the heart if it came to it. Hands up behind your head."

I carefully put my cuffed hands behind my head and lace my fingers together. We step up onto the roof. The lights are everywhere. Searchlights and emergency lights, all of them swirling and pulsing. It's like a party.

Actually, it is a party. My farewell party.

I close my eyes.

My mother's name was Blanca.

I remember that moment back at the hospital when I finally recalled her name, and for once, a memory brings me strength rather than pain. Because in this moment of anger, I can remember her love.

I think about a lot of things. Not anyone else's triggers, my triggers.

I think about my mother.

And how much I love this city.

And Thomas.

I think of the people who've risked so much for me—Larry, Mrs. Claymore, Tai, even Mrs. Fitzgerald.

I think about all the things that give me strength.

And the switch flips. Velocius becomes a kitten purring under my hand. I can master it just like that.

I open my eyes and stop cold.

Does it register with Claymore that a calm is settling over me? Has he noticed that my breathing is slowing and the fear is draining away from my body? Maybe he does. I can sense the minute changes in his body language. It's like I've transfused all my nervous tension and fear into his body.

Good.

The limo driver tries to push me forward, but in one swift

motion, I pull my hands free from the handcuffs and duck. Whatever brute-force tackling maneuver he just tried to pull has backfired in a huge way. He tumbles forward over me, flipping a somersault and landing on his face. This roof is studded with rocks in the roof tar, and it warms my heart to think about how much that must have hurt.

Before he can get to his feet, I've stepped on his wrist, forcing him to release his gun. I grab the weapon and move back out of his reach, grabbing the stairwell door before it closes.

Advantage: me.

But not for long. Right now the open door to the stairwell shields me from the sharpshooters on the roof across the street. The only thing keeping them from firing at me is the fact that they don't have a clear shot.

"Back up," I say, leveling the pistol at Claymore's heart. "Move over to the other side of the roof."

They do as I direct. I stay where I am, right next to the still-open door leading down from the rooftop, while they shuffle to the opposite side of the roof.

Claymore says through clenched teeth, "You've just ensured that your boyfriend is going to die. Shall we shoot him right now, so you can watch? Is that what you want?" It must be hard for him to talk like that—almost as if he's trying to throw his voice, so that no one watching the news footage will be able to read his lips.

"I don't think you're going to do that," I say. "How would you explain it? One of your men shooting a hostage? That would definitely be a hard one to spin."

The limo driver staggers to a standing position. I see him plant his feet like he's getting ready to charge at me. "Ah-ah-ah," I say, pointing the gun at him. "Not smart to try to rush the girl who can summon lightning-fast reflexes."

I lower the gun and step forward, away from the stairwell door. I'm now fully exposed. No more barrier between me and those men nearby with long-range rifles. Suddenly Claymore breaks out into a smile that makes my stomach turn.

"Look down for just a moment, Angel. Look down and then rethink this plan."

I glance down briefly. On my chest, my neck, and my shoulder are an array of red laser dots, the kind that rifles use to show where their bullets will strike when fired.

"It's over," he says. "You're not fast enough to dodge bullets, Angel. Know when you're beaten. Just put the gun down and we can still proceed as planned."

I take a deep breath. "Okay. You win."

I look at Thomas. Time to get this over with.

My vision blurs as the tears begin to burn my eyes. I didn't think it was going to be so hard, looking right at him while I say this. "Thomas."

"Angel."

"It would probably be better if you forget me."

"Not gonna happen—"

"You don't really get a say in that, thanks to Snowball."

Thomas's eyes are pleading now. He doesn't know what I'm going to do but he's probably starting to suspect. He's a good hacker, after all. I glance at Claymore. He's glaring at me now, not because he still thinks he has anything to fear from me, but just because he's irked that I'm dragging this out.

I look back at Thomas, knowing this might be the last time I see him. "Pick one thing to remember, okay? Focus on it. Even if it seems small and insignificant. Let it be the anchor for all the feelings you have for me. Feelings are harder to wipe out than the memories they're attached to."

"Okay," he says, gazing steadily into my eyes. "I've picked one thing."

"Good. Just hang onto that, whatever happens."

"What are you doing?" Claymore says to me. "We had an understanding."

"What am I doing? I believe it's called 'suicide by cop.'"

Thomas yells something, but the words sound mangled as time slows for me. My brain is fizzing, working at lightning speed to pick a target that will cause the fastest, most lethal response. My mind tells me to aim at the circling helicopter.

I look up and raise the pistol and as I pull the trigger—just as the sparks indicate that I've struck the underside of the helicopter—I get what I was asking for.

Time, so slow for me, suddenly speeds up. I hear the distant pop of a rifle going off, and Thomas's voice becomes clear again.

"Angel!"

I'm already throwing myself backward into the stairwell, hoping to avoid the rifle blasts coming my way.

I know I'm fast.

But apparently I'm not fast enough.

CHAPTER 29

As I fall, I manage to grab the door at the top of the stairs and pull it shut behind me. Velocius comes in very handy for multitasking.

I somersault down the stairs until I reach the landing. Above me, I hear the helicopter descend, feel the shake and thump as it comes to rest on the roof of an adjacent building.

My vision starts to curl and lengthen into tunnels. I don't know where I'm hit, and I don't want to look. Wherever it is, it's bad. I'm fighting off the shock that is trying to overtake me. I'm fighting all the natural impulses of my injured body. But I can't stop. I need to get out of here.

When I reach the fourth floor, a smell hits me—a clean, familiar smell. I know it at once. I must have smelled it every day when I was at the research center.

Rubbing alcohol.

I should keep going, but the smell is so overpowering that fresh alarm bells go off in my brain. I yank open the stairwell door and step into a corridor completely doused with rubbing alcohol. Pools of it on the floor, streaks across the walls. Through the darkness of the unlit hallway, I see empty plastic bottles strewn around. What batty thing has Mrs. Claymore done now?

I rush past the receptionist's desk and shove open the glass doors. Before I can take a full step into Mrs. Claymore's room, I hear, "Stop!"

Mrs. Claymore is standing next to the fireplace, lit by an eerie combination of emergency lights coming from outside and the dwindling embers in the hearth. She's holding onto the mantle with one hand, the fire poker in the other. Her clothes are wet. The whole room is filled with the sharp smell of alcohol.

"Don't come any closer, Angel."

I stand there panting, fighting to stay upright. "What did you do?"

"Oh, dear. You've been injured."

"Yeah. Don't tell me where. I don't want to know. But . . ." I point to the scattered bottles on the carpet and the sofa. "What is all this?"

She smiles so sadly it's almost hard to look at her. "I was thinking that they'll need a body. My husband won't be satisfied unless he's certain you're dead. I thought a fire might explain the lack of body."

"But what about you?"

"I can't go on like this anymore. It's time for me to set myself free."

"No! Not like this!"

"I'm proud of you, Angel. You're going to be the one who gets away from him. I couldn't, Virgil can't, but you . . . you're the one who can fly away. Please tell Virgil I send him all my love. And that lovely woman, Grace. She brought me hope when I had none."

"Please, please, please! Don't do this! There's got to be another way!"

"No. Let me give you the chance you deserve. Let me do this for you."

"I don't want you to do—"

But it's too late. With the poker, she gently pushes an ember out of the fireplace and bats it onto the rug, almost as if she's playing croquet.

The fire erupts, first igniting the pool of alcohol around her feet and then climbing up her legs. A split second later, the whole room bursts into flame. The heat pushes me back and I realize that it's coming straight for me. I run to the stairwell and push through the door just in time.

And now I hear my grandmother's screams. Whether my mind was editing them out until now or she managed to hold them in for a minute, they catch up to me here on the stairs. It's the worst, most nightmarish sound I've ever heard.

Until it stops.

And I think that's even worse.

Something takes over in me. Not bravery or strength. Pure animal survival instinct. Nothing to be proud of.

I stagger down to the third floor and find the room where Thomas and I hid earlier. I root through the bag of soiled clothes we left there. Robotically, I pull out a top that looks like it'll fit me. I try to peel off the scrubs I'm wearing but the fabric sticks to the bullet wound and I scream in agony. I throw a bulky hooded sweatshirt over my head instead. That'll hide the blood and obscure my size.

The window is still slightly ajar. I climb out onto the ledge and follow it around the back of the building. I then creep, climb, fall—whatever it takes to get me down to the courtyard at ground level. From there, I see a route—up onto fire escapes and down into alleys—along the backs of each building on the block.

Only once do I turn to look over my shoulder. My face is lit by the spreading fire. In front of the building, sirens are blaring and I can see an arc of water firing up toward the upper floors. But I know it's too late for Mrs. Claymore.

When I peer out from behind one of the buildings up the block from the nursing home, there's a mob of people pushing against the barricades. I keep my head low and walk until I lose track of the time and the distance.

If you survive . . . go to our meet-up spot. . . .

I walk and walk for hours, though I feel like I'm making no conscious decision about where to go. I finally arrive at the right place, in front of the City Hall subway stop. Out in the open. By the time I slip down onto a bench my arm has grown completely numb. I've been cradling it with my other hand, but now I don't have the strength to do that either. I close my eyes, not sure if I'm falling asleep or passing out or dying. I really don't care which it is.

I just want life to go away.

The next thing I'm aware of is Mrs. Fitzgerald standing over me, snapping on a pair of rubber gloves. I sit up, immediately feeling a pulling sensation in my shoulder. My arm is in a sling.

"Be careful," she says in the same matter-of-fact voice she always uses. "Don't move too fast. I don't want to have to stitch you up again."

I look down. The first thing I notice is that I'm wearing my own clothes. The second thing I notice is the pain in my chest. I pull my shirt away from my skin slightly. There's a row of stiches, maybe twenty or more.

I glance around at the room. It's completely unfamiliar. "Where are we?"

"A hotel room near Kennedy Airport," she says. "I couldn't risk taking you to your father's house or even to my office."

I put my hand over the stitches, gently passing my thumb over the black bristly ends of the stitches poking out of my skin. "How bad was it?"

"You just missed having a shattered clavicle. It'll hurt for a while but, obviously, not life-threatening. And now that you're awake . . ." She holds up a plastic squirt bottle of yellowish liquid. "We need to dye your hair."

"What?"

"You need to not look like you." Slowly my brain catches up: she's talking about a disguise. Amazing how sluggish my thoughts can be without Velocius. I suppose it doesn't help that I'm exhausted and traumatized, but that's been par for the course for a long time. "Come into the bathroom and let's get this over with. You need to get going first thing in the morning."

Mrs. Fitzgerald has me sit on the toilet and lean my head over the tub. I feel her squeeze the cold dye onto my head.

"So what now?" I ask.

"I've packed a backpack with money, credit cards, a phone,

and a passport. There's also a ticket in there for you. You'll be going to Amsterdam for a few weeks. Staying with a friend of mine. I've written the details down. You're not to call me or your father directly. My friend will relay messages to me but not for the first three weeks."

I try to take all that in but all I can think to say in response is, "What's Amsterdam like?"

Mrs. Fitzgerald works the dye through my hair, gently dabbing a few places where it drips.

"I don't know. I've never been there. Virgil thought you'd like it. If you don't, you can find somewhere else that agrees with you. You're free now."

"Free?" I say. "You mean I have nothing left."

She sort of grunts in response and keeps massaging the dye into my scalp.

"Can I ever come back here again?"

"I don't know. Maybe once we're sure that Erskine Claymore and the FBI truly believe you're dead."

When she's done with the dye, I sit up and she hands me a small box. I open it and see a pair of blue contact lenses. "Never imagined myself a blue-eyed blonde," I say.

"I'm sure there are a lot of things you never imagined," she says. Her voice is quieter than usual. Not exactly emotional, but less brusque.

I practice putting in the contacts. Since I'm not used to it, it takes me a few tries. Eventually they're both in and I look around, blinking. I notice the pile of bloody, dirty clothes—my stolen scrubs—on the floor next to the toilet.

That's when I remember. And panic.

I kneel down and start pawing through the pockets. "I had . . . there was a vial of medicine in my pocket. Did you find it? Did I drop it?"

"It's in here," Mrs. Fitzgerald says, pointing toward the bed-side table. "What is it?"

I explain to her about the drug, how it was used on Thomas and Mikey and, most important, that Thomas needs it. "I'm fairly sure Claymore's people will give him the second injection. It's just a matter of when. Claymore told me that they were going to delay until they could be sure that his memories from the entire past year had been eliminated."

Mrs. Fitzgerald peels the rubber gloves off and sits on the end of the bed. "He saw you get shot, correct?"

I nod.

"So I suppose, on a personal level, the choice is, let him forget you or let him think that you're dead. What would be the kinder thing to do?"

This is officially the most bizarre conversation I've ever had with my guardian. Grace Fitzgerald is asking me about feelings and kindness and "a personal level"?

But she has a point. "The kinder thing to do would be to spare him pain."

"Maybe," she says. "Let me rephrase my question, then. What would he want you to do?"

"He would want to remember me. Even if it hurt," I say. "That's what he told me."

She picks up the vial. "Then I'll find a way to administer it. Though I can't make any promises about how long that will take. He'll be under lock and key, for one thing."

"Yes, but you managed to sneak in to see Mrs. Claymore. If you got into that place, you can get access to Thomas."

"There's also the question of the proper dosage and the fact that this medication has been without refrigeration for several hours. Some medications degrade quickly when not kept in just the right conditions, and knowing Dr. Wilson, I'm sure this is a tricky one."

The name of Velocius's mastermind catches me off guard. "You knew Dr. Wilson?"

She removes her glasses and pinches the bridge of her nose. She takes a deep breath. "Angel. I . . . I owe you an apology. More than one, really."

"For what?"

She pulls her sweater down over her knuckles and folds her arms across her chest. The gesture makes her seem much smaller, much younger. "I don't know exactly what they told you, but I know you didn't trust me enough to reach out for help when you first realized you were in trouble. I'm sorry that I made it so easy for you to believe I'd betray you. I'm not very good with people. I'm not—"

She swallows. I want to let her off the hook. She doesn't need to say anything more. "It's okay. You never asked to be some surrogate mother to me."

I'm glad she doesn't look up at me because I feel so embarrassed by this conversation, I think I'm going to burst into flames.

"In any case, I want to apologize to you for Velocius," she says. "I'm the one who came up with the idea for it, a long time ago. I was one of Wilson's early research assistants. Dr. Ladner was my replacement when I left. I want you to know that I never would have pursued the idea if I'd had any inkling of how they'd develop it and test it."

I just look at her and pull hard on the towel draped around my neck.

"I know that when you came back here to New York, your handlers told you that you shouldn't use your skills, that it wears you out and shortens your lifespan. They don't know anything, Angel. That was just their way of controlling you. The truth is, no one knows what your potential is. No one can say for sure if there are any limits to what you can do. The government was afraid of you and tried to make you afraid of you. What I'm trying to say is, don't ever let anyone make you fear your own strength."

Strength? What a joke. I don't care if I find out I can fly. It won't do me any good now that Thomas is gone and Mrs. Claymore is dead. I've lost everyone who's ever mattered to me. If Mrs. Fitzgerald had told me this sooner, if I'd learned to understand and control my Velocius abilities earlier, maybe tonight would've played out differently. But now? What good is a superpower if you have no one left to protect? This is all too little and too late.

Mrs. Fitzgerald gets up and gathers a few things to put away in her medical bag.

"I have to get back to your father now. I'll tell him that you're all right. Your flight is at 6:30 a.m. tomorrow. Be safe, Angel."

I listen to the sound of the door latching shut. It's just a short little click, but it seems to echo in my mind for hours, long after I've rinsed the dye from my hair and stared into the mirror and fallen into a fitful sleep. I try to accept that my life in New York—the short, hopeful existence of Angel Ramos—is now over for good.

As the morning light spills into the room, I let myself go. I decide that it's all right to cry, to mourn a death, even if the person who's died is you.

SIX MONTHS LATER

grip the pair of binoculars with one hand and hold my phone
to my ear with the other. A steady, chilling winter wind cuts
through my clothes. No place does wind like Manhattan in
the winter.

"You're sure?" I say into the phone. "Completely sure?"

I can tell from the sigh on the other end of the line that Mrs.
Fitzgerald is getting impatient with me. Not that I can blame her.
She's done me a huge favor, and now she wants to get on with her
day. "You're looking right at him, aren't you?"

"Yes," I acknowledge. I'm standing a block away from Claymore Tower, watching through the binoculars as Thomas exits
the building and crosses the street.

I know it's really him. I see his red hair. I see his jawline. I
notice that his confident walk is . . . not quite the same. He's
keeping his head down, just plodding along.

I tuck the binoculars into my backpack.

"So he comes here a lot?"

"It's the same each time," Mrs. Fitzgerald says. "He goes to the top of Claymore Tower and then heads to a café at the edge of the park. Now, if you're going to do this, I suggest you get it over with instead of conspicuously loitering out in the open."

Even though I look nothing like the Angel that the world remembers, Mrs. Fitzgerald worries I'll be recognized now that I'm back in New York.

"Okay, then I guess I'll just . . . go talk to him."

"We don't know that the medication worked," Mrs. Fitzgerald reminds me, her tone at once telling me that I shouldn't get my hopes up and that she understands if I do. "We don't know what he remembers. He may just be drawn here for reasons he doesn't understand. But you'll never find out if you keep stalling forever."

End call.

Her phone etiquette is just as abysmal as ever. Over the last six months, just about everything in my life has been transformed except her.

I'll never again criticize the media, because it was the live coverage of the showdown at the nursing home that saved Thomas. And maybe me, too. All that public scrutiny threw a monkey wrench in Claymore's plan to spirit Thomas away and fake his death. It also helped that Thomas's very wealthy parents hired a bunch of expensive lawyers and even a publicity company that specializes in crisis management. They kept Thomas squarely in the public eye in just the right way so that Claymore—who has always preferred to operate in the shadows—had no choice but to back off. Upon being released from the hospital, Thomas went back to stay with his adoptive parents, out of Claymore's reach, at least for now.

And the kill shot that got me? The one those television cameras caught? Well, that's been quite a hit. Even though my body was never recovered, several ballistics experts jawed for hours on cable news shows about how lethal these rifles are, even at long range. No one, they all concluded, could have survived that gunshot.

Of course, my reputation took a beating. Claymore blamed me for the whole situation, including starting the fire that killed his wife. But I'm dead now. No need to speak ill of me. And apparently I do have some loyal supporters who are insisting that I was set up. They say that I was the victim of a conspiracy and the government is still actively engaged in covering up what happened.

Ha.

But whatever story people believe, Angel Ramos is dead. She sacrificed herself so I could start fresh with a new life.

And Mrs. Fitzgerald was right: People move on. As sensational a story as it was, other sensational stories came after. And people forgot.

We're still not sure what happened to Mikey, but Mrs. Fitzgerald has a lead. Finding out whether he got a semi-happy ending is near the top of my to-do list now that I'm back in New York.

Item one on my to-do list is now directly ahead.

I shouldn't be nervous. I've spent the past six months learning how to turn on my Velocius skills as easily as snapping my fingers. Unfortunately, none of my newly honed superpowers will help me in this situation.

The sandwich shop that Thomas has just entered is not the kind of place I was expecting to find him. Inside it smells of coffee and burned sugar and that stale lemony scent of air fresheners in public restrooms. It's the sort of café where old people come for a good deal on a bowl of soup. Nothing wrong with it, but nothing that would be an obvious draw for a rich kid with all of New York City's varied cuisine at his fingertips.

He's standing in line at the counter. I take a plastic tray and get in line behind him. My heart is pounding. I don't know what to do.

Should I just say his name?

I watch him slide his tray along, past a display of desserts. They've got slices of cake covered in plastic wrap. Sad-looking cups of fruit cocktail. He reaches up and takes a glass dish of rice pudding.

I stare down at the pudding. He looks up and our eyes meet. But there's no gleam of recognition. He just gives me a slightly embarrassed smile and then keeps sliding his tray along while I stay frozen in place.

He doesn't know me. He doesn't remember. I thought I was prepared for this possibility but I wasn't. It hurts worse than anything I've ever experienced.

Says the girl who's actually been shot in the chest.

He slides his tray up to the woman at the cash register. But instead of paying immediately, he glances back at me. "I can't help noticing that you're staring at my rice pudding. I know it's kind of a weird thing to buy, but rice pudding is the reason I come here."

I manage a weak twitch of a smile. "Oh?"

"Yeah. I can't seem to get enough of the stuff." He shrugs. "I guess I get it for the sentimental value. It reminds me of being in the hospital."

"Your hospital experiences must have been far more pleasant than mine," I say.

"Not at all. I never want to see the inside of a hospital again if I can help it, but for some reason, whenever I eat rice pudding, it cheers me up. I can't explain it."

I'm about to turn and walk away. It just hurts too much to see him.

"Aren't you getting anything?" he asks. He takes a second dish of pudding and puts it on his tray. "How 'bout it? My treat."

"Thanks, but I probably should get go—"

But looking up into his face, I'm stopped cold. Those dark brown eyes, the way he's looking at me. I forgot how unbelievably handsome he is. I can't move.

"Have we met before?" he asks. His eyes have narrowed, like he's trying to think of something he can't quite grasp. A memory. An association. It puzzles him. And Thomas has never been one to let a puzzle defeat him.

"I swear I don't make a habit of using that line, and if you tell me your name, I'll retire it forever in your honor."

I hesitate a moment. My new identity—the name that matches my blonde-dyed hair and blue contact lenses—will never stop feeling like a lie.

Even though I know I'll be breaking one of Mrs. Fitzgerald's security rules, I decide to tell him the truth. Sort of.

"Sarah."

"Would you like to join me, Sarah?"

"Why did you say it like that?"

"Like what?"

"Like, you know, Sarah. Like you're using air quotes."

"Because I don't think that's your real name. I think you just gave me some random fake name because you're thinking about brushing me off. Not that I'd blame you—you've probably been hit on by some complete creepers, and it's logical to assume I might fall into that category."

"I'm not . . . I don't want to brush you off."

Our eyes lock.

All I want to do is reach out and pull him into my arms, but I can't.

"Well, Sarah is my real name, for the record," I say. "But I will overlook your skepticism. And I still accept your gift of pudding."

He puts his hand over his heart and gives an exaggerated exhale in relief. "Thank you."

I smile. He pays and motions for me to sit down at a table with him.

This is not what I'd hoped for.

Or is it?

We're both safe now. We have a chance to start over, just like two normal people. We've been through a lot to get here. Maybe this is our consolation prize.

I'll take it.

ACKNOWLEDGMENTS

I'm grateful to Molly Jaffa, Denise Logsdon, and Alison S. Weiss for lending me their amazing brains and generous hearts during a difficult writing year.

A big thank-you to my talented Carolrhoda Lab editors, Amy Fitzgerald and Alix Reid, for putting the polish on my words and for giving this sequel a warm and welcoming new home at Lerner. And many thanks to Danielle Carnito, Erica Johnson, and Giliane Mansfeldt for making this book look so flaming fabulous.

Thank you to my #squad—Philip, Caroline, Lucy, Emma, and Gus—for providing every good thing in my life.